The

Mustang

Breaker

Other Books by Stephen Bly

Horse Dreams series
Book #1: *Memories of a Dirt Road Town*

Fortunes of the Black Hills series
Book #1: *Beneath a Dakota Cross*
Book #2: *Shadow of Legends*
Book #3: *The Long Trail Home*
Book #4: *Friends and Enemies*
Book #5: *Last of the Texas Camp*
Book #6: *The Next Roundup*

Contemporary Novel
Paperback Writer

For information on other books by this author, write:
Stephen Bly
Winchester, Idaho 83555
or check out his Web site at
www.blybook.com

STEPHEN BLY

The
Mustang
Breaker

BROADMAN
&HOLMAN
PUBLISHERS

NASHVILLE, TENNESSEE

DEDICATION

for Rina Joye Bly

• • •

Published by Broadman & Holman Publishers

Nashville, Tennessee

ISBN-10: 0-8054-3172-1

ISBN-13: 978-0-8054-3172-8

Dewey Decimal Classification: F

Subject Heading: FORGIVENESS–FICTION

1 2 3 4 5 6 7 8   11 10 09 08 07 06

1

Brownie's rear rocketed straight up as if propelled from a cannon. Develyn clamped her knees against the fender of the saddle and fought to keep her tennis shoes in the stirrups. When his back hooves slammed into the ground, she snatched up a rein and yanked it to the right.

"Stop it right now!" she hollered.

Brownie spun right.

Develyn lost her left stirrup. She felt her bottom slide out of the saddle, so she threw her body to the left. But the gelding stopped spinning, and her over-compensation flung her over the horse. Her flailing hands clutched the saddle horn. The entire saddle now slipped to the left side of the horse. Develyn clutched a handful of chocolate brown mane to keep from hitting the dirt.

Ears tucked back, Brownie lunged forward. Develyn didn't turn loose of the mane or the tilted saddle horn. Sharp pains shot through her ankles as they bounced on the river rocks.

"Stop it, I said!" she cried.

Brownie bucked again, and flipped Develyn like a rag doll over his back. Her jaw clamped as tight as her fingers. The saddle circled back into position. Her knuckles and fingers throbbed in pain. She bounced along backward, her heels slamming into the dirt and rocks on every jump.

"Please, stop it," she whimpered. "I don't want to die."

Brownie slowed his bucking, but bounced down the trail at a reckless trot.

"Bees!" Develyn groaned. "Mountain bumble bees!" With bodies the size of a quail egg, a dozen angry bees dove on the tail-swishing, wide rump of the quarter horse gelding.

At the first sting, Brownie ducked his head and thrashed his rear hooves toward the Wyoming sun. At the same moment, he spun right. Develyn slammed into the saddle, backward. She clutched a handful of mane hair, but managed also to grip the cantle and stay seated as the horse bolted up the trail.

The little swarm of bees reassembled just above Brownie's rump. Develyn tossed the handful of horsehair and grabbed the stampede string on her straw cowboy hat. Hat in hand, she leaned back over the cantle and swatted at the bees when they dove this time.

She batted several to the ground. The others retreated.

What am I doing? Now they'll attack me!

They lunged at her hat. With patience beyond her ten years, she took aim again. Three bees shot back into the air like badminton birdies.

The others veered off toward a dwarf juniper tree.

Then they were gone.

All of them.

"Whoa, Brownie!" Develyn shouted. "Whoa!"

When the horse stopped, she continued to sit backward in the saddle. She glanced over her shoulder. "It's OK, Brownie. You couldn't help it. I'm sorry I . . ." she fought to catch her breath.

"Devy-girl!"

The yell was distant, but familiar. She stared down the dirt trail at the boy on the galloping horse. She jammed on her straw hat and slid the keeper up to her chin.

"What are you doin' like that, Devy-girl?" Dewayne asked.

"Like what?"

"Backward in the saddle."

"I was swatting bees."

"Bees?"

"A swarm of very large mountain bees attacked Brownie, and I chased them off."

"I don't see any bees."

"That's because I did a good job." Develyn swung around in the saddle and hooked her toes into the stirrups.

"Hey, I got good news, Devy-girl."

She gazed at her twin brother. "This better not be a joke or something, because Brownie and me have lots to do."

He scratched his very short brown hair. "You don't have anything to do but ride."

"Hah!"

"Mr. Homer came to town today and brought a paint gelding for you to ride."

"What?"

"He said he knew how disappointed you were with your pony, so he brought you another one."

"I don't want another one."

"What? You cried and cried because you didn't get a paint horse."

"I was younger then."

"That was just last Tuesday."

"It doesn't matter. Brownie is my horse now." She leaned forward and patted the horse's neck.

"What am I goin' to tell Mr. Homer?"

"Tell him that me and Brownie have been through too much already. Tell him I've made my choice, and Develyn Gail Upton Worrell doesn't change her mind."

● ● ●

The pulsating intro of Brooks and Dunn singing "Go West" opened her eyes, but it wasn't until a long black braid swished in front of her that she remembered her location.

And her age.

"Are you ready to ride, Ms. Worrell?" Casey asked.

Develyn sat up in the plastic webbed lounge chair and shaded the bright sun with her hand to her forehead. Sweat dribbled down the back of her lavender T-shirt. "I think I fell asleep."

"Were you dreaming of a classroom of Indiana fifth-graders, or living in that big headquarters house at the Quarter Circle Diamond with your Quint?"

"I was dreaming about horses."

"That's what you always say. Are all your dreams about horses?"

"Only the good ones."

● ● ●

Develyn grabbed her distressed straw cowboy hat and a bottle of water from the wooden counter that served as the cupboard and the only shelf in her log cabin. When she stepped back outside, Casey Cree-Ryder had two horses tied to the side of her horse trailer.

"You brought Popcorn?"

Casey patted the brown Appaloosa gelding with white spots on his rump. "He needs some work."

"I've never seen you ride any horse but Montana Jack. I thought you saved Popcorn just for roping."

"Maybe we'll find something to rope."

Develyn ambled over to her taupe and white skewbald mare. "Well, My Maria . . . Popcorn has about as much chrome as you do. What a dashing pair you make."

"Yeah," Cree-Ryder grinned, "if he hadn't been cut, just think of what interesting foals they'd produce."

Develyn rubbed her horse's nose. "I just can't imagine My Maria as a mama."

"Yeah, I think the same about me, but I can dream."

"What are you talking about? You'll find the perfect cowboy one of these days."

"Dev, I don't want the perfect cowboy. The perfect cowboy wants a perfect wife. I'll take one with a few flaws, as long as he loves me like crazy."

"Well spoken, Miss Cree-Ryder." Develyn peered into the back of the silver-sided horse trailer. "We can't ride horseback to this secret place you're going to show me?"

"We could if we had three days. It's quite a few miles west of here."

"I didn't think there was anything west of here."

Casey's dark freckles waved with the smile. "Oh, sure, sooner or later you'd run into Idaho."

"I don't know why you have to keep it a secret."

"You'll see." Casey untied her horse, led him out and around a big circle behind the horse trailer, then walked him straight into the trailer. When she had his lead rope tied, she strolled out. "Your turn. I wonder if My Maria will trailer?"

"I thought you said it would be easy."

"Easy once you get the hang of it. Just show her confidence. Walk right in there beside her and she'll follow your lead. She trusts you."

"Are you sure you want me to do this?" Develyn said.

"You have to learn to trailer your own horse. You can't expect Quint to do that for you."

6

"You have me tethered to Quint already."

"Me? You're the one that dreams about him every night."

"I do not." Develyn untied My Maria and circled behind the trailer. "I've never done this before."

"Yes, well, until a week ago you hadn't danced barefoot with two dozen cowboys either. It's a season to try new things."

"Are you sure she'll follow me into the trailer?"

Casey folded her arms across the front of her sleeveless T-shirt. "Of course."

Develyn clasped the lead rope with her right hand and marched toward the open back door of the trailer where the Appaloosa gelding waited.

OK, Lord, I can do this. Just hike up here . . . step into the trailer like I've done it a thousand times before and . . .

My Maria refused to put a foot in the trailer and froze like a Remington bronze. She tucked back her ears and snorted.

"I don't think she wants to load," Develyn called out.

"Jerk on the rope. Show her who's boss."

Jerk on the rope. Yeah, right . . .

Develyn tugged hard on the lead rope. The halter stretched tight, but the horse refused to move.

"Come, girl . . . it's time to go for a ride."

"Pull harder!" Casey hollered.

With all 108 pounds, Dev flung herself forward into the trailer.

With all 942 pounds, My Maria hurled herself backward away from the trailer.

"Hold on!" Casey yelled.

With both hands seared by the friction of the red nylon rope, Develyn slid across the yellow, dry Wyoming dirt like an empty can tied to a cat's tail. When the mare stopped pulling back, Dev sprawled across the dirt like an anchor, the lead rope still clutched in her hand.

Casey ambled over and stared down at her. "Good."

"What's good about it?" Develyn choked.

"You held her."

"I burned my hands and got drug through the dirt."

"Yeah, it happens to me all the time."

"Is that supposed to make me feel better?"

Cree-Ryder reached down her calloused hand. "It makes me feel better. Come on, don't just lay around, you've got a horse to load."

Develyn struggled to her feet while Casey Cree-Ryder held the rope.

"That was exciting, wasn't it?" Casey's thick black eyebrows bounced with each word.

"Exciting? That's probably the tenth time in the past month that I wasn't sure I'd live another minute."

"You braggin' or complainin'?" Casey chided.

"What I'm saying is, My Maria is now quite tiffed at me, and she's still not in the trailer."

"Do it again."

Develyn tucked her short blonde bangs under her cowboy hat. "You have to be kidding."

"No, really. Show her you mean it. I'll help you this time."

"Good, you lead her in and I'll stand over here and take notes. I'm a good student."

"You aren't a student; you're a teacher. You need to know how to show others. You had to learn how to do yard duty when you were a rookie teacher. Now you have to learn to trailer your own horse. You lead her, and I'll provide a little persuasion."

"What kind of persuasion?"

"Go on . . . lead her up there. When I shout 'now,' you pull her up next to Popcorn."

Develyn brushed the dirt off her Wrangler jeans, then grabbed the lead rope. "Now, My Maria, I realize you don't want to go into the trailer, but you have to anyway. Honey, there are just some things in life one must do . . . like cleaning out the back seat of your car after two fifth-graders barfed all over it. It's unpleasant . . . it's unfortunate . . . but it must be done."

When Develyn stepped up into the trailer, My Maria balked again.

"Now!" Casey shouted.

Develyn smeared a trail of dust across her forehead and tossed her weight into the rope as Casey landed a two-by-four on the horse's rump.

No!

My Maria lunged back, reared up on her two hind legs, and lifted Develyn off the ground. She swung in front of the flailing hooves like a rope-tied volleyball circling a tetherball pole.

"Hang on!" Casey shouted.

My Maria reared again.

Once more, Develyn found herself dangling in the air. "Why? Why am I doing this?" she shouted. "You can just shovel up my parts and bury them in a bucket."

"Hang on! Show her who's boss."

Develyn hung on.

And My Maria stopped bucking.

"You have any other great suggestions? Because if you do, I'm not following them," Dev growled.

A short brown burro ambled up beside her.

"Oh, now you show up." Develyn fought to catch her breath. "Uncle Henry, you need to talk to this girl. She's being very, very rude."

He looked at her with big black eyes and the usual too-dumb-or-too-smart-to-care look.

"Here comes your mustang breaker," Casey announced.

Develyn glanced south at the dirt drive that led back to the cabins. "What's he doing here?"

"Came to see Devy-girl, no doubt."

"I don't want him here."

Casey shrugged. "Maybe he can help."

Develyn's neck tensed. "I won't jeopardize my safety so that you two will have an excuse to laugh."

"Are you afraid to show him you aren't perfect?"

"Why did you say that?" Develyn bristled.

"Sorry, Dev, let's just get her loaded before Renny gets up here."

"I hope you have a better idea than assaulting my horse with a two-by-four."

"While I think of it, you might want to brush the dirt off your face."

Develyn glanced at the red Dodge pickup that approached. She dropped the lead rope to the ground and tried to brush the dirt off her T-shirt.

"Grab the rope!" Casey called out.

My Maria stepped away. Develyn shoved Uncle Henry's rear end aside and lunged at the rope.

At her touch, Uncle Henry trotted right at the trailer, with My Maria at his side. When he hopped up inside the trailer, she followed him until they stood motionless next to Popcorn.

"Yes!" Casey sprinted over and slammed the trailer tailgate.

Develyn retrieved her hat just as Renny Slater stepped out of the Dodge pickup and shook his head. "I ain't never see anyone load a mustang mare like that. Ohhhweee, Devy-girl, you are good. You might want to clean up a little, but you are a Wyomin' cowboy girl . . . that's for sure."

"Renny, don't give me that dimpled cowboy flattery. Right now I feel like a middle-aged Indiana school teacher who had yard duty by herself after they served double-chocolate brownies for lunch on the last day of school."

Renny's thin blond hair curled out from under his black cowboy hat. "I reckon that's bad."

"If you ever have to choose between that and jumping in front of a train, choose the train."

Renny tugged at the sweaty bandana around his neck. "Where are the two most beautiful gals in Wyoming going today?"

Develyn hiked around and peered into the side mirror on Casey's truck. "I don't have a clue."

"Neither do I," Casey added.

"What are you talking about?" Develyn challenged.

"Oh, is he talking about us? I thought he meant Lindsay Burdett and Miss Wyoming."

Renny shook his head. "You know, Cree-Ryder, if you ever found the right attitude you could be . . ."

"Could be what, Slater? Watch yourself, I'm packin' iron . . ."

"You are?" Develyn frowned.

"Hush, girl, the mustang breaker dug himself a hole. I want to see how he gets out of it."

Renny sauntered straight up to Casey Cree-Ryder, pushed his hat back, and put both hands on her shoulders. "Listen to me. You are a dynamite of a girl. And if you spend this summer letting a little of Miss Dev wear off on you, you'll be married by next June."

"Are you proposin' to me?" Casey grinned. "'Cause if you are proposin' you'd better have a ring. I ain't agreein' to nothin' until I get the ring appraised."

Renny dropped his hands to his sides. "You weren't listenin' . . ."

"Cowboy, if I'm married by next summer I'll name my firstborn after you."

"I give up . . ." he mumbled.

"Ah, now you are tryin' to back out. Isn't that like . . ."

"Casey," Dev interjected. "Renny is a friend who just told you some nice things. Don't make a joke of it. Look him in those blue eyes and say, 'Thanks for the compliment, cowboy. I reckon me and Miss Dev both have some things to learn from each other.'"

Casey chewed on her tongue. Her chin dropped to her chest. "You didn't mean literally say it, did you?"

"Yes, I did," Develyn said.

Casey lifted her head, but kept her eyes on Renny's "Miles City, Montana, All-Around Cowboy" belt buckle. "'Thanks for the compliment, cowboy. I reckon me and Miss Dev both have some things to learn from each other.'"

Renny hugged Casey's shoulder. "You're welcome, ma'am."

"See," Develyn grinned, "that wasn't too bad."

"It was hokey. What do I have to teach you?"

"How to win in a knife fight, for one," Develyn chided.

Renny pulled off his hat and ran his fingers through his hair. "See? It's already happening. You are rubbing off on Miss Dev." He hiked over and stared into the back of the trailer. "Where are you two going?"

"Sage Canyon," Casey replied.

"Hey, you ought to ride over and take a look at . . ."

"Shut up, Slater . . . don't you go ruinin' my surprise," Casey interrupted.

"Look at what?" Develyn asked.

"Oh, there's a . . ." he started.

"Renny, if you tell her, I'll cut . . ."

"Casey!" Develyn scolded.

Cree-Ryder took a deep breath. "I will be heartbroken and depressed for a week."

"I won't risk that, Casey-girl. You two have a nice ride and enjoy the view."

"By the way, Mr. Slater," Develyn asked, "why did you come by this morning?"

"Oh, shoot, I almost forgot. Your Quint sent me a note to deliver to you."

"A note?"

"He said he tried callin' your cell phone yesterday afternoon and evenin', but you must have been out of range."

Develyn pulled her cell phone from her back pocket. "I was home yesterday, I can't imagine how it . . . rats, the power's off. How did that happen?"

Renny retrieved a white envelope from his dashboard.

"What's it say? Did he propose?" Casey pressed.

"How would I know?" Renny replied. "It's a private note."

Casey stared over Develyn's shoulder. "The last time a guy sent me a private note it said, 'Young lady, when you fell over that chair, you ripped a hole in the seat of your denims.'"

Renny sauntered toward his rig. "I've got to get on down the road. I've got some broncs waitin' for me at Bob Feller's place in Meeteetzee."

"Bob Feller?" Develyn said. "You mean, Robert William Andrew Feller, who pitched eighteen seasons for the Cleveland

Indians? The one who went 26 and 15 with a 2.18 ERA in 1946? He would have won 350 games if the war hadn't interrupted his career."

"Ouuuuuuweee," Renny laughed. "Miss Dev is a baseball fanatic. You surprise me."

"Oh, not baseball in general. Just one team. My father was an avid Cleveland Indians fan. It was all because Bob Feller was born near Van Meter, Iowa. That's where my dad was from."

"Well, sorry to say, this Bob Feller isn't Bullet Bob," Renny said. "This is an ol' time Wyomin' rancher who's worn his teeth down to his gums eating beefsteak three times a day. As far as I know, he's never been to a big league game, but he still throws a fast loop come brandin' time."

Casey handed Develyn her cowboy hat. "If I'm goin' to be like Miss Dev, I don't have to memorize baseball stats, do I?"

"No, but it doesn't hurt to hold something back, so you can surprise them later on," Develyn mused.

Casey cleared her throat. "Slater, I bet I never told you what I bought myself at Victoria's Secret in Houston, did I?"

"Casey, that's not the kind of surprise I meant," Develyn blushed.

"I'm goin' to tell him anyway . . ."

"This might be more information that I want to know," Slater remarked.

"Hush. I bought myself a . . ."

"Casey!" Develyn cautioned.

"Pair of black . . ."

"Don't embarrass yourself."

"Socks."

"Socks?" Dev asked.

"Yeah, what in the world would I do with those other things? I won a gift certificate one time in a raffle. I was hopin' to get the safari to Africa, or at least the Winchester rifle . . . but I won a $15 gift certificate at Victoria's Secret. See, I surprised you."

"You're right," Develyn said. "I'm surprised."

Casey pointed to the envelope. "Aren't you goin' to open your note?"

"Maybe she wants some privacy," Renny suggested. "Anyway, I need to go. Devy-girl, I need to talk to you. Call me if you have your cell phone working later on."

"You can't talk to her right now?" Casey challenged.

Renny stared straight at Dev's blue-green eyes. "No." His voice was soft. He slipped back into the truck and rolled back toward town with a cloud of yellow dust.

"Read your note, sweetie. I'm goin' to go . . . eh . . . let's see . . . I'm goin' to powder my nose." Casey's smile reached ear to ear. "You see, I am learning something."

Develyn walked around to the south side of Casey's truck and leaned against the front fender.

Lord, I don't know why I'm nervous opening Quint's note. It's probably just something trivial. Maybe he has to go to that range conservation meeting in Powell after all.

She slid her finger under the flap and tore the top off.

But if that's all it is, why did he lick the envelope? Maybe it's bad news. Maybe something has happened.

Lord, this is insane. I've known him for a month. I'm acting like a junior-high girl. Open the note. I think my problem is I don't know what I want him to say.

Develyn stared at the neat handwriting.

> *Miss Dev,*
> *How I missed hearing your sweet voice last evening. But I know how temperamental cell phone reception is down there. I should probably install a tower like we have at the ranch, only I know you won't be there forever! I do have to go up to Powell for that meeting, but I have a plan. Why don't you come with me? (Linds agreed to "chaperone" us.) We could fly to Powell . . . you and Lindsay could shop in Cody while I attend some boring meetings. (She'll show you all the stores where Miss Emily liked to buy her clothes.) Then, when the meetings are over, we can fly over to Yellowstone. It's about time you completed that trip you started when you were ten. No one wants to spend a summer in Argenta. We'll just be gone three days. I'm sure Miss Cree-Ryder will feed your horse. (With any luck, maybe that burro will wander off.) Anyway, Miss Dev, give me a call when you get a chance. I'll fly down and pick you up. Don't worry about packing . . . I've gathered some of Miss Emily's things in a suitcase. I know you will look wonderful in them. Call me before 4 p.m. I can have you back here in time for supper. Always, your cowboy . . . Quint*

"There, my nose is powdered!" Casey hollered as she burst out the door to the porch in front of the cabin. "What did Quint say? Is he madly in love with Miss Dev? Oh, I know that already."

"He has to . . . and you know, he wanted me to . . ."

"To what?"

"To attend a range conservation meeting with him."

"Wow, that's exciting. In some parts of Wyoming, that's the same as being engaged."

"Hush! Don't use that line on me."

"What's the problem? Is it good news or bad news?"

"The problem is, Miss Cree-Ryder, I don't know if it's good or bad."

"You want me to read it?"

"No."

"Yeah, I didn't think so. Do you still want to go for a ride?"

"Of course I do. After all that work I went through to trailer My Maria . . . I want the ride. There's a great mysterious vista to experience."

"Not as mysterious as that note."

"I'll tell you about my note as soon as you show me the vista."

"Show and tell?" Casey laughed. "You do sound like a teacher."

"Is that supposed to be a put-down?" Develyn squeaked open the passenger door on Casey's pickup. She climbed up and stood on the running board. She punched her fist into the clear Wyoming sky and shouted, "I am a fifth-grade schoolteacher and proud of it!"

When she heard clapping, Develyn ducked inside the cab and slammed the door.

"Here comes Cooper," Casey said as she started the engine.

"I know . . ." Develyn replied. "He must think I'm an idiot."

"Do you care?"

Develyn scowled at her dark-skinned friend, then turned to watch the gray-haired cowboy approach.

He tipped his black, beaver felt hat. "Miss Casey . . .

Miss Dev. Don't know what the conversation was about, but I'm glad you like being a schoolteacher."

"We were just teasing around," Develyn admitted. "Didn't mean to yell that loud."

"This is central Wyomin', Miss Dev. You can yell all you want to and no one will care."

She found herself reading the creases of his eyes. *How old is he, really?* "Is your brother OK, Coop?"

"He's spent much of his adult life in jail. He's OK. Doesn't want to speak to me again, but that will change as soon as he needs something. Are you two going for a short ride, or on down the road to a rodeo?"

"We'll be back by late afternoon. Why?" Develyn asked.

Cooper Tallon scratched the back of his neck and glanced over at Casey.

"Look, I've already powdered my nose. I could sing real loud or jam my fingers in my ears if you need some privacy."

He shook his head. "Wear orange, Miss Cree-Ryder."

"What?"

"You ought to wear more orange."

"I hate orange."

"It would look great on you."

"Did you come clear over here to rag on me?"

"No. I came over here to tell Miss Dev that I still hope we find time to sit down on the porch some evening and visit. If we are summer neighbors, we ought to know each other a little."

Develyn smiled. "Cooper, I'd love that."

"Tonight?"

Develyn glanced down at the note in her hand. "No . . . I don't think so."

"Tomorrow?"

"I have to decide about the next couple of days."

He turned back toward his cabin. "It was just a thought. I surely won't pester you about it."

"No, Cooper, really . . . it's just . . ."

"Miss Dev, you just let me know when and if your social calendar is free."

"That was cold, Coop."

He turned back to her. "I reckon it was. There are a lot of social graces I'm rusty on, but that's no excuse. I would enjoy the visit any time we get a chance."

●   ●   ●

Casey's pickup bounced down the driveway to the dirt road. It wasn't until they passed the Sweetwater Grocery that Cree-Ryder spoke. "I like staying with you, Ms. Worrell."

"What prompted that?"

"If I'm at home, the most excitement I have in a week is gettin' kicked in the gut by a snotty two-year-old filly. But you? You get a note from Quint, a drive-by from Renny, and a walk-over from Cooper Tallon. All before eight a.m."

"You want all three of them?"

"Are you giving them away?"

"No, it's just everything's getting complicated. I think I'll keep one."

"I know which one," Casey beamed. "It's a simple choice. Pick the one with the big Wyoming ranch."

Develyn wadded up the note in her hand. "It's getting much more complicated than you think."

2

"Stop!" Develyn shouted.

Casey Cree-Ryder pulled over. "What's the matter?"

"I want to read that sign back there." Develyn unclicked her seat belt and shoved open the squeaky door.

"It's some sort of oil field sign."

Develyn grabbed her water bottle and hiked back through the soft yellowish dirt to the sign. Casey trailed along behind, a toothpick perched between her full lips.

Rubbing the back of her sweaty neck, then downing a swig of water, Develyn read the sign. "WARNING: Do not proceed if siren sounds or lights are flashing."

"What is this?"

Casey shrugged. "I told you. It's just some oil field sign."

"They have warning lights and sirens in the middle of the wilderness? Does oil flood down the road or what?"

Casey yanked off her cowboy hat. Her thick black bangs dropped to her eyes like a curtain. "I think this is a gas field."

"Are there refineries around here?"

"Natural gas." Casey shoved her hat back on. Her thick black braid drooped almost to her waist. "If it blows out in the atmosphere, it can settle down like invisible fog and ah, well . . . I reckon at that point it becomes a weapon of mass destruction."

Develyn took a deep breath. "Are we allowed in here?"

"As long as the lights aren't flashing." Casey took her arm and led her back to the truck.

Develyn glanced back over her shoulder. "Have you ever seen them flash?"

"I've never even heard of them flashing. I think it's one of those worst-case scenarios the government dreams up. These companies aren't going to let a squirt of that gas escape. It's their income."

They crested a rise and dusted their way down the draw when Develyn heard a buzz. When she jerked her head back, her hat tumbled into her lap. "What was that? Is that the gas alarm?"

Casey waved her long black braid like a pointer. "It's your cell phone, Ms. Worrel. Relax, girl. What's the matter with you?"

"I didn't think we'd get reception out here."

"Yet, you bought your cell anyway."

Develyn fumbled for her phone. "I hope it's not Quint."

"So that's it. Is that why you are uptight? There's something you don't want to tell him. Hmm," Casey grinned. "What was in that note? I reckon a gas field disaster is the last of your worries."

Develyn pressed the cell phone to her ear. "Hello?"

"Hi, Devy-girl. You riding the range today?"

"Lily! I'm glad it's you."

"It's nice to be welcomed."

Casey leaned across the bouncing pickup and hollered. "Hey, Lil' . . . you marry that lawyer yet?"

"Is that Casey?" Lily asked.

Develyn cleared the dust out of her throat. "Oh, yes."

"Tell her I'm not close to being married, but I do have a date tonight."

"Where are you off to?"

"An Alan Jackson concert in Indy."

"You are kidding. Without me?"

"Dev, you ran off to Wyoming to chase cowboys."

"I did not."

"Where are you right now?"

"In the middle of a natural gas field in Casey's pickup headed for Sage Canyon."

"What's at Sage Canyon?"

"I don't know. It's a secret."

"Whose secret? Your Quint's?"

Develyn lurched forward when Cree-Ryder hit the brakes to avoid a male pheasant that winged his way across the dirt road-way. "No, it's Casey's secret. Where are you, Ms. Martin?"

"Doing yard duty at Riverbend Elementary. You do remember that you are a teacher here?"

"How's summer school this week?"

"Besides Dougie Baxter stuffing towels in the toilet and flooding the hallway again?"

The truck hit a pothole and tossed Develyn to the ceiling and back. "Yes, besides that."

"Quiet. Of course, Tiffanee Percy is missing Ms. Worrell."

"She's a cutie."

"She's cuter now, with her hair cut short . . . just like Ms. Worrell."

"Oh, dear. I hope that's OK with her mother."

"Mom thinks it's wonderful. It's her daddy who pines over losing that waist-length hair. You know men and long hair, even on their daughters." Lily laughed. "What am I saying? All those cowboys love your short hair."

"Tell Tiffanee 'howdy' for me. Tell her to finish reading *Anna Karenina* by the first of August."

"She reads Tolstoy?"

"Lily, that girl reads everything in print. Long Russian novels keep her occupied and away from the short, trashy ones."

"Honey, I've got to get back to class in a minute, but I need to talk to you about something."

Develyn sat up and stared out the open window. "What's happening in Crawfordsville?"

"It's Dee."

Develyn's stomach felt wrung out like a wet rag. "What's my prodigal daughter doing?"

"Dev, she's OK. She's been working backup at the Beef

Haus. Maybe it's nothing. Listen, I might be out of line, but I have to tell you."

"I'm dying, Lil, what is it?" Develyn rubbed her temples with her fingertips.

"Honey, I've seen Delaney three mornings in the last week, and she's been sick every time."

"Sick?"

"Says she has the flu, but July in Indiana isn't the flu season."

Develyn stared out the window at the passing sage. *Lord, this would be a very good time to have peace that passes all understanding.* "She told me she isn't pregnant, if that's what you're hinting."

"That's why I didn't want to tell you. Look, girls make mistakes; we know that. I just wanted you to know. Maybe the subject will come up. You could say 'Lily told me you had the flu' and let her take it from there. Honey, I'll do whatever you want. I just had to say something."

"Thanks, Lil. You are a priceless friend. I'll check with Dee."

"Sure, Devy-girl. Let me know. I'll stop by and check on your cats or something this evening. Maybe I'll learn more."

"Before or after the concert?"

"Oh, yes, before the concert. I suppose my evening is rather busy. Oops, there's the bell, and Timmy O. just kicked the soccer ball off Jennifer Carnine's head."

"Heaven help Timmy!"

"I wish you were here, Ms. Worrel. Bye, honey."

"I bet you do. Bye, sweetie."

Develyn folded the phone and tucked it in her jeans pocket.

"And?" Casey prodded.

"Oh, summer school is summer school. All the normal things," Dev murmured.

"That's not what I'm asking. Is Delaney sick or pregnant or both?"

"She's not pregnant," Develyn snapped.

Casey stared out the front window. "You want me to change the subject?"

"What I want is a simple life," Develyn snapped. She leaned back against the pickup seat. "I'm sorry, Casey. That came out wrong. But there are some days I so envy you."

"You envy me? Which part? The part about being a Native American, Irish, Mexican, African-American mixed-breed? Or is it that I have no family? Maybe you are envious of the fact that unless there is another immaculate conception, there is no way I could be pregnant."

Develyn watched the distant rim of mountains to the north. "I'm sorry, Casey. I love your singleness of focus. You work with your horses and you enjoy it. That is what I envy."

"Oh, good, for a minute I thought you were jealous of my long black braid." A grin broke across Casey's round face.

"Do you know what I envy most? You make quick decisions. I let things eat away at me for days and weeks and years, and never decide anything in a hurry."

"You decided to spend the summer in Wyoming rather quick."

"Yes, and it turned out to be a great thing. That's my point."

Casey slowed down to turn. "But you still have hassles."

"Yes, but they are my fault." Develyn held on to the armrest as the truck and horse trailer lurched forward. "Are you sure this is a road?"

"I didn't say it was a road. It's just the way to get to where we're going."

"You see, I would still be parked back there wondering which way to turn. I need to make quicker decisions."

"Are you talking about Delaney . . . or Quint . . . or the trail to Sage Canyon?"

"Yeah," Develyn mumbled.

"Yeah, what? You aren't talking about your daughter now, are you?"

"I won't know anything until I talk to Dee," Develyn said. "So I suppose I'm thinking of my uncertainty over Quint Burdett."

"The mysterious note?"

Develyn flattened the wadded note on the leg of her jeans, and handed it to Casey.

"Are you sure you want me to read it?"

"I'm not even sure I wanted to read it."

Develyn waited several moments as they continued to bounce down the rutted dirt path.

Casey flipped her toothpick over with her tongue, then cleared her throat. "OK, what have you decided? Are you going with Quint to Powell?"

Develyn traced a question mark in the dust on the dashboard. "I wish I knew. Miss Cree-Ryder, what would you do?"

"Do you want to know what I would do if it were me? Or what I think Ms. Develyn Gail Upton Worrell should do?"

"Both."

The rutted trail ended. Casey drove across untracked prairie, then stopped in a clearing in the sage. "Here's where we unload."

"How can you tell? It looks like no one has been out here since the days of the Oregon Trail."

"That's what I love about Wyoming. It's still a wilderness." Casey shoved open her door as if expecting it to stick.

"You didn't answer my question. What would you do about the trip to Powell?"

"Dev, I need to ponder how to say some things. Give me a little time. I don't want you to shoot me if I blurt it out wrong."

"I won't shoot you." Develyn climbed out of the truck. "I didn't even bring a gun."

"I did."

● ● ●

My Maria followed Uncle Henry out of the trailer. With both horses saddled, they rode west off the embankment, down into a dry creek bed and into a stiff wind. Cree-Ryder yanked her battered felt cowboy hat down low in the front so that her braid swished in unison with her horse's tail. Develyn followed, but My Maria twitched her head often and needed a constant kick to keep up the pace. Uncle Henry trailed along behind, never losing sight of the others.

Devy-girl, you ran, but you couldn't hide. You're in the middle of Wyoming, but you still have decisions to make. Choices to eliminate. A daughter to understand. Lord, I hope that Delaney isn't pregnant. But I don't know if that is for my sake or hers. If she has sinned, she must confess it and I know you will forgive. I know this is wrong, but if she is pregnant, it will provide everyone more ammunition to say what a failure I am as a mother. Perhaps I am a failure and refuse to admit it.

Should I have shrugged off Spencer's infidelity? Then, at least, Dee would have been happy. Would he have died anyway? Would I be the rock-solid widow who hung in there to the end? The martyr? I couldn't, Lord. You know I couldn't. I needed more faith, I suppose. That was one time I acted quickly.

"You got it figured out yet?" Casey called back.

"Look," Develyn pointed to the north. "Antelope."

"We've passed several hundred pronghorn antelope this morning. Are you changing the subject?"

"I'm refocusing."

"What does that mean?"

"I'm tired of reliving the past. I'm going to live this day to the fullest."

"Good. Are you going to live tonight to the fullest too? And where will you be?"

"That's tonight, honey. I don't even know where I'll be an hour from now. My whole life is a surprise, a mystery. Come on, my beautiful bronze friend. Let's race to that lone cedar over there."

"It's not a cedar; it's a pinon pine."

"So much the better." Develyn kicked her heels into My Maria's side. They bolted up the incline. By the time they reached the rounded peak, the paint horse was at a gallop. The saddle slapped into Develyn's back side, and she transferred most of the weight to her knees.

She felt the stiffness in her neck relax as she gulped in the dry prairie air. *This is it, Lord. This is what I need. I don't want to make life-changing decisions. Not for me. Not for Delaney. You created this day, and I want to enjoy it. I want to catch every sound . . . wonder at every sight . . . and feel every bruise! Take care of me, Lord, because I'm doing a poor job of it myself.*

She reined up next to the scrubby little tree that was the only object taller than sagebrush on the horizon.

"I win!" she shouted as Casey rode up.

"You have the fastest horse. You didn't fall off this time."

"Yes, isn't that amazing?" Develyn gazed across the broad valley that stretched before them. "What's on the horizon?"

"The rimrock at Sage Canyon."

"We're almost there?"

"Don't let clean air fool you. It will take two more hours."

"Not if we race."

"You can't run horses all day, Devy-girl. These two need some walking in between. Are you in a hurry to turn back to the rig?"

"Nope. I was contemplating staying out here forever. No one could find me that way."

"Do you believe that?"

"Eh, no, not really." The wind stiffened. Develyn tugged her hat down lower in the front.

"Come on, then . . ." Casey led the way off the hill.

Develyn pointed to the west. "Is that a river down there?"

"A creek, not a river."

"What's it called?"

Popcorn stumbled, but Casey kicked his flanks. The Appaloosa bolted ahead. "I think Parker Creek. Maybe it's Crazy Woman Creek . . . Parker empties into it somewhere along here."

"Crazy Woman Creek? Is that why you brought me here?" Develyn laughed.

"No, I'm taking you to Sage Canyon."

Develyn rode up alongside Casey. "I love the name. I wonder if you lived here, would your address be Crazy Woman Creek, Wyoming? It wouldn't surprise my mother at all."

"You thinkin' of buildin' in here?"

They loped down the rolling prairie. "No, but look around. What do you see, Casey?"

"Absolutely nothing. No people, no cattle, no fences, no oil pipe, no houses . . . nothing."

"Yes, isn't it wonderful?" Develyn said. "No kid next door repairing his motorcycle. No meetings to attend at school every night. No garden club to impress with your flower bed. No sixteen-year-olds racing up and down the street. No twenty-year-old clerk at Target trying to hit on you. No traffic jams. It must be a wonderful feeling. Do you think this is the way Adam and Eve felt?"

Casey kicked Popcorn and picked up the speed. "I reckon they felt better than this, honey. Being naked in a lush garden with the man the Lord created for you sounds a whole lot better. Nothin' personal, of course. I enjoy your company."

Develyn's hand flew up over her mouth. She started laughing. "Yes! You are right again, Miss Cree-Ryder. You do have a way with words."

"What you mean is, I just blurt out what's in my mind without worrying about what others will think of me."

Develyn galloped up alongside Casey. "Yes, I suppose that's right. I wish I could be that way more."

"Yes, and then, maybe, you could have what I have. Wouldn't that be swell? A five-year lease on 160 acres of ground, twelve horses, an old pickup, two horse trailers, one of which has a camper that serves as my home. Oh, boy, Ms. Worrell . . . if you could only have what I have."

"Casey, what would you like to change in your life? I mean, you complain about all of that, yet it seems like you enjoy life."

"You know what, Dev? Meeting you and being your friend this summer is one of the best things that ever happened to me."

"Casey, that's a wonderful thing to say."

"But it's also made me unhappy with my life."

"Oh, dear."

"No, it's a good thing. I just realize that I'm ready for more."

"You mean find a husband, start a family . . . get a regular job and all of that?"

"Yeah, but nothing too routine," Casey grinned. "Let's face it, Dev . . . the man who marries Casey Cree-Ryder will be a brave man, indeed."

"And a fortunate one."

Casey reined up and faced Develyn. "Why do you say that?"

"Sweet Casey, you are the most loyal person I've ever met. You give everything to a relationship. You will make some lucky cowboy feel like he's king of the world."

"Wow, this is so cool." Casey cantered on down the slope. "Keep goin', you're on a roll. Tell me how wonderful I am, even if it's a stretcher."

Develyn laughed and rode up to the edge of the shallow, narrow creek. "I love it, Casey. You always say what's in my mind. Let's see how good you are at guessing. What's in my mind right now?"

"You want to pull off your shoes and soak your feet in the water."

"Close."

"I know, I know . . . you want to slosh around in the creek barefoot so you can feel the mud squish between your toes!"

"See . . . you do know what I'm thinking."

"If you plan on going to Powell with your Quint, we'd better make this a short stop."

Develyn slid down off My Maria and tied her to the stump of a dead cottonwood. She sat on the stump and pulled off her tennis shoes and white cotton socks.

Uncle Henry splashed out into the six-inch-deep creek.

Casey unbuttoned her jeans.

"What are you doing?" Develyn challenged.

"I don't want to get my Wranglers wet."

"But it's only a few inches deep. We can roll up our jeans."

"Not, me, Devy-girl." Cree-Ryder let her jeans drop to the dirt.

Develyn stiffened her back. "I am not wandering around in my underwear, no matter how remote we are."

"Neither am I." Casey tugged up her long T-shirt to reveal running shorts. "I came prepared."

"Whew . . . for a minute I was worried . . ."

Casey waded into the stream. "That we were going skinny-dipping in six inches of water?"

Develyn took two steps. Mud mashed the soles of her bare feet. "I wasn't sure."

The water was cool but not cold.

"This feels so good."

"It reminds me of running my fingers through a bowl of chocolate pudding."

"Pudding?" Develyn questioned.

"Sure, every kid's done that, right? It's a tradition like chewin' snoose on the first day of high school, or dropping a square of Jell-O in the rich girl's gym shorts."

"I've taught school over twenty years, and I've never heard of those."

"I reckon you have different traditions in Indiana," Casey mumbled. "So, what does the mud remind you of?"

"It takes me back to when I was eight. I was walking home from school after a rain storm. Dewayne . . ."

"Your twin brother?"

"Yes, Dewayne jumped in the puddles and tried to splash water on me. I wanted to get even, but I had on some new white tennis shoes."

"So you pulled them off and splashed in the puddles?"

"Yes, but I liked the feel of the mud between my toes so much that I never did try to splash him. I walked all the way home barefoot, then sat on the fire hydrant to pull my shoes on, so my mom wouldn't know."

"But your feet were all muddy."

"I ruined the shoe color, but my mother made me wear them all year anyway. I felt like a martyr, but it was worth it. I love this feeling. Didn't you have times when you hiked in the mud?"

"Sure, I got bucked off on a sandbar while crossing the Yellowstone one time when I was fourteen. I had to hike to shore and spent three hours catching a horse from hell."

"Oh, dear. I was hoping you had a more pleasant memory."

Casey splashed a circle around Develyn. "How high can you jump?"

"What kind of question is that? I don't jump well."

"I can jump pretty good for a well-rounded girl," Casey grinned. "You want to see?"

Develyn backed away. "What are you talking about?"

Casey splashed over to her. Then she leaped straight up out of the water, tucked her feet under her, then slammed them back into the creek. Water and mud sprayed all over.

"You . . . you . . . you did that on purpose!" Develyn stomped back, but only splashed water up her own jeans. She reached down and with her open hands plastered Cree-Ryder with water and mud.

Moments later, soaked with creek water and shrieking with laughter, they stopped.

"This is crazy, Casey," Develyn hooted. "I'm a middle-aged Indiana school teacher in the middle of absolutely nowhere having a water and mud fight."

"Where else could prim and proper Ms. Worrell have a mud fight?"

"That's true."

"I think you might want to clean up before you have your big weekend with Quint."

"I need to clean up before I get back on My Maria."

Casey took her hand. "It felt good, didn't it?" She led Develyn to the creek bank.

"It was wonderful."

"It seemed like a fitting exercise at Crazy Woman Creek."

Develyn nodded. "Yes, for five minutes I didn't have a worry in the world, except splashing water on you. Thanks, Casey. You're a great therapist."

"That's me: Dr. Cree-Ryder."

"Doctor of what?"

"Splashology."

"I love it."

Casey tugged her along the creek bank. "Come on, the clean water's upstream."

They stood in the clear water and washed their arms and legs.

"Casey, tell me what you would do about this deal with Quint."

"Do you really like him?" Casey asked.

"I think I do."

"What do you mean, you think you do?"

"I like him."

"Does he like you?"

"I think . . . no, he does like me. He's told me that."

"If it was me, I wouldn't go. Because if we like each other and that could lead to . . . you know, foolin' around. It's not that I'm all that pure and holy; it just scares the crap out of me."

"What?"

"Dev, this is kind of hard to talk about. And I haven't had anyone to talk to. But, when I was young I . . . eh, there were three of them, and they grabbed me . . ."

"Casey, no! Oh, no . . ."

"And I've been scared to death to get too close to a man since. That's why all the humor and threats." Casey's voice softened. "I've wanted to be different than I am. And I believe the Lord will help me change. But I'm not there yet. I'm sorry, Dev. Why did I blurt that out?"

Develyn hugged Casey's shoulder. "That's alright, honey. You can talk to me." She let out a sigh. "You're right about one thing. You have to have someone to talk to. I should know. This has been the first summer I've been able to face some things about myself. And you are probably right about the trip to Powell. I shouldn't go."

Casey led Develyn out of the creek. "That's not what I said. I gave you the reason that I wouldn't go. You have more will-power and experience than I do. I mean, you were married twenty years. You know what you're getting into. Who am I?"

"Being married twenty years only makes me old, not wise or self-disciplined. But I know what you mean. So what's the verdict? I know I have to decide on my own. But you are a really good friend, and I respect your advice. What do you think I ought to do?"

Casey tugged on her dry jeans. "You have to decide if you want to play Barbie with Ken."

"Is that what this is?"

"Quint wants to treat you like a Barbie doll. You are his beautiful plaything that he can dress up and pretend is his Miss Emily. He can lead you around and show you off. He wants to tell you where to go, what to do, what to think."

"That's . . . that's . . . that's not . . ."

Casey sat on the stump and tugged on her socks. "Not what?"

"It's not completely true. He's a very nice man. He still grieves for Miss Emily, but he needs to move on. Lindsay told me that. She thinks I'm just the one who can help him."

"Would you marry him, just to help him?"

"Marry? I'm not talking about marriage."

"Oh? You have never thought about that? You and Quint never talked about marriage?" Casey challenged.

"Only in a roundabout way. He asked me if I'd miss teaching after we were married."

"I think that's talking about it, alright." Casey grinned as she pulled on her boots. "What did you tell him?"

When she stood, Develyn sat on the stump. "Something

came up, and we didn't get a chance to finish the conversation. But we will."

"What will you tell him?"

Develyn wiped water and mud from between her toes. "I'd like to teach a few more years. It's what I do best."

"You mean, find a job out here? This is the boonies. Maybe you could get your pilot's license and fly to Casper every day to teach."

"It's not that simple." Develyn's socks felt wet as she pulled her tennis shoes over them. "I'd lose all my Indiana retirement."

"I don't think Quint Burdett's wife would have to worry about retirement."

"Maybe not. But it's a part of what gives me confidence in myself. And I need that."

"So, you don't want to teach in Wyoming?"

Develyn rolled down the cuffs of her wet jeans. "It's not even that easy. Wyoming schools are not going to hire a middle-aged teacher with a master's degree and all the credentials I have."

"It would cost too much?"

"Sure. They could hire a twenty-three-year-old fresh out of the University of Wyoming for about half the salary."

"So you would have to abandon teaching," Casey shrugged. "It would be like me giving up horses, I guess."

"Could you do that?" Develyn challenged as she squeezed the water out of the legs of her jeans.

"No one has ever asked. I suppose it depends on how much I needed the guy."

"Needed?"

"If my life was incomplete, unfulfilled, headed nowhere . . . sounds like my life story, doesn't it? . . . Anyway, if that's the way life was . . . then I think I could walk away. How about you, Dev? Is your life incomplete, unfulfilled, headed nowhere?"

"This summer seemed that way. But no, I'd have to say that isn't me."

"Then maybe you don't need to marry him," Casey offered.

"If I were to marry, Quint would be the type. He's tender, yet decisive. He's hard-working and yet has the respect of his men. He has a solid Christian faith and a well-disciplined life. He is quite predictable . . . steady . . . dependable."

"Dev, you do what you want, and I'll volunteer to be in your wedding party, if you'll have me. But it seems to me he wants to control your life. I don't think you'd be happy with that, but what do I know? No one on earth, not even my own mother, ever wanted to control my life. Maybe it's nice to have someone pick out your clothes, lead you around, and tell you where to shop and what to buy."

"Quint doesn't treat me that way . . . does he?"

"He's a really nice, rich, Christian man who is a controlling kind of person. If that's your type, you couldn't do better. Just get used to sequined blouses and being called Miss Emily from time to time. You will have to live up to his image of you, but I think you can do it. There, I'm through. Dev, you are a special friend, and I am not the one to give you counsel. Look at me. I'm a mess. I don't even know how you got all of that out of me. I'd let you pour a bucket of water over my head, if we had a bucket."

"You probably made more sense than you know."

"I did? Good, 'cause I was afraid you'd pull out your gun and shoot me."

"I told you I'm not carrying a . . ." Develyn paused. "Do you really have a gun?"

"Relax," Casey laughed. "I left mine in the truck."

Develyn brushed her damp blond bangs back. "Do I have mud in my hair?"

"Your hair, your shirt, your face, your jeans. You look good with a little darker skin."

"I suppose you think I'd look good with a long black braid."

"Sweetie, you would look as absurd with a long black braid as I would with short blonde hair. We're stuck with what we got."

"That's a good philosophy of life. But we do have some choices about the men in our lives."

"That's easy for you to say," Casey laughed. "You have choices. I have the simplicity of not having any to choose from. You ready to ride? We barely have time to reach the rim and back so you can go on your trip."

Develyn tightened the cinch on My Maria, shoved her left foot in the stirrup, and pulled herself up into the saddle. Her jeans felt wet, cold, and stiff against her legs. They rode straight west through scattered sagebrush toward a distant ridge.

"I'm glad we're out here today, Casey. It's great to get away and have time to think things through."

"And play?"

"Yes. I'm thinking you need to move to Indiana so we can have more times like this. I need more wide-open-space think time."

"Would you like me to move several Wyoming counties with me?"

"Do you mind?" Dev laughed.

"Or you could just move to Wyoming. I wonder if Quint would let me come visit from time to time?"

"Of course he would. Cuban, Tiny, and the boys won't mind as long as you don't tote guns and knives."

"You'd think of all men on earth, that cowboys would understand a girl's need to carry a gun. Listen, just in case you don't marry Burdett, you should buy yourself a little place out here. Then come back every summer and unwind. Doesn't that sound like a good idea?"

"Hmmm, you might be right. I would enjoy the peace and quiet."

My Maria broke into a fast trot, and the buzzing sounded again.

"Is that the gas warning?" Develyn called out.

Casey loped up beside her. "It's your cell phone, Devy-girl. What is this gas warning phobia of yours?"

Develyn fumbled in her pocket. "There can't be any reception out here! I have to go out on my front porch to use it at home in Indiana. I'm not going to answer it."

Casey raised her thick black eyebrows. "What if it's Delaney?"

Develyn reined up and sighed.

3

"Miss Dev, where are you?" The tone sounded stronger than mere inquiry.

Develyn surveyed the rolling brown prairie and matching brown burro. "Riding west from Crazy Woman Creek." Develyn thought of Quint's tender gray-blue eyes.

"What in the world are you doin' out there, darlin'?"

She glanced at Cree-Ryder, who slipped to the ground and yanked on her cinch. "Casey and I went for a ride. She said there's a . . ."

"Sometimes I think you let her influence you too much," he snapped, followed by a short pause. "I'm sorry, Miss Dev. I don't mean to be harsh. I got to missin' you real bad."

"That's sweet."

"So that's why I flew down here." There was an echo in his voice, as if inside a phone booth or the cab of a pickup.

"Where are you?" Develyn pulled her feet out of the stirrups and laid them alongside My Maria's neck as Casey tightened her cinch as well.

"At your cabin in Argenta."

She eased her feet back down. "What are you doing there?"

"Looking for you, of course."

"Quint, I didn't know you were coming down. I think I told you that this was a riding day for Casey and me."

"I surmised you would go out at daylight and be back by now."

Develyn couldn't hold back the chuckle. "What have I ever done to give you that idea?"

"Breakin' daylight was always Miss Emily's favorite time to ride."

"Schoolteachers only learn about daybreak from textbooks. But it's a nice day for a ride. The wind hasn't been too bad."

"Miss Dev, here's what I was thinkin'. We could fly up to the ranch for the afternoon and then go on up to Powell tonight for supper. Why don't you turn that wild horse mare around right now? I'll fly into Casper and pick us up some Chinese for lunch and be back here about the time you get in. We can grab a bite to eat while you're rubbing her down and then head up to the ranch."

Develyn licked her chapped lips. "Quint, we haven't reached our destination yet."

"Miss Dev, which would you rather see . . . me or more Wyoming sage?"

"Quint, this is . . eh . . ."

46

"I know it's crazy. I feel like a teenager at times. I haven't been this much in love since me and Miss Emily were young. I can't believe it myself sometimes. I always thought it was a gift of the Lord to have Miss Emily. And now to find another so identical in every way. I'm double blessed, honey. Listen, I'll go to the Imperial Dynasty and get you some Thai asparagus pork on crisp Sri Lanka noodles. Do you think Cree-Ryder is staying for lunch, or does she have somewhere to go? A you-and-me lunch sounds mighty nice right now."

"Thanks for all the suggestions, but today is trail ride day, and I want to finish . . ."

"Miss Dev, you worry too much." His voice was choppy, impatient. "You have the rest of your life to ride through Wyoming. You don't want to see everything in the first summer. I'll fly you out that direction one of these days. Do you think you can make it back here in an hour and a half?"

"No." The firm tone of her own voice surprised her.

There was a long pause.

"Sorry, Quint, that came out way too harsh."

"When will you be back?"

"I'm not sure. I assume it will be after dark."

"How will we make it to . . ."

"I appreciate the offer to go to Powell," she interrupted. "And even the shopping with Linds in Cody. I do want to get up there someday and see the museum. But I have these riding plans today, so I'd better skip the trip this time."

"If I hadn't phoned, would you have left me hanging? When were you planning on telling me this?"

"I wasn't sure how long this trip would last. Quint, I just need this ride to think some things through."

"Honey, what's wrong?"

"Nothing, Quint. You asked me if I'd like to go on the trip. I needed to think about it. It just doesn't work out today. I'm sorry."

"Something's wrong," he insisted. "What's going on? If I did or said something inappropriate, you'll have to let me know."

"Quint, everything's fine. You know how little I've gotten to ride over the years. It's so nice to be out here. That's why I came to Wyoming. I don't need to shop in Cody. There's nothing I want to buy."

"Oh, don't worry about the shopping. You can ride in Powell. I've got friends with a huge indoor arena. They could even give you some team penning lessons. You might enjoy that. You could ride all the time I'm at my meetings."

"I would love to learn more, but we have indoor arenas in Indiana. What we don't have is hundreds of miles of untamed prairie. It feels so good to be riding out here. Tell Lindsay I'm sorry. We'll do the shopping thing another time."

"No problem there. Lindsay can't go. Some unexpected foreign dignitaries are flying into Cheyenne, and the governor wanted her to be part of the reception committee."

"Lindsay isn't going?"

"It can be some peaceful you-and-me time. Doesn't it sound romantic? How about it, Miss Dev? The purdiest school teacher in Wyomin' isn't goin' to turn down this lonesome cowboy, are you?"

"Oh, how I like that western drawl. You cowboys are ever so charming."

"Then you'll go with me?"

"No, but you are charming. Enjoy your meetings, honey. Call me when you get home."

"Something is going on, and I want to know what it is. Look, I can fly out there and land this sucker on a roadway. Are you near a roadway?"

"Don't fly out here. Let's talk when you get back from Powell. The reception isn't too good, and we're about to drop down a draw."

"Miss Dev, I'm sorry if I sound pushy. You are so much like Miss Emily that I assume things about you that I shouldn't."

"Don't worry, Quint. There is nothing wrong . . . you are being you . . . and I'm being me. That's what the Lord wants us to do, right? I'll talk to you Monday. Bye."

"OK, Miss Dev. You know I love you as much as I know how."

"Yes, I know. Bye, Quint."

Dev shoved the phone back into her pocket. *Yes, he loves me as much as he knows how, with a heart that still belongs to Miss Emily.*

"Wow!" Cree-Ryder exclaimed as she remounted Popcorn. "I can't believe you shined him on like that."

"I didn't shine him on."

Casey kicked the Appaloosa, and they trotted west. "Of course you did. Riding out to Sage Canyon is the Wyoming equivalent of 'I have to stay home and wash my hair.'"

Develyn slapped the reins. My Maria bolted up next to Cree-Ryder. "He was pushing me."

"Of course he was. You're a beautiful lady, Develyn Worrell. You got a cowboy that's anxious to be with you. You must be used to that."

Develyn tugged the front of her straw cowboy hat down, then chuckled. "Casey, I haven't been around an anxious male since my honeymoon. I'm not even sure Spencer was anxious then. Just nervous."

"Oh, I'm often around anxious cowboys," Casey hooted. "Of course, they're always anxious for me to leave."

They rode side-by-side for several moments. The wind made a soft hum through the sage, and the crunch of hooves on crusted dirt added to the rhythm.

"Devy-girl, why did you decide not to go with him?"

"Because of the Thai asparagus pork on crisp Sri Lanka noodles."

Casey shoved her hat back. "What does that have to do with anything?"

"Quint was going to fly into Casper and pick up some Thai asparagus pork on crisp Sri Lanka noodles for lunch."

"And you don't like those?"

"I don't have any idea if I like them or not, but neither does Quint. That's the point. He assumed something, and didn't bother to ask."

"So, he was playing Barbie with you?"

"That's what it felt like."

"And Barbie rebelled?"

50

"Casey, you need to know that Quint is a very nice Christian man who is trying his best to get over a crushing grief. He just doesn't know how, but that's not his fault. He is kind and considerate and respectful. He's built a lifelong pattern of doing things; it's just not my pattern. At least, not yet. He really is a wonderful man."

"But he's not the right one for you?"

Develyn dropped the reins around the saddle horn and stretched her arms to the sky. She took a deep breath. "Not today. I may change my mind tomorrow. But today, I needed splashology more than grief therapy. I need to be right here with my best friend west of the Mississippi."

A wide smile broke across Casey's round, brown face. "I like that, Dev. But I hope you know what you are doing."

"Sweetie, the last time I knew what I was doing was when I posted grades at the end of the term. From then on, I've been trapped inside a pinball machine bouncing off one flipper to another."

"So what happened on the phone? I heard you tell him no to Powell. Was there something about Lindsay not going?"

"Yes, she had to be in Cheyenne. That would have made it more awkward. I needed this time away today to think about things, and he couldn't even give me that."

"You don't seem all broken up over it. How are you feeling?"

"To tell you the truth, Dr. Cree-Ryder, if I had a tub of Gatorade I'd pour it over your head right now."

Cree-Ryder twirled her long black braid. "To signify victory?"

"No." Dev galloped past her. "To get even with you for all that splashing."

* * *

An hour later, Casey Cree-Ryder reined up near the crest of Sage Canyon. "This is where we tie off the horses."

Develyn pointed to the west. "We can't ride to the rim?"

"Not blindfolded."

"Why would we want to be blindfolded?"

Casey slid to the ground. "Not we . . . just you. I told you I have a secret to show you."

"I didn't bring a blindfold." Develyn jammed her left foot in the stirrup and swung her right leg over My Maria's rump as she dismounted.

"I did. It's a tea towel, but it will do," Casey said.

"I can't believe this."

"Just wait, Devy-girl. I'll show you something you can't believe."

Uncle Henry plopped down on his side in the shade of some sage, while Popcorn and My Maria stood tethered to a large granite boulder.

Develyn could see the ground drop away just past the rise and a distant rim on the western horizon. "Is it some kind of valley?"

"Turn around." Casey tied the tea towel over Develyn's eyes. "It's Sage Canyon, remember?"

"But I don't . . ."

Casey spun her to the west. "Faith, girl. Now's the time to prove that you trust me."

Develyn took a deep breath and let it out slow. *Lord, I've known Casey for five weeks, and I'm letting her lead me blind to the edge of some remote canyon. It seems like I'm stumbling from one crazy stunt to another.*

Develyn shuffled along. Cree-Ryder's hands guided her shoulders. "This is freaky."

"A few more steps, Devy-girl." Casey's hand felt warm and sweaty as she took Develyn's arm. "Now, reach down there. What do you feel?"

"A big rock?"

"A petrified log. Sit down on it like it was a bench."

The cold hard rock bench pressed into her damp jeans. "I don't know why you have to . . ."

"Just wait, Devy-girl. I'm sorry the clouds have moved in and blocked the sunlight. When I pull the towel off, you'll see a deep valley. That's Sage Canyon. We're up on the east side of it on the rim rock. It drops straight down . . . don't get freaked . . . we're safe. But look straight against the base of the rim on the other side of the canyon and describe what you see."

"I hope it's a Starbucks, because I could use a latte right now."

"Are you ready?"

"Casey, why are you drawing this out?"

"It's a surge of extreme power. I have you under my control."

"Take off the tea towel, for Pete's sake."

Casey yanked at the towel. "Ta-dah!"

Develyn rubbed her eyes. "Are you kidding me?"

"Surprised, huh?"

"But . . . but . . . but . . ."

"Now, there's a schoolteacher's exhaustive vocabulary for you. You sound like an outboard motor."

"What's it doing out here?"

"Nothing for the last one hundred and eight years."

Develyn shook her head. "It's . . . it's . . . it's a castle!"

"They call it a mansion, but with the round stone turrets, it looks like a castle."

Develyn stood, hands on hips. "Who put it here?"

"They say that Count Antoine Pierre LaSage built it for his French wife in 1892. But the locals just call it Sage Mansion, if they know about it at all. This is technically LaSage Canyon."

It looks abandoned." Develyn pulled her hat off and ran her fingers through her short blonde hair.

"I heard that the family moved out before 1900. The wife hated Wyoming, but they couldn't go back to France. They were a part of the Mexican thing with Maximillian, and ended up without a country. Some say they moved to Montreal, and others claim Martinique. Anyway, ever since World War II, this has been oil company land and off-limits for anyone. Very few people know it's back here."

Develyn stared at the three-story Victorian house with white stone turrets and wrap-around veranda. "Even from way up here, it looks huge. So, it's just a big, empty castle in the middle of the wilderness?"

"They say all the outbuildings . . . shop, barn, corrals and all . . . burned down years ago. That's all that's left."

"What's inside?"

Casey plopped down on the petrified log and shoved her hat back. "I don't know anyone who's gone down there. It's inaccessible for most folks. Besides, it takes so long to get here to view it, it's time to turn around."

"I want to go see it," Dev insisted.

"Yes, well, I'm sure you do, sweetie. But the oil company that owns this part of the state has blasted away the old roadway that was carved into this side of the canyon. So from up here you either hang glide off the rim . . . or rappel down a rope."

"Are you telling me there is no way to ride a horse down there?"

"I'm telling you there is no way that I know of."

"Ah, hah! We'll just have to find one. I can't believe there is some place in Wyoming where we can't ride a horse."

"Dev, even if we did get down there it would be so late in the day, we couldn't make it back to the truck before dark."

Develyn paced in front of the seated Cree-Ryder. "We could stay all night in Sage Canyon."

"We didn't bring any gear, and with those clouds circling above we aren't goin' to sleep out on the prairie."

Develyn pointed her finger at the building. "I'm not leaving without seeing that castle."

Casey frowned. "I can't believe Ms. Conservative Indiana Schoolteacher is saying this."

Develyn raised her already upturned nose. "And I can't believe that Ms. Hang-Loose Bronze Bombshell is afraid to ride down there and check it out."

"I'm not afraid."

Develyn grabbed her arm and tugged her to her feet. "Then come on."

Casey raised one thick black eyebrow. "Did you call me a bronze bombshell?"

"Yes." Dev wrinkled her nose.

"No one has ever called me a bombshell before."

"Sweet Casey, someday you'll realize how cute and alluring you are. If you ever stop carrying guns and knives, maybe the men won't be scared spitless of you. Now, are you coming with me, or do you want to wait in the truck until I return?"

"Wait for you? I'd be arrested for second-degree murder if I left a city girl like you out here. Indiana schoolteacher abandonment is a crime in Wyoming. But what is your great plan for reaching the castle? You goin' to teach that paint horse of yours to fly?"

Develyn waved her arm to the left. "Does that stream flow south?"

"Yes."

"Then we'll ride south." Develyn shoved her hands in the damp back pockets of her jeans. "Then we can swing around until we come to the stream. All we have to do is follow it north until we reach the castle."

"There are two problems with your theory. First, this is a long canyon. It would be noon tomorrow, at best, before we got there."

"You got any plans for tomorrow?"

"And even if we had a tent, sleeping bags, and food for us and the horses, it wouldn't work. Down at the base of this canyon is a natural gas pumping station. It's huge, with a chain-link fence, attack dogs, razor wire, and everything. It blocks off the mouth of the canyon. Ever since 9/11, they've tightened security down there. This is one of those places a terrorist would love to blow up. I'm afraid there is no way down to the mansion." Casey poked her thumb toward the horses. "It's time we got back to the truck."

"What is this with you? You always complain that I never want to go anywhere. You sit around the cabin and whine that I never take you anyplace. So, now I propose some exciting adventure, and you just whimper around about wanting to stay home and watch reality TV or something."

Casey laughed and threw up her hands. "Oh, so this is your idea of a big date?"

"You told me yourself that you have never been to LaSage Mansion. Perhaps bronze bombshells don't have the courage of us plain mousy types."

"There's nothing mousy about your blonde hair."

"Nor real, either. The point is, you are all talk and no show."

"Oh, it's a dare, is it? Now you are casting aspersions on my racial mixture . . . my cowboy girl bravado . . . my hard-nosed attitude."

Develyn folded her arms across her mud-splattered, lavender T-shirt. "I'm merely stating that I'm surprised at your reluctance. Perhaps you should have stayed at the store and watched the soaps with Mrs. Tagley. I don't want you to ever complain again about your life being boring. Now run along, honey, and wait in the truck. My Maria, Uncle Henry, and I will go down there and have a grand adventure without you. Lock the doors and take yourself a nap. You can read it all in my best-selling autobiography or see it in the Hallmark movie."

Casey laughed so hard that she clutched her sides.

"Dev, you are terrific. You do know how to be loose and tease. This is a whole side of you I've never seen. I love it, girl. Wow."

"I always get a little spacey after I finally make a big decision. There is something so wonderful and freeing about it."

Casey put her arm around Develyn's shoulder. "All of this silliness because you decided not to go with Quint to Powell?"

"It's a little bigger decision than that." Develyn slipped her arm around Casey's waist.

"You mean?"

"Yeah, that's what I mean."

"Poor Quint . . . he had his heart set on Miss Dev."

"No, Casey, his heart was still on Miss Emily. It was the rest of his body that wanted Miss Dev."

Casey dropped her arm to her side. "I can't believe you said that. I mean, that's the kind of thing I'd blurt out, but not you."

"We seem to have a role reversal. Come along, my brown wimpina, we are visiting the LaSages tonight. They are expecting us for tea at 4:00 p.m., and you know how testy they are if we're late."

Casey Cree-Ryder drew her braid across her upper lip like a mustache. "I don't have anything to wear."

"Don't wear the black scoop-necked formal. It's much too revealing. The countess will be livid."

Casey stared down at her clothes. "I was thinking of perhaps wearing the basic navy blue sleeveless T-shirt."

Develyn raised her eyebrows. "The mud-splattered one?"

"Yes."

"You'll be the hit of the party."

"Oh, good." Casey led Develyn back to the horses. "Do you think the LaSages will serve slugs and salmon eggs?"

"Yes, of course."

Casey untied the horses. "I won't eat them."

Develyn pulled herself up into the saddle. "Then you'll just go hungry, young lady."

They rode to the north, a few feet parallel from the canyon rim. Uncle Henry scuffed along, fifteen feet behind.

"Dev, look . . . setting aside all the laughing and teasing, there really isn't any way to get down there."

"What about that old adage that horses have four feet for balance and can go where humans can't?"

"Yes, but even with twelve feet, there are some inclines you can't go down."

"Where is the old roadway?"

"Follow me."

Within minutes they sat horseback staring down at an avalanche of boulders that dropped off the rim for a thousand feet.

"What is that?" Develyn asked.

"That's the old roadway."

"Road? The ruins of Pompeii look better than that."

Casey nodded to the east. "Now, can we go back?"

Develyn stood in the stirrups. My Maria shifted a little to the right. "Are you sure there isn't some other way?"

"The only thing I'm sure of is that there is no way down except through the oil company gate."

Uncle Henry trotted up between the horses, then leaned against Develyn's leg.

"Why don't we circle the entire canyon?"

"Dev, it would take too long. We would be stuck out here in a thunderstorm at night."

"I just can't give up on the idea."

"Let's turn back."

"Casey, I don't want to go back."

"You mean, you don't want to take a chance that Quint is waiting for his Miss Dev?"

"That's not what I said."

Casey tugged on the collar of her T-shirt. "Why don't we ride back to the truck, trailer up, then go into Lander or Riverton? There's a good pizza place in Lander. We can hang out there until it's safe to go home."

"You make it sound like I'm trying to avoid Quint. I really want to see the mansion, that's all."

60

"You can prove that it has nothing to do with Quint."

"How?"

"Let's go home."

"Go home?" Develyn moaned.

At the sound of her words, Uncle Henry plodded forward, stepped around each boulder, as he plunged off the side of the cliff.

"Honey, I didn't mean go down there," Develyn called out.

The burro continued to meander forward.

"Uncle Henry, you get back up here right now!" Dev shouted.

Casey rode over next to her. "He's not minding you, mama."

"If we turn around, he'll have to follow."

"Or maybe that's his home down there," Casey said.

"The mansion?"

"The canyon. Rumor has it that the count just packed up some of their clothes and deserted the place . . . furniture, livestock, and everything."

"Where did Uncle Henry go?" Dev asked.

"He's behind those boulders, see?"

Develyn prodded My Maria to the edge of the canyon. Instead of stopping, the horse eased down the side of the cliff.

"What is she doing?" Develyn called out.

"She's following Uncle Henry. Whenever she gets scared, she follows Uncle Henry."

Develyn clutched the saddle horn and leaned back. "Can My Maria make it down this grade?"

"I hope so, Devy-girl, because she can't turn around, that's for sure."

"What are we going to do?" Develyn hollered back up the cliff.

"We?" Casey yelled. "I think I'll just go back to the truck. This is too scary to watch."

"Casey!"

"OK . . . OK . . . I'll follow until we find a place big enough to turn around."

My Maria's horseshoe slipped on the granite rock.

"Oh, no!" Develyn cried out.

The horse regained her footing.

"Hang on, Dev, you're doin' fine," Casey called out from somewhere behind.

"Fine? Any moment now I expect to plunge to my death. This is a lot steeper than I thought. What am I doing here? I'm just an Indiana schoolteacher."

"A crazy schoolteacher."

"Crazy, but not brave like a bronze bombshell I know."

"Devy, this bronze bombshell is scared to death. I don't mind going to heaven, but being mangled on the rocks while the buzzards pluck out my eyeballs is not my idea of dying with dignity."

"This is not funny!" Develyn hollered. "What are we going to do?"

"Hang on and pray that Uncle Henry knows what he's doing."

"Casey, don't let the buzzards pick at my bones."

"Look at him go. Uncle Henry seems to know every place to put his foot. All we have to do is have the horses step where he's stepping."

"Look at him? I'm not going to open my eyes." With reins laced around her fingers, Develyn clutched the cold, leather-covered saddle horn with both hands. She slid forward in the saddle until her thighs pinched tight against the fork of the saddle. Her wet jeans rubbed her raw. She tried to lean back on the cantle and keep the toes of her tennies jammed into the stirrups.

Lord, I don't know how to have an adventure. I spend my entire life doing the safe thing. Then I lose all sense of reason and do something like this. Why can't I just have little . . . mostly sane . . . adventures? Why did I have to jump head over heels . . .

Develyn flipped open one eye and spied Uncle Henry's rump a few feet in front of her.

Bad choice of words, Lord. Maybe Mother is right. Maybe I don't have a lick of sense . . . whatever that means. There has to be something between a safe life and a terrifying one.

I'm not sure if I'm talking about my life or my relationship with men.

"Are you doing OK, Devy-girl?" Casey called out.

My Maria slipped. Develyn gasped. Then the paint horse regained her footing. "I'm just . . . talking to the Lord . . ."

"Yeah, I'm praying too. I haven't prayed this much since riding in a yellow cab in New York."

"You've been to New York?"

"I go there every year for the opera season."

"What?"

"Sure, last year it was *Candide, Orlando,* and *The Pearlfishers.* This year it will be *Carmen* and *Madame Butterfly.* But my favorite is Puccini's *The Girl of the Golden West.*"

"You don't really go to New York for the opera, do you?"

"No, but it took your mind off dying for a minute, didn't it? I went to a horse show once in Madison Square Garden. How many times have you been to the Garden?"

Develyn blinked open an eye, gasped, then slammed it shut. "I really . . . don't . . . think . . . this . . . is . . . a . . . good . . . time . . . to . . . talk."

"Yes, it is. Close your eyes and hold on to the saddle horn. My Maria will make it down on her own, or she won't. But either way she has no intention of listening to you. So let's talk about cities. Do you like Chicago?"

"I like the north side and the lake front . . . but I've gone to Chicago all my life. There and Indy."

"How about L.A.? Ever been there?"

"No, have you?"

"Nah, but I've been to Dallas and Houston. I like Dallas best."

"I like Houston. Have you ever been to Miami?"

"No, but I've been to Orlando."

"I don't like Miami too much, but I like the Keys."

"I'd like to go to Seattle some time."

Develyn felt more relaxed even as My Maria stumbled step by step. "So would I. Ever since I saw . . ."

"*Sleepless in Seattle?*"

"Yes. I love that movie."

"The kid is annoying, but I love the movie anyway," Casey said.

"I like the scene . . ."

"Where Meg Ryan . . ."

"Is standing in the . . ."

"Roadway . . ."

"Staring at Tom Hanks . . ."

"And the traffic is whizzing . . ."

"By, and their . . ."

"Eyes meet and then . . ."

"She takes off . . ."

"But they know."

"Yeah," Develyn sighed. "They know . . ."

"Look at . . ."

"At the hearts on the Empire State Building?"

"No!" Casey shouted. "Open your eyes, Dev!"

"Oh . . . no!" Develyn hollered. "Uncle Henry . . . wait."

Loose gravel littered the last half of the descent. Uncle Henry tucked his rear legs under him as he began to slide.

"Can he do that?" Develyn said. "Can we do that?"

"I hope so, because we can't go back up unless Uncle Henry leads the way."

My Maria stopped. Dev's feet, still in the stirrups, were shoved up by the horse's neck. "I don't know what to do."

"Spur her forward."

"I'm not putting my feet to her flanks. I'd tumble over her head."

"Then slap her backside."

"And turn loose of the horn?"

"You can't stay there. Uncle Henry slid on down the hill."

"Hill? This is like jumping out of a fifty-story building."

"More like a hundred-story building, but who's counting? Give me a second, and I'll ride down and slap My Maria."

"No!" Develyn hollered. "I'll do it. If I'm going to die, it will be my own responsibility. I don't want you to live with that guilt."

"Guilt? I'll be just as dead, sweetie."

Develyn laid back until the Cheyenne roll of the cantle mashed into her lower back. She stared straight up at the clouds that now blocked the Wyoming sky. "Now would be a very good time for the Lord's return."

"Are you going to wait for him?"

"No. But I don't want to rush things anyway."

"Did you ever go to Disney World?" Casey asked.

"I went to Six Flags, instead."

"Did you ever sit at the top of one of those rides, and just before it drops off into certain death, you said 'what am I doing here?' and yet you did it, and you lived through it all and everything?"

"No."

"You never went on a scary amusement park ride?"

"Never. What's your point?" Develyn said.

"Forget it. Kick her neck with the heels of your shoes and shout 'giddyup.' I'll see you at the bottom."

"Are we goin' to die, Casey?"

"Nope. Look at Uncle Henry. If you had been riding him, you'd almost be there by now."

Develyn reached up and tugged her hat down in the front, then grabbed the saddle horn again. "Bye, Casey . . ."

"Bye, Devy!"

"Giddyup!" Develyn slammed the heels of her tennis shoes into the paint horse's neck.

My Maria lurched forward as wind and dirt blasted her face. Develyn fought to stay in the saddle. The paint horse slid, then tried to stand, then stumbled, then slid some more. Develyn thought she might be screaming something, but she couldn't hear anything. A roar like an imploded building crashing to the ground. The dust was so thick she could not see My Maria's head, so Develyn clamped her eyes and mouth shut.

When she could hold her breath no longer, My Maria stopped. Develyn slid forward, her belt buckle caught on the saddle horn. The paint horse snorted and staggered forward.

"Devy!"

"Casey? Where are you?"

"Do you see any angels?"

"No."

"Do you see any of those other guys?"

"No."

"Then I think we're alive. We're on level ground, at least level rock. Climb down and lead My Maria straight ahead."

Develyn tugged the horse only a few feet as the dust started to drift to the east, and she spotted a dirt-covered

Casey Cree-Ryder. Popcorn now looked like a solid brown horse. Only Casey's tongue and eyeballs looked clean.

"We did it, girl!"

"Yes!" Develyn yelled. "We lived through it!"

"Look up there."

"Oh, my word," Develyn gasped. "What . . . what happened to the old roadway?"

"It sloughed off. We rode an avalanche down the mountain."

"How did we do that?"

"You mean you don't do that back in Crawfordsville?"

"I don't even ride the whip at the Montgomery County Fair, let alone an avalanche. The old roadway is gone."

"Only halfway down."

"How will we get out of here?"

"Oh, now you ask that?"

Develyn searched the narrow valley. "Maybe we could slap Uncle Henry in the rear and tell him to go home."

"We told him to go home, and this is where we ended up."

"Am I as dirty as you?" Develyn asked.

"You look very good all brown. It beats that pathetic white skin of yours."

"What are we going to do now?"

"We're going to call on the LaSages, remember?"

"Like this?"

Casey smeared her cheeks. "We'll ask to use the ladies' room to freshen up a tad."

Develyn pointed across the canyon floor. "Uncle Henry's over by those green trees. Shall we ride?"

"My Maria and Popcorn need a break . . . let's walk . . . or stagger. There must be a spring that feeds those trees. Maybe we can wash off there."

"Let's go look at the mansion before it gets dark."

"Sure, and what do we do after dark?"

"I've got no idea."

"Dev, are you sure this beats going to Powell with Quint Burdett?"

"I don't know how I will clean up, where I will spend the night, or how I will get out of here. I don't know when I'll get my next meal or whom I will talk to next on the cell phone. There are a million things I am not sure of, but there is one thing I do know. I'd rather be right here, bruised and filthy, than flying off to Powell tonight." She pulled off her cowboy hat and felt a handful of dirt tumble down the back of her shirt. "However, I do hope the LaSages don't mind if company drops in."

It seems strange that the LaSages would invite us for tea, then aren't here when we arrive." Casey peered though the yellow chez curtains that stretched inside the tall windows of the mansion.

Develyn strolled down the veranda. "You don't suppose we have the wrong day?"

"Shoot, Devy-girl, I think we have the wrong century." Casey smeared the dirt on the window with the hem of her T-shirt. "Hey, this is the living room."

Develyn held her hat in her hand. "It was probably called the 'great room' back then. Wouldn't it be fun to look at the whole house?"

Casey smashed her round nose against the window. "I don't think there's any furniture."

"Not after one hundred years." The wooden porch squeaked under Develyn's tennis shoes. "I'm going to try the back door. There has to be another way in."

"It has a big staircase. I can see that. This house is so totally out of place. How in the world did they get all the materials back here in 1890?"

"I suppose if you have enough money, you can do anything."

Casey glanced back out into the canyon. "But why here?"

Develyn licked bitter yellow dust off her narrow lips. "If they needed to hide out from anyone, this would be the place."

When Casey glanced up she had dirt on the end of her nose. "You make it sound like international intrigue."

"That beats a story about successful sheep ranching. As long as we're pretending, we might as well have some adventure."

Casey leaned against the window again. "Did you ever live in a house with a wide, curving stairway?"

"I've lived in a two-story house, but the stairway was rather boring."

"I lived in a barn loft for two years, but I had to climb down a ladder or rope," Casey murmured.

Develyn strolled the veranda to the north and left Casey at the window. *Casey is so matter-of-fact. Living in a barn loft and climbing down a rope? She makes it sound so routine and ordinary.*

Finding a clean spot on her T-shirt, Dev rubbed the window.

This must have been the kitchen. It's twice the size of mine in

Indiana. It looks a lot like Quint and Lindsay's. But there is nothing in it except that island and a cookstove . . . at least I think that's a cookstove. Empty kitchens look bigger.

She hiked around to the west side of the house. Fifty feet behind the house, wild rose bushes sprawled and clung to the side of the canyon.

They must have jammed the house against the cliff to break the wind. Or to keep anyone from sneaking up on them. It's strange to see rose bushes out here. But they cover up the canyon wall . . . the rock is broken and jagged, but it all looks smooth covered with roses.

I'm sure this whole canyon is beautiful in the spring when the creek runs full and the meadow is green. I wonder how far it was to the neighbors? And who does a French countess visit with, anyway? I wonder if she was ever lonely and cried herself to sleep at night? I've spent way too many nights crying myself to sleep.

The wide back door had eight panels, all with cracked and peeling white paint.

Lord, I haven't cried myself to sleep since I came to Wyoming. I like that. Not that my problems have disappeared. I still feel guilty about Spencer's death. I'm still worried about my Delaney. I still don't know if I will spend the rest of my life alone. But I don't lie awake at night staring at the dark ceiling. I hope the countess enjoyed Wyoming as much as I do.

Develyn studied the weeds in the backyard.

I wonder if she had a manicured garden? That looks like an archway in the roses. An archway to what? Maybe it's just a façade to convince her she had a bigger yard. Did she stroll out here in the summertime and pretend she was in Paris? OK, maybe not Paris . . .

but it must have reminded her of something. You can't just move to a foreign land without shaping some of it like home. But if she had been in Mexico . . . and Martinique . . . I wonder where her home was?

The veranda stretched to the back door, then the house jutted out. The round glass door handle felt cold. It was so slick Dev couldn't tell if she turned it, or if her hand slid over it.

Without any sound, the door jerked open.

A gauze-draped woman glared at her.

Every hair on Develyn's body stood straight up. She fought to breathe. "Oh, my word! Oh, Lord Jesus . . ." she cried.

"If you're applying for the maid position, come back when you are properly attired," the woman growled, with a raspy voice, then slammed the door.

Develyn hugged herself hard to try to keep from shaking all over. Her teeth chattered. She felt tears flood down her dusty face.

I don't want to be here, Lord . . .

The door flung open again.

A brown face and familiar long black braid greeted her. "Whoa, for a second there, I fooled you, didn't I?"

"Casey! You scared the life out of me!"

Cree-Ryder glanced down at Develyn's jeans. "Are you sure that's all I scared out of you? These curtains make a good shawl, don't you think?"

"This is not funny, Casey."

"Now, Ms. Worrell, stop being such a schoolteacher. You've been saying that I'm not adventuresome, that you wanted to do something exciting, right?"

"I didn't want to be that excited."

"Well, don't just stand there. Come on in and look around."

Develyn stepped into a small room with empty floor-to-ceiling shelves. "How did you get in?"

"I used my best attribute."

"Which is?"

Casey wiggled. "I threw my hips against the front door and it popped open. Sometimes it's good to be built like a quarter horse. Not often, but sometimes. It's a dusty mess in here."

"I am sure under this blonde hair coloring, my hair is now—thanks to you—totally gray."

"I don't want your life to be so boring."

"Boring? I was only teasing, and you know it." Develyn tried to hold back, but couldn't keep from laughing. "I haven't had a boring minute since I met you."

Casey grinned. "You braggin' or complainin', Devy-girl? Look at this? What do you think this is?" She pointed to a large deep shelf with ropes hanging alongside it.

"It's a dumbwaiter. You pull those ropes and the shelf goes up like a little elevator to the upper floors."

"No foolin'? You mean, like breakfast in bed and all?"

Develyn wiped thick dust from the dumbwaiter and studied her finger. "I suppose so."

"Hey, that's cool."

Following Casey, Develyn strolled through the kitchen with a twelve-foot ceiling. The great room was bare, but it was lined with rich dark paneling and a gigantic rock fireplace. "Oh, my, this must have been quite a room in its day."

With daylight dying outside, each room turned musty, dark, and empty.

Casey headed for the wide mahogany staircase. "Wow, this is the kind of stairway Miss Scarlet would descend. I wonder how Countess LaSage felt as she scurried down this sucker."

"I don't imagine the countess ever had to scurry anywhere."

"I think she scurried out of Mexico when the French were driven out."

Develyn laced her fingers in front of her rib cage. "Maximillian von Hapsburg was executed in Mexico in 1867. Napoleon III had pulled the French troops out before then. They didn't build this mansion until the 1890s. They were up to something for those twenty-five years. Perhaps they ran contraband out of Africa."

"Oh, so the schoolteacher is coming out. I prefer something more refined. Perhaps there was court intrigue. Or supporting the wrong side in the revolution."

"What revolution?"

"It doesn't matter," Casey grinned.

"I just wonder how old she was when she moved to Wyoming. I will have to Google this next time I'm online."

As if practicing karate, Casey led the way, slicing through occasional cobwebs. The second floor consisted of six large, empty rooms.

"This one leads out to the tiny balcony over the front door."

"That makes this the ladies' parlor, the sitting room," Develyn explained.

"How do you know that?"

"Many houses from that era were built this way. The ladies in the house would sit here and read or sew as they awaited dinner."

"Where would the men be?"

"Down in the drawing room, the one with all the shelves, smoking pipes and cigars."

"Devy-girl, did you ever smoke a decent cigar?"

"I'm not going to fall for that bait."

"I think this is the biggest house I've ever been in."

"I'm still amazed that it survived this well. Other old buildings we've seen in Wyoming are about to fall over," Develyn added.

"With that rim of the canyon so close to the house, it gets dark here early."

"Yes, and they must have had only kerosene or oil lamps. All this natural gas so close, but undiscovered."

"That's just like me!"

"Natural gas?"

"Great value so close, yet undiscovered." Casey marched through the rooms again. "Listen, Ms. Worrell, I do have two serious questions. How in the world do we get out of this canyon before it's pitch dark?"

"And the second question?"

"How did they get up to the third floor? There's no stairway."

"Perhaps the stairway collapsed."

"If it did, there should be some ruins, or a hole in the ceiling where it used to go through . . . or something."

"There has to be stairs somewhere."

"You find them."

Casey and Develyn circled the rooms two more times, then returned to the central parlor. "This room on the south side must have been the main one," Dev said. "It has the dumbwaiter. Maybe they never finished those rooms upstairs."

"Then why the curtains on the windows? And even if unfinished, there would be a stairway someplace. No one would haul building materials this far for a façade . . . would they?"

"Oh, you know the Countess LaSage. She always seemed a little strange."

Casey waltzed around the empty room. "Do you remember the time she showed up at the costume ball dressed as an eggplant?"

Develyn slipped her arm into Casey's. "Or how about the time she fired her entire kitchen staff because of burnt toast?"

"Speaking of burnt toast." Casey waved her thick black braid. "How about the time she appeared as a ghost at the back door and scared the heebie-jeebies out of that blonde choregirl!"

"Choregirl? Don't get personal," Develyn said.

"The dumbwaiter!" Casey shouted.

"The dumbwaiter, what?"

"That's how they got to the third flour. It's like a citadel in a castle, the fortress within a fortress. Does the dumbwaiter go up from here?"

Casey and Develyn scampered to the open cupboard with ropes. When Casey tugged on the rope, the shelf rose higher and higher.

"It does go up!" Casey exclaimed.

"I'm sure they could transfer goods from every level. But it's not an elevator."

"But it could be a temporary one."

Develyn pulled off her straw cowboy hat and scratched the back of her head. "What are you talking about?"

"One of us should get in there while the other one cranks her up to the third floor."

"What?"

"Come on, Dev, how many times do we get a chance to take our life to a new level?"

"Is that what that saying means? Just who do you think should crawl in that hole?"

"Naturally, the strongest one should pull the ropes and the lightest one ride."

"You want me to risk my life in a tiny coffin held up by one-hundred-year-old rotten ropes?"

"I want you to have the joy of discovery."

"What am I going to discover?" Develyn folded her arms across her chest.

"Fabulous jewels . . . or . . . dead bodies . . . or both!"

"I don't think I like this, Casey."

"You know it has to be this way. I can't crawl in there. I'm just too, eh . . . ."

"Shapely?"

"Yes, and you're too much of a wimp to pull me up. The only way we'll find out what's up there is for you to hop in."

"Or we could leave and just assume it is as empty as the rest of the house."

"Oh, I couldn't do that to you."

"To me?"

"Devy-girl, you know for a fact all winter long you'd lay awake in your king-sized Indiana bed and . . ."

"Queen-sized . . ."

". . . and say to yourself, 'If only we had checked out that third floor. My entire life would have been different. If I had only listened to that attractive and very charming African-Irish-Mexican-Native American bronze bombshell."

"That's what I'm going to think all winter long?"

"Yes, I'm quite sure of it."

Develyn hiked over to the dumbwaiter and peered in. "Casey, this is beyond crazy."

"Of course it is. What's your point?"

"I could hurt myself. What if the ropes break?"

"You can only fall one floor. That's no worse than jumping off the roof of your house. Everyone's done that."

"I never did that."

"What do you do on Halloween in Indiana? Anyway, trust me. You won't get hurt."

"Why is it that every time I've been told, 'trust me,' I've been hurt?"

"That's because of the people you used to hang around with. Now that you have raised your quality of friendships, you will have to develop more trust."

Develyn pointed to the shadows in the yawning mouth of the dumbwaiter. "What if there are spiders up there?"

"Yeah, well, if you just want to speculate on the unknown . . . what if Leonardo DiCaprio is up there waiting for you with champagne and caviar?"

"Eh . . . DiCaprio doesn't do it for me. He's way too young."

"Would you prefer Mel Gibson with grande-breve latte and a low-carb Subway sandwich? Or Sean Connery with Ensure and a bowl of Jell-O?"

"I'll take Mel."

"There you go. Hop in, Ms. Worrell. Mel awaits you."

"Do you promise me nothing totally gross will happen?"

"I cannot imagine anything disastrous."

"I can." Develyn crawled into the dumbwaiter and tucked her knees under her chin. "What am I supposed to do when I get to the third story?"

"Holler down what you see."

"You want me to lower the dumbwaiter down and pull you up?" Develyn asked.

"No way. You aren't going to get me in there!"

"Not even for DiCaprio?" Develyn teased.

"Not even for DaVinci." Casey tugged on the dusty, rough hemp ropes.

The little closet darkened, the air stagnated and the pulleys squeaked as Develyn lurched upward.

I don't like to be confined. You know that, Lord. In the middle of the boonies of Wyoming I crawl into a box smaller than a coffin. This is insane. This is not working. I've got to get out of here. Right now!

Just as Develyn kicked her feet forward, the squeaking stopped. The dumbwaiter slammed against the top beam. Her feet forced a cabinet door open, and twilight broke across her. She crawled out into a huge room that looked as if it encompassed most of the entire third floor.

It's furnished! This room . . . this suite is still furnished!

She heard Casey yell something, but it was so muffled she couldn't distinguish the words. There was a thin layer of yellowish dust over everything in the room.

She surveyed a high bed with tall white posts trimmed in gold, wardrobe closet, dressers, a sitting desk, and big leather chairs. A silver and black dress with full skirt hung, yellow-dusted, on a wooden peg in the far wall. She found oil lanterns, a cherry-wood pen set, with black ink . . . long dried. Oriental rugs spread across the wooden floor. Pewter-framed photographs stood as a witness to former occupants. On the wood paneling at the far side was an oval oil portrait of a beautiful dark-haired lady in royal attire. Develyn tiptoed over and studied the brass plate at the bottom of the frame.

Lord, I feel like I'm intruding. This is the countess' private room. These are her things. This was her life. It's like a time machine. I halfway expect her to walk out of the closet and ask what I'm doing here. What am I doing here?

She heard bangs and shouts from the second floor.

Casey! I have to find the stairs.

A polished mahogany door on the west side of the room revealed a steep staircase. Develyn crept down the darkened stairs. The only light came from the open third-story door behind her. When she reached the bottom, she groped the wall and found a cold brass door handle. She turned it slowly and flung it open. "Ta-Dah!" she hollered.

A strong arm slapped around her shoulders, threw her against the wall. A hunting knife waved in front of her nose. Then the strong arms dropped away from her.

A wide smile appeared. "Devy-girl, you scared me to death."

"I scared you? Casey, where did you get that knife?"

"I always carry a knife."

"Where do you carry it?"

"Don't ask." Casey peered up the stairway. "Is Mel Gibson up there?"

"Not hardly."

"Are there spiders?"

"I didn't see any."

"What is up there?"

"You'll have to come see. Why didn't we find this doorway?" Develyn asked.

"The door handle must have fallen off. Or got stolen. With recessed hinges, it just looks like the paneling."

"All her things are still up there," Develyn whispered.

"The countess?"

"I believe so." When they reached the room, Develyn waved her arms. "Just look at everything."

Casey shoved her cowboy hat back. "Is that her picture?"

Develyn folded her hands in front of her, like a schoolteacher on the first day of class. "No, I believe that is Empress Eugenie. She was the . . ."

". . . Scottish/Spanish royal who married Napoleon III, and went into exile with him to England after he was defeated by Otto von Bismarck at the Battle of Sedan on September 2, 1870," Casey finished.

"Eh . . . yes, I think so . . ." Develyn murmured. "How did you know that?"

"I watched *Jeopardy* a lot when I was a kid." Casey stalked around the room. "Wow, is this cool or what?"

"Miss Cree-Ryder, I think you're a straight-A student hiding behind a rough-and-tumble wilderness girl routine."

"I didn't get straight A's," Casey shrugged.

"It wouldn't have surprised me . . ."

"I got a lousy B+ in trig on my last quarter, thanks to good old Mr. Whitney."

"Tough subject?"

"Nah, I seldom needed to crack a book. I think it had something to do with letting the air out of the tires of his old VW . . . and the dead raccoon in his trunk."

"You did that?"

"I don't want to talk about that. Let's just say he deserved it." Casey strolled to the dresser. "Shoot, he probably deserved to be in jail." She plucked up an ivory-handled brush and blew dust clouds off it. "Maybe we should finish looking around. Because I still don't have a clue how to get us out of this canyon, a fact that doesn't seem to concern you at all." She brushed her bangs and grinned in a dirt-filtered mirror.

"We'll use the secret trail up the back of the canyon."

"What secret trail?"

"There is always a secret trail out of a box canyon. Didn't you ever watch those B westerns when you were a kid?"

"What's a B western? Ronald Reagan was president when I was a kid."

Develyn studied the dress hanging on the wall. "You know what, Miss Cree-Ryder? We ought to stay here tonight."

"In this house?"

"In this room." Develyn opened a bright red and green Chinese fan in front of her face. "I don't think the countess will mind."

Casey picked up a glass lantern and sloshed the oil. "Do you have a match?" She tugged open a drawer. "Oh . . . here!" With a flip of the wrist the long stem match was lit, then the soaked wick of the lantern. "We didn't exactly come prepared for an overnight stay. We really need to go."

"Casey, you've always been so negative. Even when we were little girls, you never wanted to sleep in the tent in the backyard."

Casey laughed. "I love it! What a hoot you turned out to be, Ms. Worrell. I would have liked to have grown-up with you around, provided we were closer in years. Actually, I was born in a tent."

"You were?" Develyn pulled open a dresser drawer and surveyed the neatly folded silk scarves.

"Over at Wounded Knee, in South Dakota."

"You mean, during the siege and all?"

"The official siege started February 27, 1973, and lasted seventy-one days. I was born after that. Mother got there too late, but said she was going to camp right there until the baby was born. I think it caused a ruckus, but the government was shy about doing anything. I was born in a teepee."

"OK, so maybe the tent camping thing was a bad joke. But let's just stay here. Will your truck and trailer be alright out there on the prairie?"

"Sure, it's a trailhead, and there are always some rigs parked there in antelope hunting season."

"How about the horses?"

Cree-Ryder jammed on a huge hat full of silk lilies. "What do you think?"

"Oh, it's you, honey. By all means, wear that to the royal ball."

"Yeah, right." Casey pulled off the hat. "We could picket the horses in the backyard and toss the tack on the porch. Uncle Henry will wander around, but he won't go anywhere without mama."

Develyn scooted across the room and grabbed Casey's arm. "Let's do it."

"Devy, there are two small problems. First, we don't have any clothes to change into. We'll get hypothermia or something if we don't put on something dry. I don't know about you, but my clothes are still splashed."

Develyn tugged open a huge wardrobe closet door. "No clothes? Hmmm. And the other problem?"

"We don't have any food, sweetie. Why don't you phone Quint and have him parachute down a care package from the Imperial Dynasty in Casper?"

"I am not calling Quint for anything," Develyn snapped.

"Is that what this is all about? Hiding out from Quint?"

"No. Well, not entirely. I'm not hiding. I just don't mind having something else to do." Develyn peered at the dresses in the wardrobe. "Did you ever want to pretend you were a countess?"

Casey waved her black braid at Develyn. "Why do I get the feeling you will be the princess and I will be your lady-in-waiting?"

"No, we are sister countesses."

Casey pointed to her dark brown skin. "If we are sisters, then our mama has been fooling around."

"Casey, this is just pretend. No one can see us, so we can be sisters if we want."

"Well, sis," Casey grinned, "which one of us goes out to tend the horses?"

"That's your job."

"Why?"

"Because you are younger, and I have to fix up our room. I'll shake out the quilts and dust a bit."

Casey headed toward the stairs. "Perhaps you can ring for the servants to send up supper in the dumbwaiter."

● ● ●

Develyn had three lanterns burning, including one at the top of the narrow stairs, when Casey returned. "You're soaked."

"It's raining," Casey reported.

"How are the horses?"

"Uncle Henry stomped up on the back porch, so My Maria and Popcorn followed him. They'll be OK. I slapped the hobbles on them. If it stops raining, they will probably eat the tall weeds in the backyard." Casey surveyed the room. "You've been a busy countess."

"I shook out the comforter, then swept and dusted, but it's still musty." Develyn pointed at the far wall. "I discovered that cupboard is full of firewood."

"Oh, do we get to burn the place down?"

"I lit a match and it did draft up the chimney. I think it works. I think we should build a fire."

"You didn't find any supper?"

"No, but I found this." Develyn swung open a closet door.

"Clothes?"

"Yes."

"You aren't expecting us to dress up like nineteenth-century Victorian countesses, are you?" Casey laughed.

Develyn pulled out one of the dresses and held it to her chin. "Of course I am."

"There is no way this Native-American, Mexican bod can fit in one of those."

"How about your African American-Irish bod?"

"I don't think so."

"Look what else I found."

Casey strolled over next to Develyn. "What is that?"

"A wasp-waist corset."

"Oh, no, I like my bumble-bee waist just fine. You are not getting me in one of those."

Develyn pulled a purple dress from the wardrobe closet. "Isn't this the most elegant, dusty dress you've ever seen?"

"It will look very good on you, but you are not getting me in a corset."

"It's for you."

"Why me?"

"I don't have the . . . eh . . . curves for it."

"You mean you are too flat-chested?"

"That's not the way I wanted to put it, but that's about it. Come on, let's try them on. It will get our minds off of eating."

Casey held the purple dress up in front of her. "OK, but I will not wear that corset thing."

● ● ●

Cree-Ryder hung her damp jeans over the back of a wrought-iron dressing table chair that was parked in front of the fireplace. "Do you know how long it's been since I've worn a dress of any kind?"

"You look beautiful."

"It always feels weird when I undo my braid and comb my hair out."

"Casey, you have to-die-for hair."

"I don't know if it's Native American hair or Mexican hair . . . but I do like it. Do you think it's alright if we wear the jewelry too?"

Develyn pointed to the open jewelry box. "Let's wear whatever we want, then leave everything exactly as we found it. It has laid here for a hundred years. It's about time someone enjoyed it, even if only for a few minutes."

"I wonder if the countess had double-pierced ears?" Casey stabbed on two sets of earrings, then pranced in front of a tall mirror. "How would you describe this dress?"

"I'd say it's a suit of fine imported challie, trimmed with velvet to match the color of the design. The skirt has three small flounces around the hem, each with a piping of velvet. The waist has folds of challie and purple velvet down the front, with small violet velvet bows. There are shirred pieces of the challie coming from the sides of the waist and in front with a piping of bright pink velvet," Develyn lectured.

"How did you know all of that?"

"I made most of it up. I can't tell you how many buying trips I made with my mother when she owned a dress shop. I'd have to sit there and listen to salesmen give their pitch over and over."

"But not these kind of dresses."

"No, but some things never change."

"What are these poofy-sleeves called?"

Develyn raised her upturned nose. "My dear, those are called . . . 'poofy-sleeves'!"

Casey continued to stand in front of the mirror. "Other than not coming close to being able to button it in the back, it's OK."

"When you go to the royal ball tonight, make sure you stand with your back to the wall. No one will know."

"Stand against the wall?" Casey chided. "Oh, sure, that's easy for plain white bread like you. No one will care. But the prince will want to dance with the bronze bombshell. And if he puts his hand on my back . . ."

"Is that a problem?"

Casey's eyes widened. "Only if the princess sees him do it!"

Develyn bowed before Casey. She cleared her throat, then spoke with a deep voice and phony accent. "Countess, would you consent to dance with me?"

Casey curtsied, "Certainly, my lord."

Develyn took a step forward and put her left hand in Casey's right. Her right hand rested on Cree-Ryder's almost bare back.

"Oh, my," Dev giggled. "That's quite a different style of dress, countess."

"Yes, it's the rage in Paris this season. It's called LeBak Unbuttoned."

"Well, if it has a French sounding name, it must be OK."

They waltzed around the room several times, then over to the bed and collapsed across it on their backs.

When the giggling stopped, Develyn sat up. "Casey . . . this is incredible. I'm a forty-five-year-old schoolteacher from Indiana who was so close to going crazy I took off for the summer to get away from everything. My daughter barely speaks to me because she thinks my hardness caused her father to have a heart attack and die. My mother keeps insisting that I'm a total failure. Before coming out here I hadn't had a date in two years. My entire life has consisted of teaching fifth-graders, feeding cats, and sitting in a dark living room feeling sorry for myself."

Casey continued to lie on her back. "Is this going somewhere?"

"Well, here I am in the middle of Wyoming in an abandoned mansion, dressed up in nineteenth-century Victorian garb, having the time of my life. Doesn't that sound a bit strange?"

"Develyn Gail Upton Worrell, your life has been like this ever since I met you."

"Then it's all your fault."

"I'm the sidekick, honey. I'm just here for a few laughs, so you can rescue me from peril."

"Rescue you?"

"That's what sidekicks are for, Devy-girl, to allow the heroine to be brave and daring."

"This brave and daring heroine is going to build a fire. We need to warm up this room enough to dry out our other clothes."

"We aren't wearing these on the ride back to the truck?" Casey pulled herself off the bed and followed Develyn across the room.

They stood by the fireplace and watched the flame pop out of the dry firewood. Casey shoved on another log.

"OK, now that we've played dress up, I'm still hungry."

Develyn glanced around the room. "We just need a different game. Let's look for the hidden treasure."

"What hidden treasure?"

"This room is so private no one has found it for more than a hundred years. Maybe they had a secret compartment where the letters of French court intrigue are hidden."

"Or French gold?"

"Or French perfumes."

"Or French fries, or French toast . . . or even a jar of French dressing!" Casey plopped down on the edge of the bed. "It beats doing nothing. Let's see, countess, where is your secret hiding place?"

Develyn flopped back on the bed.

"What are you doing?"

"That fire feels so good, I'm going to take a nap."

"And make me do all this treasure hunting by myself?"

"Do you mind?"

"Don't expect a 50/50 share of what I find," Casey whined.

"You may have 60 percent, unless it's something good to eat."

"In which case we toss it out in the middle of the floor and fight for it like dogs," Casey chuckled.

"That sounds fair enough. But you can't use your knife."

"Which one?"

"You have two knives?"

"I didn't say I had two. I just said I had more than one."

Develyn closed her eyes. *I've never even seen a knife fight. I'll just let Casey win.*

● ● ●

The hay scratched her back, but the saddle blanket made a good pillow. Develyn pulled the lap blanket up to her shoulders.

I don't know why they always fall asleep in the hay in the movies. It's not very comfortable. Dewayne said there are rats in the hay, but if it had rats, then I'm sure Brownie wouldn't eat it, and he loves it.

She opened one eye and peered through the moonlight at the brown horse.

I know they say you are old, but that only means you are wise. I think maybe you are the wisest horse in the whole world. Maybe Daddy will let me take you home. I could ride you back to Indiana. . . . We could stop every night and sleep under the stars and I could sing, and you could watch over me.

But I don't sing very good, Brownie. Dewa can sing good, but we don't want him to come with us. Brothers can be such a pain. Do you have any brothers? I don't know if horses even recognize their own family. I guess they recognize their mother . . . everyone recognizes his mother.

Sometimes I think my mother hardly recognizes me.

Lord, why am I such a disappointment to her? It's like when I let my heart run where you've made it to run . . . I always disappoint her.

I can't be like Mother.

She knows all the rules of life, and has a heart to keep them.

I don't know all the rules. And sometimes, I don't even want to know. Life is like the fancy silverware that grandma uses. Sometimes it's like all my life I've been eating dinner with a salad fork.

That's what I love about being out here in Wyoming and riding horses every day. There is no one to tell me how wrong I am.

Lord, I love my mother. But we are so different. I hope when I grow up, she'll be proud of everything I do.

Develyn rolled on her side. The hay didn't poke her now.

It smelled musty.

But soft as an old comforter.

A very old comforter.

● ● ●

"Hey, what's going on up there? You're trespassing on private property."

Develyn sat straight up on the tall feather bed. Casey Cree-Ryder, in Victorian dress, stood at the back in the shadows.

"What's happening?" Develyn whispered.

Casey pointed toward the front window. "I think we've been discovered."

"We saw someone in that upper room!" a man's voice hollered from the dark. "This is the central Wyoming Security Patrol. You are ordered out of the building."

"Stay away from the windows," Casey whispered.

Develyn crawled off the bed and slid over next to Cree-Ryder. "I was asleep. What happened?"

"You mumbled a lot in your sleep."

"I was dreaming. This isn't a dream, is it?"

"I think they are security from down at the gas refinery. Maybe they patrol this area every night. What are we going to do?"

"I don't think I want to go down and talk to them dressed like this."

Casey slipped her arm around Develyn's shoulder. "I'm sure not. The back half of this dress is more embarrassing than a hospital gown."

"Is the door down at the bottom of the stairs closed?"

"And locked."

"Then they might not know how to get up here."

"We seen you in that room when we drove up!" the man's voice shouted.

Develyn leaned toward the window. Casey held her back. "Shhhh. Listen."

"Someone's in the house?"

Casey nodded.

"Burleigh, what did you find?"

A voice filtered up from the little balcony below them. "Ain't no one in here, Rudy."

"The light's still on . . . you got to go up the stairs."

"There ain't no stairs. I'm on the top level."

"Like heck you are. There's a lantern lit in the room above you."

"There ain't no room above me. That's just a false window into the attic."

"Burleigh, go up there. I'm lookin' at the lit room right now."

"This is weird, Rudy."

Casey leaned over to Develyn. "Let's show him really weird. Did you ever go to church camp?"

Develyn studied her dark brown eyes. "Yes. What does that have . . ."

"You remember standin' out in the forest with a flashlight so you could shine it on your face and scare the heebie-jeebies out of someone walking by in the dark?"

"I never did that."

"You are the type that didn't . . . and I'm the type that did it to your type. Anyway, let's do it to them."

"OK, we appear in the window and then what?"

"Turn out the lamps and let them flicker off. Then see what they do."

Develyn nodded at the side window. "Can we wear those curtains for veils, like you did at the back door?"

"Sure."

"There ain't no floor higher than this one," the voice from inside the house yelled.

"Rudy, come down here. Let me show you," the other one insisted.

Develyn and Casey stayed out of view until they both had the thin white gauze curtains draped over their heads like a shawl.

"What's the plan?" Develyn whispered.

"Appear at the windows at the exact same time. Scowl. Then allow the lamps to flicker out. We'll back away, and see what they do next."

"We're in enough trouble already."

"Yes, but it will buy us time. While they are trying to figure it out, we can change clothes in the dark," Casey said. "If we are going to be arrested, I want to be wearing my jeans and boots."

"Arrested?" Develyn shook her head. "I don't want to get arrested."

"Honey, it's a little late to worry about that. This mansion visit was your idea, remember?"

They jockeyed themselves near the windows, both carrying oil lanterns.

"You see, Rudy. See that light up there."

"And I say you can't get up there because . . . "

Casey nodded to Develyn. The ladies crept in front of the windows, each with a lantern, waist high, in front of them.

"There she is!" a man's voice shouted.

"Burleigh, do you see that? There's one in both windows."

"What the . . . no . . . no . . ."

"Them lanterns went out. There was two of them, wasn't there?"

"You didn't see anything, Rudy."

"I surely did, I saw . . ."

"What did you see?"

"Two gals lookin' like . . . eh . . . ghosts . . . and . . ."

"You didn't see anything. I didn't see anything. You got that?"

"But . . . but . . . that one was the countess. She was a woman of color, you know."

"We didn't see a thing," the other insisted again. "Do you want to go back to Gates and tell him that there are two ghost women livin' in the mansion on a floor that has no stairs?"

"Eh, no . . . I thought you was going to tell him."

"I didn't see anything. What could I tell him? You tell him."

"I . . . eh . . . didn't . . . well, come to think of it, I didn't see anything either."

"And you didn't smell that smoke coming out of the chimney?"

"What smoke?"

Develyn peeked through the darkened window at the truck taillights as they drove south along the creek bed.

"Yes!" Cree-Ryder shouted. "She was a woman of color . . . a bronze bombshell!"

Light the lanterns. Fetch my silk gown. Ring Maude in the kitchen to bring me up some tea. Please be a sweetie and draw me a hot bath," Casey ordered. "I want the peach bubble bath tonight."

Develyn and Casey rolled on the bed laughing.

"I haven't had this much fun since a junior high slumber party," Develyn giggled.

"I haven't had this much fun, ever!"

"Casey, no one will believe this scene."

"I don't even believe it. Wait until you try to explain this to your friends in Indiana."

Develyn reached over and slipped her hand into Casey's. "I think you'll have to come visit me, just to be a witness."

Casey squeezed tight. "Is that an invitation?"

"Countess Cree-Ryder, my humble Crawfordsville abode is always open to you. I'd love to have you come visit, anytime."

"Good. I'll arrive by Thanksgiving and stay through Christmas. I like big presents and lots of them. Now, what do you think?"

"I'd be delighted."

Casey stared at her for a minute. "I believe you would, sweet Devy-girl. I've never in my life had anyone want me to stick around for weeks."

"Well, you met her now."

In the dark, they continued to lie on the bed.

"You got room for ten horses in your backyard?" Casey said.

"No."

"That's OK, I'll keep them indoors. They're all house-broken . . ."

Develyn bounced up off the bed. "What?"

Casey pulled herself up. "You are so easy to tease, Miss Dev. Listen, I won't bring horses, and I won't stay for six weeks, but I'd love to come visit you sometime this fall or winter."

"Casey, I meant it about the Thanksgiving-to-Christmas invite."

"I know you did. But what will your husband say?"

"My husband?" The word exploded from Develyn's mouth.

"I figure you'll be married by then."

"I told you that Quint wasn't the one."

Casey struck a match and relit one of the lanterns. "Oh,

sure, he's not the one. That only leaves a million other cowboys who are chasin' you Miss Dev."

"I think your dress is too tight. It's making you delusional."

Casey strolled around the room. "Well, before I pass out like that chick in *Pirates of the Caribbean,* we better plan our escape. Those two security guards will be back as soon as it's daylight. I suggest we try to sleep, get up about 4 a.m., saddle up and ride away from the house. Even if we can't find a trail out of the canyon, we can be a long way from the mansion."

"Do you think they will come back before then?" Develyn peered out the front window at a black Wyoming sky.

"Nope. They aren't about to admit they saw ghosts."

Develyn tugged off the musty silk dress. "With all the excitement, I hope we can fall asleep."

Casey posed in front of the big mirror. "I feel like Ella having to leave the ball at midnight."

"Ella?"

"Cinder-Ella. She carried the cinders and was named Ella. What do they teach in the fifth grade in Indiana?"

"Not enough, I can see."

● ● ●

Develyn sat straight up in the hay when Brownie bit her bare toe.

But it wasn't hay.

Nor Brownie.

Nor a bite.

"Ouch!" The dim light from the lantern barely reached the bed.

"Time to get up, Devy-girl."

"Casey, it's still dark."

"Yeah, but daylight will break by the time we saddle up the horses. It's time to ride back to reality."

"It's cold in here."

"I let the fire go out. Didn't want smoke in the chimney."

Develyn pulled on her tennis shoes, then straightened the comforters on the bed. "Is it raining still?"

"No rain. In fact, the wind has been blowing since midnight. I think the ground is dried out."

"Is it cold?"

"Down here it's not too bad, but up on top of the rim it will be windy and feel cold."

Develyn stared in the mirror and tried to comb her hair with her fingers. "Tell me again why we rode off in T-shirts and didn't bring our jackets."

"Because we were going to turn around and ride back to the truck. I didn't have any idea Miss Develyn would act like a teacher-gone-wild and ride off a cliff."

"So, this is all my fault?" Develyn jammed her straw cowboy hat down on her head.

"Of course it is. And it's one of the most cherished memories of my life. You know the instant when this adventure became a lifetime moment?" Casey asked.

"When he said, 'The Countess was a woman of color?'"

"Yes! That's when all of this exploded with meaning."

"Well, Countess Cree-Ryder, shall we go for a morning ride?"

"Quite."

"Shall I have the servants come along with tea and biscuits?"

"Oh, sweetie, let's just ride alone today," Casey giggled. "I get so tired of servants waiting on me hand and foot." She shoved a wool bundle toward Develyn.

"What's this?"

"Our one souvenir. I found these two wool lap blankets under some bedding. They are still in usable condition."

"We are going to ride with a blanket across our laps?"

"Nope. I did a few alterations. Pull off your hat and slip it over your shoulders like a poncho."

"Just like Clint Eastwood?"

"Yeah, do I get to be the good, the bad, or the ugly?" Casey laughed.

Develyn slipped her head through the slit in the wool blanket, then jammed her hat back on. "Honey, we are both good!"

"Yes, we are cute too."

"Let's see . . ." Develyn stared at herself in the mirror. "Thirty hours since our last shower . . . twenty-four hours since fresh clothes . . . not even a comb for our hair. Dirt on our faces, dusty blankets for coats, and no idea in the world how to get out of this canyon. Oh, we are cuties, alright."

"Remember, a journey of a thousand miles starts with a single steep step, so don't trip. Take my hand," Casey offered.

"What for?"

"We need to turn out this lantern, and leave it up here."

"Do you think we can find our way downstairs in the dark?"

"I've got cat eyes," Casey boasted.

Develyn clutched Casey's strong warm hand as they eased down the stairway toward the second floor.

There was a simultaneous crash and explosive "Ouch!"

"What happened?"

"I ran into the door," Casey said.

"What about your cat eyes?"

"They ran into the door too."

Enough daylight broke in the east that when they reached the back porch, Develyn spied My Maria and Popcorn munching tall brown weeds in the backyard.

"They look content enough," Develyn said.

"That's because they don't know what's goin' to happen later on."

"What is going to happen later on?"

"I don't have a clue," Casey shrugged.

They saddled the horses as sunlight flooded the canyon.

"Where's Uncle Henry?" Develyn asked.

"I figure he'll show up when his mama calls him."

Develyn yanked the cinch tight and led My Maria around in a circle. "Which direction are we headed?"

"North. That is the opposite route of the gas plant and locked gate."

Develyn pulled the cinch even tighter. "Uncle Henry? It's time to go, baby!"

"Well, look at that." Casey pointed to the wild-rose, vine-covered rock canyon wall behind the house.

Develyn turned to see Uncle Henry's head peek out of the roses. "Honey, what are you doing back there?"

"How did he get behind the roses? It's like solid rock."

"There's an old vine-covered archway. Maybe it was a cave or a shrine or a fancy outhouse."

Casey led Popcorn over to Uncle Henry and parted the bushes. "I don't believe this," she blurted out.

"If there are dead bodies, I don't want to hear about it," Develyn groaned.

"I can't believe you were right, Ms. Worrell. There's a narrow trail carved straight up this cliff."

"Really? And Uncle Henry found it? I told you!" Develyn shouted. "The countess wasn't going to get pinned in. It's her escape route."

"It looks very narrow."

Develyn pushed her hat back and cleared her throat. "Enter through the narrow gate. For wide is the gate and broad is the road that leads to destruction, and many enter through it. But small is the gate and narrow the road that leads to life, and only a few find it. That's in Matthew 7 someplace."

"Verses 13 and 14," Casey replied. "So, we are choosing the narrow gate?"

"What are our choices?" Develyn asked.

"This possible trail out or being arrested."

"That's what I thought, O sarape-clad bombshell. Lead on Clintina . . ."

"Don't push me, blondie," Casey growled. "If you would just tell me the name on the grave, I would leave you here with this beautiful mansion . . ." A smile broke across her face. "All we need is that annoying, repetitive theme song and we could be the *Thelma and Louise* version of *The Good, the Bad, and the Ugly*."

The trail up the canyon behind the roses proved to be steep and slow. It turned out to be a rock ravine no more than three feet wide, as they zigzagged up the slope of the canyon wall.

"Daylight never reaches down here," Casey called out. "But neither does the wind."

"Do you think the count had this trail made?"

"It could have been an old Indian trail, but he certainly used it for an escape."

Develyn surveyed the rock, no more than two feet from either side of her head. "I think I'm getting claustrophobic. It's like a crowded elevator in a tall building. You can only take it so long, then you want out to get some fresh air, even if it's not your floor."

"Don't get weird on me Devy-girl. We have quite a ways to go."

"What if it doesn't go all the way to the top?"

Casey glanced at Develyn. "There's a cheery thought. I guess we put these horses in reverse and back down."

"No, really, Casey. What if this is just a fissure in the rocks and it peters out and we are wedged in here?"

"Put your feet up on My Maria's neck."

Develyn stared ahead at Casey's braid. "Why?"

"It's gettin' narrow up here, girl. You don't want your legs pinned in."

"Casey, this isn't funny."

"Honey, I'm not joking. Put your feet up. If we get stuck you can take your cell phone and call Harrison Ford to fly his helicopter over to rescue us."

"My cell phone! Yes . . ." Develyn crammed her hand into her jeans pocket.

"Devy, there is no way possible a signal could drop down in here. And who would you call? Quint?"

"No, I can't call him."

"The sheriff? Do you want to tell him that you broke into the LaSage Mansion?"

"I'll call . . . eh . . ."

"Cooper Tallon?"

"No, no. He came out after me before. I can't admit I'm a complete ditz who gets lost every time she rides on the prairie."

"Then who?"

"Eh . . . I could call . . . Renny!"

"The mustang breaker. What do you expect him to do?"

"He'll figure out something."

"In the meantime, keep prodding that paint horse. We might make it out yet."

Develyn banged her cell phone against her knee. "It doesn't matter," she called out. "There's no reception."

"Well, what do you know, a dead spot. It's a wonder someone isn't down here building a cell tower and putting ads on TV."

"How's Uncle Henry doing?" Develyn called out.

"He's on up the trail a ways, trying to lead us."

"Why did you stop?"

"Popcorn's stuck," Casey admitted.

"Are you serious?

Develyn's chin dropped as Casey stood up on the saddle. Cree-Ryder pulled a wide-bladed knife out of one boot, and a thin-bladed one out of the other.

"What are you doing?"

Casey stabbed the wide blade in a crack in the rock and pulled herself up about a foot off the saddle. "I'm going for a stroll." She sliced the narrow knife into another crack on the other side of the crevice, then pulled herself up a little further. "I'll just go up top and see what I can see."

"And leave me here?"

"You can come along."

"Casey, I'm scared."

With one boot jammed in one side of the ledge and the other boot on the opposite ledge, Casey inched up. "Yeah, I'm scared too."

"Don't leave me down here, Casey."

"Dev, relax. I'm right here. Let me get up to daylight and see what a fine squeeze we are in. Just keep talking to me."

"Casey, I feel like my life's in a rut!"

"Yes, it is honey. A granite rut. I wonder if this is how that phrase began? I think you should leave that comfy house in Indiana and go out and spend the summer in Wyoming where there are wide-open spaces. You'll have room to breathe, nothing to do, and a chance to meet charming people."

"Yeah. Right." Develyn studied the brown rock walls just wider than her shoulders. "Is anything ever normal in Wyoming?"

"I thought Normal was a town in Illinois."

"Spencer grew up in Normal."

"Your ex? Was he normal?"

"Maybe, but I hope not." Develyn patted the cold rock ledge. "Think about it. Every day in Wyoming is too windy or too still, too wet or too dry, too thrilling or too threatening. When is it ever normal here?"

"The last full week in September. It's called Normal Days . . . and everyone stays home and promises to do nothing," Cree-Ryder hollered. "But no tourists are allowed. None of them are normal."

"Hey, are these the kinds of rocks that have snakes?"

Cree-Ryder paused on a ledge about eight feet above the horses. "This is the wrong time of the year for that."

Develyn adjusted her blanket serape and pushed her hat back. "There are no snakes in the summer?"

"Oh, there are plenty of snakes." Casey grunted as she climbed higher. "This is the wrong time of the year to ask that question."

"If I see a snake, I'll die."

"That should save some needless venom. You aren't going to get bit. I'm almost to the top."

"Well, I'm not."

"Devy, I'm going to be out of sight just for a minute . . . provided I don't fall on my head . . . just wait."

"Like I have a choice?" Develyn screamed. Tears trickled down her dusty cheeks. *Lord, why can't I have a peaceful day? They are either the best of times or the . . . OK, no Dickens quotes. . . . Lord, I'm not sure what I want. I just know what I don't want, and I don't want to be stuck down here in this rock tomb. This is crazy. I shouldn't be here. I should have listened to Casey, turned around at the rim, and returned to the truck. Then I'd be in my little cabin, just lifting an eyelid and smelling a hundred years of history hang in the air. But if we had turned around, I would have missed the mansion . . . the night . . . the dresses and the security guards. . . . I could have played it safe, but I would have missed the dance. . . . OK, I won't quote Garth Brooks, either. This summer, I just want to relax and have fun. I just don't know how.*

I'm forty-five years old.

It's time I learn.

"Casey?" Develyn called out.

She waited a moment.

"Casey?"

I'm alone. Did she abandon me? "OK, Ms. Worrell . . . you're a fifth-grade teacher . . . nothing panics you." She reached forward and stroked My Maria's neck. "Honey, we can't move forward until Popcorn does, and he seems to be a little chubby around the girth, so let's encourage him to move. Perhaps if you bit him on the rear end."

Then he would kick you and you'd buck and I'd hit the rocks and I'd be trampled by two panicked horses with nothing left of me but bloodstained rocks and a grease spot. And if I crawl up there and slap his backside, he'll pound my head like an aluminum can run over by a semi . . . so . . . from a distance . . .

"Casey!"

Develyn's feet were still up on My Maria's neck.

I wonder if I threw rocks at Popcorn, would he kick his way free, or would he just get more stuck? There are some rocks up there. If I stood in the saddle like Casey, I could reach them.

Of course, I'm not like Casey.

Moving one foot under her and then the next, Develyn crouched on the saddle. Then she squatted. She stood, hunched over, holding each side of the cold rock crevice.

She shuffled her feet to the widest part of the saddle seat.

My Maria shifted her weight.

"No! No, honey. Stand still for mama!"

I'm mama to the horse and mama to the burro. Where's my Dee? My Delaney. That's what I miss about my summer. I miss my girl. It is the first summer in twenty years that I haven't been with her.

Lord, I trust you listen to crazy women, because this whole scene is nuts. I'm trapped in a granite ravine, somewhere in Wyoming, praying for my daughter. Lord, I pray Dee can come out and spend the rest of the summer with me. I want her here. I can't believe it took me six weeks to figure that out.

On a ledge to the left she scooped up several jagged, egg-sized rocks. Still standing straight up on the saddle, she lobbed a rock at the backside of the Appaloosa gelding. The stone tumbled off his rear. Popcorn snorted and flinched, but didn't move.

"Perhaps this is not the best idea," she mumbled. "Perhaps we should . . ."

The sound coming from behind her rattled like a muted castanet.

My Maria pranced.

"Whoa, baby, whoa. It's just a . . . ah . . . oh, no, Lord . . . no, no, no . . . Casey!"

Develyn scanned the rocks, but couldn't see the snake.

The rattling continued.

"Popcorn, get your fat behind on down the trail right now!" *I am not going to be snake-bit. Not today.* With strength she hadn't used in years, Develyn sailed the rock straight into the horse's rump and screamed, "Giddy-up!"

Popcorn gave a wild kick, lurched forward, and stomped up the trail.

My Maria gave pursuit with Develyn still standing in the saddle. "Wait . . ." She walked her hands along the jagged rock walls to keep her balance. "Wait, honey . . . whoa . . . stop . . . no!"

Develyn leaned forward and flexed her knees with each jolt of the horse's hooves on the rock. The skin on her hands and knuckles scraped and tore as she scrambled to keep from falling. My Maria was at a near trot.

"Slow down! I can't keep this up."

The rock wall rubbed the fenders of the saddle as the paint mare slipped between the parallel ledges.

I'm going to fall on my head and die with snakes slithering over my broken, painful, terrorized body.

No, I'm not. Lord, I want to see Delaney. I need to be with my daughter. I am not going to munch it today! It doesn't fit my schedule.

Develyn found the rhythm of My Maria's gait and let each step impact the bend in her knees. She pulled her raw hands back from the rocks and continued to ride standing in the saddle.

"There has to be a rim up here somewhere, girl. Just keep this pace until the top."

Sunlight broke down into the ravine as the trail zigzagged, then they broke out into a prairie of rolling hills and sagebrush.

"Yes!" she shouted.

Cree-Ryder led Popcorn over to her. Develyn's hat was ripped, and the blanket serape was covered with dirt.

Develyn slid down in the saddle. "I made it out!"

"You rode standing in the saddle?"

Develyn held out her hands. "I didn't have a choice. I kind of got ripped up. There was a snake, and I was in a hurry."

"I can't believe I witnessed an Indiana schoolteacher ride out of that canyon standing in the saddle."

"Did you get a good photo of it?" Develyn grinned. "I might use it on the cover of my memoirs."

"I'm afraid you'll have to sketch it from memory."

"You are a mess, Ms. Cree-Ryder, what happened?"

Casey waved her arms as she talked. "I hiked down the trail toward you. Uncle Henry was already on top. About halfway to you, this crazy Appy tried to run me down. It was all I could do to hold on to the headstall, and he drug me up the trail."

"That was my fault. I frightened him, and he took off."

"What did you do?"

"I told him if he didn't get his big rear out of there soon, I would trailer him with a llama all the way to Indiana and put him in a petting zoo for fifth-grade boys who wanted to learn how to wear spurs."

"Dev, what did you really do?"

"Blasted his behind with rocks and screamed. It feels good to be out of there, Casey."

"Yes, well, you might be the only one in history to ride a horse all the way up that fissure."

"Since the countess?"

"Ever. You see that little shack and corral over there?"

"Is that a house?"

"At one time it was a carriage house."

The wind whipped Develyn's face. She tugged her hat down. "For whom?"

"I think the count and countess kept horses and a carriage up here in case they needed to sneak away. They must have walked up here."

"You think so?"

"Yep."

"You mean, Develyn Gail Upton Worrell just rode a horse up a western trail that no one has ever ridden before?"

"Most likely. You're a trailblazer, Devy."

"You know what is so great about a crisis? It feels so wonderful when you finally get out of it."

"You talking about Quint again . . . or the trail up the canyon wall?" Casey challenged.

"Both, Ms. Cree-Ryder. Can you lead us back to the truck from here?"

"I can do that, if you promise no side trips."

"There you go again . . . always holding me back."

"Come on, Ms. Worrell, there isn't a cowgirl or a cowboy in the world that could hold you back from anything."

● ● ●

They rode straight into the yellow sunlight of a cloudless Wyoming day. The showers the night before had cleaned the air and swept the prairie free of tracks. The wind, now at their backs, had dried the mud enough that it would not collect in the hooves of the horses. Casey Cree-Ryder led the way. Uncle Henry trotted next to Develyn and My Maria.

"OK, Ms. Worrell, what do you want to do today?"

"Eat until I'm stuffed. Take a long, hot bath. Wash my hair. Sip on a Starbucks while I get my fingernails done, then I'd like to lie out in the sun, read a good book, and nap."

"Really?"

"It sounds wonderful."

"I've never had anyone do my nails. I'm not the fancy nail type person."

"You should try it once, just to see if you'd like it."

"Would you go with me? I mean, I'd feel like cat at a dog show if I went by myself."

"Let's do it. Let's go get all pampered."

"How much will it cost me?"

"It's my treat," Develyn insisted.

"I don't want to do my toes. No one on earth sees my toes."

"What's wrong with them?"

"I've been horse-stepped so many times, every toe has been broken more than once. The doctor once said he's seen riots more orderly than my toes."

"OK, no toes," Develyn said.

"Where will we go?"

"Where can we go and soak in a tub?"

"You mean, rent a tub?"

"Or a whirlpool, or a hot springs."

Casey turned around in the saddle and put her hand on Popcorn's rump. "Thermopolis! That's the whole reason for the town. They have a big hot springs just north of town and everything."

"How long does it take to get there?"

"Are we going today?"

"Yes."

Casey scratched her neck. "Maybe a couple hours from here. Not much more than an hour, after we get to the rig."

"Then that's where we're going."

"We aren't going back to the cabin?"

"Nope."

"Are you still running away from Quint?"

"Of course not. I'm just thinking of something peaceful to do. And I want to call Delaney as soon as I get a signal."

"Devy, it can't be much later than 7:00 a.m. in Indiana. When does Dee become functional in the mornings?"

"About 11:30. I'll wait. Casey, do you think three of us can squeeze into the cabin?"

"Sure, I've slept a dozen cowboys in a cabin that size."

"Cowboys?"

"There is nothin' in the world safer than bein' the only girl with a dozen ranch cowboys. They will pulverize any inappropriate behavior. But there is nothin' more dangerous than being with one ranch cowboy. Anyway, you are talking about Dee, I suppose."

"I wanted to invite her to come out."

"That would be wonderful. I'd love to meet her. Is she just like you?"

"She is absolutely nothing like me."

"Does she look like you?"

"Actually, she looks like you, Casey . . . only white."

"Poor thing, she can't help having pathetic skin. She must get it from her mama. Hey, this is exciting. Do you think she'll come?"

"That's the big question."

"Does she like to ride?"

"Harleys."

"Motorcycles . . . wow, she isn't like you, is she?"

"She is stubborn and opinionated and has a tough time saying 'I'm sorry, I made a mistake.'"

"I like her already!"

"Lots of time in the last few months, she has utterly hated me."

"She still blames you for her father's heart attack?"

"I think so. Part of it's her struggle. I think she wished she had time to tell him more, and now that's taken away. Anyway . . . there are always two sides to a story, and you've only heard mine."

"What more is there to know?" Casey pressed. "He was a jerk who more than once cheated on you, including with your daughter's eighteen-year-old friend."

"And I, sweet Casey, don't have any idea if I know how to love and take care of a man."

"Whoa, that's a radical thing for a woman married over twenty years to say. Is that why you ran away from Quint?"

"I didn't run away. I just backed away quietly."

"Whatever. Who am I to talk? I don't know how to take care of a man for twenty minutes."

"You just haven't found the right one, sweetie."

"That's what I've told myself for thirty years."

"Today, we don't have to find a man. We just need a soak in the hot springs, get a latte and a manicure."

● ● ●

The sun rose quickly, and the wind was at their backs most of the way. The trail led them away from Sage Canyon, and all they could see was rolling sage prairie, antelope, and the distant Big Horn Mountains to the north. As they swung to the south, a few oil wells and natural gas pumping stations popped up on the horizon.

Develyn followed Casey down to a narrow stream. "Is this Crazy Woman Creek?"

"Yep."

"Do we need a splashology stop?"

"I think we are muddy enough, don't you?"

"We are a mess. Do you think we can sneak into Thermopolis without anyone seeing us?"

Casey dove her hand under her serape and scratched. "Nope."

"At least we won't see anyone we know."

After walking the horses a while, they remounted and started up a gradual climb.

"Countess, are we about there? My backside feels like hamburger."

"Oh, it is so difficult to get hearty servants these days. Back in the old country, the help was much . . . wait a minute . . . for my Cree grandma, this is the old country."

Uncle Henry let out a bray, then trotted ahead of them.

"Does he sense we are getting close?"

"Either that or he smells the smoke."

"What smoke?"

"You don't smell the campfire?"

Develyn stood in the stirrup and took a big gulp of air. "No."

"How sad. You white girls can't sing, can't dance, can't smell, can't jump, and have pasty skin and hair that has to be colored to be attractive."

"And, my bronze bombshell friend, your point is?"

"It's a miracle that you find anyone to marry you."

"Casey, you don't know how true that is."

Cree-Ryder crested the hill in front of her. "There's a campfire, and it's right next to that red Dodge pickup.

"You don't have a red Dodge pickup." Develyn galloped up next to Casey. "Renny? What's he doing out here?"

"I doubt if he's looking for me, Ms. Worrell."

"I'm not going to let him see me like this. I haven't had makeup in two days."

"I haven't had makeup in ten years."

"Yes, but you are a natural bronze bombshell."

"Point well-taken. Pull that blanket over your head. I'll do all the talking."

● ● ●

Renny Slater squatted next to a sage fire. He glanced up, but didn't stand. "Mornin' ladies, you out early . . . or did you ride all night?"

Uncle Henry trotted up and scratched his head on Slater's side-view mirror.

Casey Cree-Ryder swung down out of the saddle and tied Popcorn to her horse trailer. "You cookin' breakfast, Slater?"

"I had me a couple of eggs and some ham. You want me to stir you up some?"

"How many eggs do you have left?" Casey asked.

"I've got ten left," he replied.

"Cook 'em all," Develyn groaned as she eased herself out of the saddle.

"You saddle sore, or did you get run over by a train?"

Develyn slapped her hands to her hips. "Slater, if you want to live to see noon, you will not mention my looks again this morning, is that clear?"

"Yes, ma'am," he grinned, revealing two deep dimples. He broke eggs into the black iron skillet.

Casey tied up My Maria, and the ladies pulled the saddles from the horses.

"Did you come out here looking for us?" Develyn asked.

"Yep. This was my assignment."

"Assignment?"

"Quint Burdett called. Said you failed to come in, and he got a delirious phone call."

"Delirious?"

"Said you were babbling on incoherently. He was worried about you when you didn't show up by dark."

"I told him I wasn't coming back."

"Well, he called me up and since I was in Lander, I was to start this way at daylight and check out the trailheads. He asked Tallon to scout east of Argenta, and Cuban and the hands at the ranch swept south from the headquarters."

"And Quint?" Casey said. "Where was he going to look?"

"In Powell, I reckon. Anyway, he had some kind of a rangeland meeting up there."

"He surely was worried. He sent all of you out, but went to the meeting?" Casey asked.

"I think he's the state chairman. He said to call as soon as any of us had word."

"Incoherent?" Develyn grumbled. "I thought I made myself perfectly clear."

"Oh?" Renny one eyebrow. "Is this a lover's spat?"

"Not lovers," Develyn replied.

"I should have known." He beat the eggs in the skillet. "By the way, would you want to tell me where you've been all night? I've seen bronc riders catch a foot in the stirrup and get drug around the arena that looked cleaner than you two."

"Slater, you might as well crawl into that fryin' pan," Cree-Ryder said. "You'd be safer in there."

"We had a really delightful time at a slumber party," Develyn announced.

"Yes!" Casey added.

Renny pointed his fork at the package of meat. "How much ham do you want?"

"The whole hog," Casey replied.

He unsnapped the sleeves of his shirt and rolled them up to his elbows. "I take it they were short on refreshments at the slumber party?"

Develyn could taste the thick aroma of frying meat. "Yes, and we were out longer than we planned, but we weren't lost, just enjoying the Wyoming prairie."

"I trust you got out of that rainstorm last night."

"We were quite snuggly," Develyn bragged.

"There isn't a room or a house between here and the highway twenty-five miles west of here. Where did you stay?"

"Now, Renny." Casey squatted down next to him. "Girls don't have to give away their secret rendezvous sites."

"You're right, but I'd better phone Quint and tell him you are secretive but not delirious this mornin'."

"Did he really call us delirious?" Develyn asked.

"Just you, Miss Develyn. He thinks Cree-Ryder is crazy all the time."

Casey laughed. "I'm glad he sees some things accurately. You got some forks for us to eat those eggs with? If not, we'll just eat them with our fingers."

"Renny, I'll phone Quint. You get ahold of Tallon and Cuban if you can. I don't want them wasting the day."

Slater turned over the sizzling ham. "I've got to go back to the highway for my phone to work."

Develyn pulled her phone out of her pocket. "Looks like I have a signal. I'll be right back. This needs to be a private conversation, incoherent or not." Develyn hiked toward Casey's horse trailer, then turned back. "Renny, Casey and I are going up to Thermopolis after breakfast and soak in the hot springs, then get our nails done. You want to go with us?"

"Two beautiful cowgirls are inviting me to soak in the hot tub?"

"Hot springs," Casey corrected.

"I'll go, but only on one condition."

"What's that?" Develyn replied.

"I don't have to get my fingernails painted."

Burnt, tough, and drenched in Tabasco, they were the best eggs Develyn had ever eaten. While the makeshift poncho dragged the dirt, she squatted next to the small sage fire and scraped her tin plate clean. Her straw cowboy hat blocked the morning sun. The back of her hand served as a napkin. She reloaded the plate.

"You cook a good breakfast, Renny," she mumbled between bites.

He stood, then shook his head. "Ms. Worrell, no one at that Riverbend Elementary School in Indiana would recognize you right now."

"You think the hat would fool them?" She fanned away the smoke with her hand and motioned Casey to pass the tin coffee cup they shared.

"Plus the mud on your face, the matted hair, and that wild look in your cat-like eyes."

She turned to Casey. "Countess, have you got any idea what this peasant cook is babbling about?"

"No idea in the world." Casey pointed her hunting knife at the black iron skillet. "You want to wrestle for that last piece of ham?"

Develyn rubbed her upturned nose with her fingertips. "Sure. Guns or knives?"

"Bare knuckles."

"Sounds fair. I suppose we slug it out until one of us is unconscious."

"Wait!" Renny squatted down and cut the ham slice into two pieces. "There, you can each have one."

Casey stabbed one with her hunting knife.

Develyn reached over and plucked the other one up with her fingers. "You know, I've always heard that men get a thrill out of watchin' two women fight. I can't understand why he panicked."

"Are you questionin' Renny's manliness?" Casey jibed.

"Oh, no, never tick off the cook. That's lesson number one, when you're on a trail drive." Develyn folded the ham and scooped up more of the eggs, then jammed a big bite in her mouth. "Hmmm hpmth, clemp nah whtmp isnna."

Casey laughed. "You might want to try that again when you've chewed your food."

"If Quint could see me now, he would be convinced that I am having a mental meltdown."

"Is that what he said on the phone?" Casey asked.

"He said I should call Lily, because she's the only one who could talk sense into me."

"Is that your pal back home?" Renny asked.

"Yes, she's been there for me for years."

Casey stabbed a bite of ham with her hunting knife. "What else did ol' Quint say?"

"Let's see . . . he said maybe I need to get this idealized cowgirl thing out of my system. Make sure I don't do anything I'll regret later. And eat my vegetables."

"He said that?" Casey motioned for the coffee cup.

"He said it was important to eat right when under stress. That and a few other things."

"What other things?" Cree-Ryder asked.

Develyn continued to shove food in her mouth. "Renny, don't some men look for a wife who is just like their mother?"

"I reckon so. My mama's a fine lady, that's for sure."

"What other things did dear ol' Quint tell you?" Casey interrupted again.

Develyn wiped her hands on her poncho. "But I have never heard of a woman looking for a man who was just like her mother."

Casey waved her knife over the sage fire. "Are you ignoring me?"

"You saying Quint is like your mother?" Renny pressed.

"Sometimes he seems to want to control my life just like my mother."

Renny sipped coffee from a blue tin cup. "I think people like that are well intentioned. I reckon they surmise they are making your life better."

Casey stabbed the knife through Develyn's poncho and pinned it to the dirt. "What else did Quint say?"

Develyn pulled out the knife, wiped the blade on her jeans, then tapped the tin cup. "Renny, darlin', would you be a good cowboy and pour us another cup of coffee?"

Slater shook his head. "Maybe Quint is right about you."

"Well?" Casey pressed.

"He said the usual. He loved me, missed me, and just knew that everything would settle down after we are married." Develyn took the steaming tin cup from Renny. "Did you ever put Tabasco in coffee?"

"Yeah," he nodded.

"Is it good?"

"No."

She sipped the coffee and passed it to Cree-Ryder. "He's still countin' on you marryin' him?" Renny asked.

"So it seems."

Cree-Ryder took a sip and handed the cup back to her. "What did you tell him?"

"That I didn't think marriage was on my summer calendar."

"Wait a minute," Renny said. "You mean you are not goin' to marry Burdett?"

Casey flipped her black bangs out of her eyes. "Of course she's not. That leaves you an open barn door, mustang breaker."

"That's not what I meant."

130

"What did you mean?" Casey probed.

"I just meant, I thought Quint is quite a catch."

"I'm not sure who was catching whom. Do goldfish like being goldfish?" Casey blurted out.

Develyn studied her last bite of ham. "Where did that come from?"

"It seems to me that Quint wants you to be his pretty goldfish. So I wondered if goldfish enjoy swimming around and around in a confined area havin' ever'one stare at them."

"Quint is not that bad," Develyn said. "It's just that I got caught up in a fantasy that I need to back away from. You know, this is really good ham, in a honey-burnt sort of way."

"I think she's changing the subject," Casey said.

Develyn opened her mouth wide and waited.

Casey fed her the last bite of ham, still speared on the tip of her hunting knife.

"I'm here for the summer," Develyn explained. "I go back home in a few weeks. I didn't mean for everything to take on such a serious note."

"That is good news. I'm about as nonserious an hombre as rides the Wyomin' range." Renny stood up. "Let's pack up and get you to the hot springs."

Develyn smiled. "Countess, is he saying we need a bath?"

Casey sniffed the air. "Yep, Devy-girl, some men are picky that way."

● ● ●

When her cell phone rang, Develyn had to undo the seat belt to tug it out of her jeans. The voice on the other end was insistent.

"This is your conscience calling."

"Hi, Lil! I was going to call you today."

"Where are you?"

Develyn glanced around the cab of the pickup. "Where are we?"

"Twenty-three miles south of Thermopolis," Renny replied.

"We're . . ."

"Yes, I heard Mr. Burdett. Of course, I don't have any idea where Themopopolis is."

"Thermopolis," Develyn corrected. "And that wasn't Mr. Burdett."

"Who are you with?"

"Renny and Casey. We're going into town to get a bath."

"Wait a minute. I get a phone call from Quint Burdett about how concerned he is about you, and now I find you going to a bath house with a different cowboy?"

"We're going to the largest mineral hot springs in the world and sharing it with Boy Scouts from Tacoma and senior citizens from Sun City. What is this about Quint phoning you?"

"I was out on yard duty when my cell phone rang. I only tote it around hoping my wayward pal, Ms. Worrell, might call me. But it was Quint Burdett. He was worried about you and asked if I'd talked to you lately."

132

"Wait a minute. Quint phoned you on your cell phone?"

"Yes."

"But that's an unlisted number."

"I assumed he got it from you."

"He most certainly did not. How did he know your number?"

"Honey, are you accusing me of something?"

Develyn leaned forward in the truck seat, in an attempt to gain privacy. "No, I'm accusing Quint Burdett of something. What did he want to know?"

"If you had a habit of running away from important decisions."

"He asked you that?"

"I think that was the jist of it."

"What did you tell him?"

"About Ms. Worrell, who decided in ten minutes to take off for the whole summer to follow a wisp of a little girl's dream about Wyoming and recklessly spend the summer of her forty-fifth year chasing cowboys? I told him you were a quite responsible and sensible schoolteacher . . . most of the time."

Develyn lowered her voice. "I am not chasing cowboys."

"Hah!"

"Who was that?" Lily asked.

"Casey."

"She knows I'm right."

"You can't believe anything she says. She also thinks she's a French countess."

"A princess?"

"A countess. It's a long story. What else did Quint say? I'm getting ticked about this."

"He seemed like a nice enough man. I think he's sincerely worried about you. He reminds me a lot of . . ."

"My mother?"

"Funny you should mention that. Delaney said she tried to phone you last night. Your mother phoned from Austria. There's been a slight accident."

"What kind of an accident?"

"David, bless his heart, was on a chair in a hotel room in Vienna, trying to pin a blanket over the window so that . . ."

"So that Mother can sleep in the dark. Yes, she always makes him do that. What happened?"

"He fell off and broke his arm."

"Oh, no. Poor David."

"And so he was at the hospital overnight, and the tour group went on without them. They'll have to stay a few more days and link up with the next group."

"Is David alright?"

"I think he's resting up."

"I bet he is. A trip with my mother could wear out a battalion of Marines. How's Delaney?"

"I think she's feeling better. I haven't seen her much in the past few days. Just trying to finish up summer school."

"Has it been six weeks?"

"Almost. It seems like six years since I've seen you last."

"Lily, why don't you come out and see me?"

"Delaney and I have discussed flying out to Wyoming."

"Really?"

"Yes, we wanted to be there for the wedding."

"Wedding? There isn't going to be any wedding."

"Hah!"

"Was that Casey again?" Lily asked.

"Yes."

"Are you in Mr. Slater's pickup truck?"

"Yes. We left Casey's rig and the horses at her friend's place in Shoshoni. We're riding to town with Renny."

"Are you sitting in the middle?"

"Of course."

"Hah!" Lily mimicked.

● ● ●

Develyn held out her hands to Casey. "Look at this."

"The pathetic white color, or the wrinkly skin?"

"The shriveled skin, O bronze bombshell countess."

"That's not shriveled. Those four ladies from Arizona are shriveled."

"They are all in their eighties."

"But you are clean, that's the important thing."

"Yes, but I have no makeup. No eye shadow. No foundation. No mascara. I am almost too embarrassed to go get my nails done."

"Are you too embarrassed to get a latte?"

"No," Develyn grinned. "We'll find one that has a drive-thru."

"So, you don't want anyone to see the real you?" Casey challenged.

"Heavens no."

Casey dried off her waist-length, thick black hair with a fluffy white towel. "Maybe that's been my problem. I've always let the guys see my natural beauty. Perhaps I need to deceive them a little."

"I am not deceiving anyone," Develyn snapped. "I'm just trying to look my best, that's all."

"Whatever. I guess it's sort of addictive." Casey tossed her towel into the wire basket in front of the locker. "You've been doing it so long, you can't imagine otherwise."

"Of course I can go without my makeup. I just choose not . . ."

"Do it."

"What?"

"Let's see Develyn Worrell go one week without a tiny bit of makeup."

"Not even get our nails done?"

"Nope."

"You are not talking lipstick, too, are you?"

"Of course I am."

"But my lips are so weak," Develyn whined.

"What's your point? You and me are still going to ride every day, right?"

"Yes, but . . ."

"And you insisted that you aren't chasing cowboys."

"That's right."

"So, who is it you are trying to impress? Uncle Henry? My Maria? Me? We love you just like you are."

"Are you challenging me to a week without makeup?"

Casey folded her arms. "I'm daring you. And I'll do the same."

"You seldom use makeup anyway."

"And your point is?"

"It should be an equal sacrifice. I know! I'll go a week without makeup and you . . . have to wear your hair down."

"A whole week?" Casey gasped.

"24/7. Of course, if you don't want to, we can . . ."

"I'll do it!"

"You will?"

"Yes. So, that's settled."

"I can't believe I let you talk me into that."

Casey stared at the locker room mirror and jammed on her cowboy hat. "I look like the queen of Mule Days with my hair down under my hat." Casey tossed a sack over to Develyn.

"What's this?"

"A couple of University of Wyoming T-shirts. I didn't think we wanted to go out into beautiful downtown Thermopolis in our muddy T-shirts."

"Thanks. Hey, we'll look like twins."

"In your dreams, Devy-girl."

"You can't fault a lowly maidservant for wanting to look like the countess."

"How true. Come on, my dear." Casey grabbed her arm. "I mustn't keep the little people waiting."

• • •

Renny Slater lounged against the front of his red Dodge pickup next to a tall, thin cowboy with short hair and brown skin.

"Oh, no!" Casey groaned, then spun around.

"What's the matter?"

"See the guy talking to Renny?"

"Yes, who is it?"

"Jackson Hill."

"Who's that?"

"He's the guy I wrote secret love notes to for two years."

"What? You never told me about that. Did you two go out?"

"No. I never let him know they came from me."

"Wow . . . when was this?"

"I was nineteen and he was twenty-one. We were doing all the Wilderness Circuit rodeos that year. I'd sneak a note in his gear bag during his ride."

"You wrote a cowboy love notes?"

"I was immature."

"It sounds very romantic."

Casey shrugged. "He never wrote one back."

"How would he know who to write it to?"

"He could have left one in his bag, you know, just in case I looked."

"And he never knew it was you?"

"Nope."

"Then what's the big deal?" Develyn grabbed Casey's arm and spun her around. "Come on."

"But my hair is combed down."

"I don't get the connection."

"He might not recognize me."

"Is that good or bad?"

"I don't know, Dev. What should I do?"

"What's the worst thing that can happen?"

"I could scare him off by my looks."

"Now you know exactly how I feel without makeup." Develyn tugged Casey toward the red pickup.

"I hope he doesn't remember me," Casey murmured.

"He's cute."

"Yes, and you ought to see him with his . . . eh, never mind. He's probably married by now."

"How long since you've seen him?"

"Eight, maybe ten years."

"Good grief, girl, what are you worried about? Come on, shoulders back, head up . . . strut a little."

Both men glanced up.

Jackson Hill's brown eyes widened. "Wow, Casey Cree-Ryder. You look great, darlin'. I haven't seen you in forever." He slapped his arm around her shoulders and gave her a hug.

She rolled her eyes at Develyn and gave a sheepish hug in return. "Hi, Jackson, are you still ridin' broncs?"

"No, I've been runnin' a pack string up in Glacier Park. Just got a few days off. How about you? You chasin' barrels on the circuit?"

"Not much. Training a few horses for rich girls, that's all."

Hill glanced over at Develyn. He tipped his black Resistol. "I don't believe we've met, ma'am."

"This is . . ." Casey blurted out.

"I'm her mother," Develyn announced.

He blushed and stuck out his hand. "Glad to meet you, Mrs. Cree-Ryder. Sorry for the stare, you two don't look anything alike."

"I need my makeup," Develyn said.

Renny Slater laughed. "She was teasin' you, Jackson. This is Develyn Worrell. She's a schoolteacher from Indiana and a friend of ours."

"I'm glad you cleared that up. I don't feel so bad about staring."

"Sorry to tease you, Jackson," Develyn smiled. "I get ribbed so much out here, I'm starting to do it myself. Of course, I am old enough to be Casey's mother."

Jackson Hill pulled off his cowboy hat and held it in his hand. "But you age well, ma'am."

"Thank you, cowboy." Develyn glanced at Casey and mouthed the words, *I need my makeup.*

"Casey, I don't reckon I've ever seen you with your hair down like that. It's always been in a braid. How long have you been wearin' it down?" Jackson asked.

"About ten minutes."

"Well, I like it, that's for sure."

"Jackson, the three of us were heading out for an early supper. You are certainly invited," Develyn offered.

"I already invited him," Renny said, "but he turned me down. Of course, now that he knows I got me a pair of purdy ladies, he might change his mind."

Jackson stared straight at Casey. "I surely wish I could. I promised my boss I'd evaluate a string of horses he wants to buy from an ol' boy north of Riverton. I just stopped here to use the phone and line up the appointment. When I ran across Renny and he said Casey was around, naturally I wanted to stay and say howdy. But I need to head out, because I'm not sure how long it will take me to find this ranch."

"Whose ranch?" Renny asked.

Hill pulled a scrap of paper from his shirt pocket. "Henry Starfoot. He's on the Rez."

"I don't think I know his place," Renny pondered.

"Casey knows where it's at," Develyn boomed.

"I do?" Casey gulped.

Develyn shoved her elbow in Casey's ribs. "Starfoot . . . remember? The other night you were talkin' about some girls that used to do well in the All-Indian rodeos and you mentioned a Starfoot girl."

"But . . . but . . ."

"You said there were a thousand antelopes on that road back to their place. I'm sure it will come to you once you get down there," Develyn insisted.

"It will?" Casey shot her a quick glare.

"So, why don't you ride with Jackson down to see the horses, then he can give you a lift to Shoshoni to pick up the horses and Uncle Henry."

"Your Uncle?" Jackson asked.

"No, her burro," Casey murmured. "I still don't . . ."

"Grab a burger on the way out of town. You two can get caught up on things," Develyn insisted. "How long has it been since you've seen each other?" She looked straight at Jackson.

"About ten years, I reckon. I'd enjoy having you come along, Cree-Ryder. You can even bring your guns and knives if you want to."

"Whoa . . ." Develyn replied, "there's one confident cowboy."

Casey had a panicked look in her eyes. "But I sort of promised you two that I would . . ."

Develyn slipped her arm into Slater's. She rolled her eyes at the mustang breaker. "Renny, honey, I am trying my best to get us a little private time."

Slater patted her hand. "I know, mama, it's hard to push them out of the nest when they don't want to go."

"You trying to get rid of me?" Casey protested.

"I think they were hoping to be alone," Jackson said.

"Have fun," Develyn urged.

Casey marched right up to Develyn. "Boys, I need to talk to my mother alone for a minute." She tugged Develyn across the parking lot, then lowered her voice. "What do you think you are doing?"

"Getting you a date with the cutest cowboy under forty that I have seen since I got here."

"A date? Going to look at pack horses is a date?"

"In some parts of Wyoming, it's tantamount to being engaged."

"Do you want to be alone with Renny? Is that what this is about?"

"I want you to be alone with Jackson Hill. Renny and I will be fine. He's a good friend."

"I don't know where that Starfoot ranch is, and you know it."

"Fake it, Casey, and have fun."

"But . . . but . . . what are we going to talk about? I mean, how should I be?"

"Talk about anything you like. Be yourself, Casey. Be that wonderful, beautiful countess that you are."

"I can't believe you are doing this to me."

Develyn led her back to where the men stood next to the truck. "Sweetie, you are goin' to thank me in the morning."

"Is it all settled?" Renny asked.

"Almost," Develyn said. "Jackson, are you married?"

"What?" He stared at Renny, then at Casey. "Is she teasing me again?"

Casey shook her head.

"Eh, no, ma'am. I'm not married."

"Have you ever been married?"

"Develyn!" Renny cautioned.

Jackson shook his head. "No, ma'am, I ain't never been married. However, I was engaged to Barbara Belton for two days one time."

Renny howled. "Who wasn't?"

"OK," Develyn said. "One more thing, will you promise to see that she gets back to our cabin by midnight?"

"Do you mean midnight tonight or tomorrow night?" he grinned.

"I like this boy," Develyn laughed. "Tonight."

"I'm almost thirty-two, and I feel like a sixteen-year-old on prom night," Jackson said. "Your mama is tough, Casey, darlin'."

"Don't get her riled . . . never underestimate the wrath of a fifth-grade teacher," Casey said.

"No foolin'? My mama has taught fourth grade in Sheridan for thirty-five years."

"A schoolteacher's boy? Hmmm . . . in that case you can stay out until 12:30," Develyn announced.

The four strolled to Jackson's white Dodge pickup. After Casey slid into the truck, she rolled down the window. "You know, I should be the one telling Renny to get you home early."

"Now, don't get to meddlin'," Renny said.

"Well, if you don't get her home in time, Quint Burdett will have the entire Wyoming National Guard activated to look for her."

"Do you have your cell phone?" Develyn asked.

"Yes, and I have a quarter, just in case I need to use a pay phone to have you come pick me up."

Develyn folded her arms across her chest. "I'm being overprotective, aren't I?"

"Yeah, you shove me out and then want strings attached."

"I have heard that line before."

Casey raised her thick, black eyebrows. "From Delaney?"

"Yes, so it must be true." Develyn glanced at a grinning

Jackson Hill. "Take care of her. And I wasn't really joking about 12:30."

He tipped his hat. "Yes, ma'am. Shoot, it will take that long for us just to catch up since June of 1996."

"It was May of '96," Casey corrected.

"Nope, you're wrong." Jackson reached down to his boot and pulled out his wallet. "It was June 26, 1996."

"What was June 26?" Casey asked.

He pulled out a faded, folded page from a steno notebook. "See here . . . June 26, 1996."

"Oh, my word, no . . ." Casey sobbed. "You saved them?"

He nodded. "Thirty-eight of 'em."

"Those are the notes you put in his gear bag?" Develyn choked.

"I kept ever' one, then reread them on lonely nights. I didn't know who had written them, but I knew if I held on to them long enough, I'd find out."

"When did you learn that it was Casey?" Develyn asked.

"Two minutes ago, when she started to cry."

"You didn't know until then?"

"I hoped it was her, but I didn't know." Jackson Hill put his hand on Cree-Ryder's shoulder. "You don't have to go with me, if you don't want to."

"Are you trying to get me to leave?" Casey sobbed.

"That would break my heart. I really want to visit with you."

Casey wiped her nose on the back of her hand. "Then let's leave before I shoot you or kiss you. I don't want witnesses either way."

The truck roared out of the parking lot.

Renny put his arm around Develyn's shoulder. "That's quite a story, Ms. Worrell. You'll have to fill me in on what I don't know."

"I'm still stunned that a man would carry those anonymous notes for ten years."

"Dev, darlin', you have no idea how lonely life can be on the road. It's memories like that which sustain a man."

"But for ten years?"

"If you are pinin' over a girl you know, you can find a cure within six months to a year. But an unknown gal only gets better with every passing memory. I guarantee you Jackson would have carried that note until his dyin' day, if he hadn't found out it was Casey."

"I can't believe how quick a situation can change."

Renny took her arm and led her back to his truck. "Nor can I . . . Devy-girl."

● ● ●

"So, I said to Etbauer . . . 'Billy, you're holding that rein too short' . . . and he said . . . 'Renny, I am short'!"

Develyn glanced around at the crowded steak house. Every conversation in the building suspended, waiting for Slater to finish the story. He sat up and glanced around. "Am I talkin' too loud again, darlin'?"

She shook her head and grinned. "You are just being Renny Slater. Everyone loves your stories." She cut a small bite of rib-eye steak and stabbed it with her fork. "You ought to write down some of these tales."

"Me? Write? Devy-girl, I haven't written much more than my name in twenty years. You're the schoolteacher. Maybe I could get you to write them down. Anyway, nothing spectacular ever happened to me."

"Is that so?" she pressed. "You mean to tell me that riding a horse over a cliff in Wind River Canyon and surviving isn't spectacular?"

"Just 'cause not many folks have done somethin', doesn't mean it should be written about. Shoot, Miss Dev, I was just lucky."

"Lucky? You punctured your lungs, broke your ribs, dislocated your collarbone, and broke your wrist." Develyn glanced at her reflection in the blade of the knife. *If only I had some makeup.*

Renny took a swig of iced tea. "I just sprung my wrist."

"And laid in that stream until daylight. I'd say that was worth writing about."

"Devy-girl, to be honest, I reckon we all have different adventures in life. But I think I enjoy mine more than the next guy. Ever' day is worth living. You just don't know what that day will bring."

"You goin' to quote Forrest Gump and tell me life is like a box of chocolates?" The steak tasted sweet, juicy, and hot.

"No, ma'am, for me, every day is like a bronc I've never ridden before. You screw your hat down tight. Grab that rope rein with a vise grip, jam your boots in the stirrups, then you lean back and nod, 'outside'."

"The gate swings open, and the day begins. Some days you get bucked off on the second jump. Other days you ride that mean sucker until the crowd stands to cheer. And lots of days, you make your ride, but don't get much of a score. Then you fall in your bunk ever' night with the thought: wait until tomorrow. So you get up and start the adventure all over again."

She scraped a fork full of baked potato. "You sayin' that life's a rodeo, cowboy?"

"Yes, ma'am . . ." He tipped his black beaver-felt cowboy hat. "You can either get sick worrying about it, or just stay in shape and enjoy one day at a time. How about you, Miss Dev? How would you describe your life?"

"I live a schoolteacher's life."

"What does that mean?"

"It means I have all my lessons planned out for the entire year, and a good day is when I complete the lesson plan on the day assigned."

"But what about the surprises?"

"They are constant grief and annoyance."

"I notice in Arizona, Florida, and other states, some towns make a big deal out of how many days of sunshine they expect to have each year. So, following your lesson plan philosophy of life, how many good days do you expect to have in a year?"

Develyn stared out the window toward the parking lot. *Lord, why are you doing this to me? Why do you challenge me to think my life through? I don't want to answer him.*

She cleared her throat and laid her fork on her plate. "I'd say I have about fifty-two good days a year, three spectacular days, fifty-two bad days, three horrible days . . . and about 255 mediocre days."

"Whoa, I wasn't expectin' such a detailed account."

"Renny, in my lesson plan book, I use a red felt-tip pen and draw a star for every good day . . . a blue X for bad days . . . and nothing for a mediocre day. I know what the record is."

"How about these summer days, since you came to Wyoming?"

"I don't judge them at all. They all seem to be good in their way."

"There's your secret. Don't judge them at all. No more marks in your lesson plan book for life."

"Renny, I'm a very organized person."

"I didn't say no more plans. I said no more predetermined judgment. When do you make your mark in the lesson plan book at school?"

"At the end of the day, before I go home."

"But how do you know for sure it's been a bad day? Maybe all the returns are not in yet."

"What do you mean?"

"Jesus was crucified on a Friday, and some of the women who had traveled with him, including his mama, were there. If you surveyed them on Friday night, how many of them would say that was a lousy day?"

"All of them, I suppose."

"Now here we sit at the Tapadera Inn, eatin' steaks and butter-drenched baked potatoes, corn on the cob, and apple pie waitin' for us. Lookin' back from where we are right now, would you say that the Friday Jesus was crucified and died for our sins was a good or a bad day?"

"It was a glorious day for us. That's why we call it Good Friday."

"There's my point. Even the worst of days might turn out in the long run to be the best of days."

"OK, Mr. Slater, I am overwhelmed with cowboy logic. Where is all of this leading?"

He pushed his hat back. "How about you driving with me up to Graybull tomorrow and helping me break a two-year-old filly?"

She wiped the white cloth napkin across her narrow lips. "What has that got to do with your great philosophy?"

"It means you'll take a risk on havin' a good day."

"How long will it take?"

"Eight hours."

"You ride a bucking horse for eight hours?"

"I hope I don't ride a bucking horse at all. I've got a method of calmin' 'em down, so that by the time I climb on board there is no buck in them. I think you'd learn somethin' about horses . . . some about Renny Slater . . . and even some things about Ms. Develyn Worrell."

Develyn sipped on her iced tea, studied his dimpled grin and his large brown eyes. "I'd like that."

"So would I."

"Renny, you are easy to be with. Some day, I plan to forgive you for sticking that thistle under My Maria's saddle at the auction."

"I was hopin' you had forgotten about that, darlin'."

"Oh, no, there are some things a girl never forgets."

"Like a boy remembers his first horse, and a girl her first kiss?" he offered.

"Or her last kiss."

"Are you pinin' for Quint?"

"No, no . . . not really. Can I be brutally honest with you, Mr. Slater?"

"You goin' to embarrass me?"

"I just might. But it won't be on purpose. You asked me about my first kiss . . . well . . . I have never been kissed much. My ex-husband was not the kissing kind. It didn't accomplish his goal. I believe his comment was, 'Why waste time with the appetizer, when it's the entrée that I'm after?'"

Renny glanced around the room, then rubbed his chin. "Eh, well . . . I reckon that is one man's philosophy."

"Are you embarrassed, Renny?"

He flashed a dimpled grin. "No, Miss Dev, not me. But them two ladies over in the side booth under the fake flowers is blushing like they laid in the sun too long."

"They were listening to me?"

"Everyone's listenin' to you."

"We're quite a pair of talkers, Mr. Mustang Breaker."

"I reckon we are." He leaned across the table. "Now, let me tell you somethin'."

She lowered her voice. "You aren't goin' to embarrass me, are you?"

"I don't think so."

"Rats."

"I like you, Devy-girl."

"I like you, too, Renny. I never have to pretend to be perfect when I'm with you. That's a nice freedom you give me."

She leaned over and whispered. "Are you going to tell me you haven't kissed very much either?"

He patted the top of her hand. "No, ma'am. In fact, I just might be the best kisser in Wyomin'."

"Oh, then, well good."

"What I wanted to tell you is that I don't believe I've ever been around a lady who was as good a listener as you."

"How's that?"

"Most gals have their own agenda. They want me to talk about their subject or just sit still. My ex-wife is a very sweet lady whom I haven't seen in ten years. She's happy with a new husband and kids, so I hear. But I don't think she ever listened to anything that was really on my heart since the night I proposed to her. She planned out my life and had me jump through the hoops. Some days I was tired of jumpin' and just wanted to have her sit still and listen. But that never worked out. Thanks for listenin' to me."

"Renny, I'm glad we had some time alone to visit. When are we leaving to go to Graybull in the morning?"

"I'll pick you up about 5 a.m. or so."

"Oh, dear. Make it 'or so' please. I'll hardly have time to put my face on."

"You know you don't have to paint it up for me. I like it today."

Develyn's hands went to her face. "I forgot! Oh, dear, what a dumb promise I made to Casey. I must look old and pathetic."

"To tell you the truth, Devy-girl, you look good." His eyes seemed to lock on to hers. "You look real good."

D on't give him anything you don't want to give him."
Casey peered out from under the bedcovers at the back
of the cabin. "Yes, Mother. We're just driving down to Laramie.
He has some ol' college pals to look up. One of them is an
assistant professor at the University of Wyoming."

Develyn stared at her reflection in the mirror. "Why did
I let you talk me into this 'no makeup' thing?"

"You look perky as always."

"Casey, no woman looks perky at 5:45 a.m. And I had to
beg him to wait until 6:00. Renny wanted to leave at 5:00."

"Well, Jackson loves my hair down, so I don't suppose
keeping the promise will be a problem for me."

"What do you like best about him?"

"He's nice to me. Really nice. You know . . . polite, considerate. Do you know what he did? He opened the door of the pickup for me."

"That's what a gentleman does."

"Dev, that's the first time anyone ever opened a door for me."

"He's a good-looking young man."

"Did you see his brown eyes? They are dreamy, aren't they?"

"I have to be honest. I didn't look in his eyes."

"I stared at them for hours. You can learn volumes by looking into a man's eyes."

"So, I hear."

"I was so worried all the way home about how to tell you I wanted to go to Laramie and wouldn't be riding with you. Isn't it cool the way the Lord works things out?"

"Casey, is it just me, or does life move at a different pace out here? Two mornings ago we rode out, and I was trying to figure out Quint. Yesterday morning we snuck out of LaSage Canyon. And now, you are headin' off with Mr. Dream Cowboy."

"And you are drivin' off with the biggest flirt in Wyoming."

"I like Renny."

"Every woman in this state likes Renny. But that's OK. He's a nice guy, Devy-girl. I told you that from day one. The Lord has done a number on that mustang breaker. But he's rodeo through and through."

"What does that mean?"

"He's always goin' down the road. There is always some big thing just over the hill. He can't stay in any one place too long.

It's a mentality. A lifestyle. In the old west days, he would be called a drifter. Like most roughstock riders, he has an eight-second attention span."

Develyn giggled. "Just like fifth-graders."

"I suppose. Just don't expect something from Renny that he can't give."

Develyn brushed a comb through her short blonde hair. "Yes, Mother. How do I look?"

"Darling, of course. You always look darling."

"I didn't look darling yesterday morning."

"That's true." Casey swung her feet out of bed, then stood. She wore an oversize Frontier Days T-shirt that hung just past her panties. "Can I borrow that purple shirt of yours with the cowboy hat silhouette on it?"

"Sure, honey, but we aren't exactly the same size, you know where. It might be a little snug."

"I certainly hope so."

"Casey Cree-Ryder, let me clarify my earlier injunction. Don't you be givin' away something the Lord doesn't want you to give away."

Casey shuffled across the slick linoleum and hugged Develyn's shoulder. "And, sweet Devy-girl, don't you go giving away anything the Lord doesn't want you to give away."

Develyn stepped back. "I'll be with Renny all day."

"Rule number two in dealing with cowboys: Never underestimate cowboy charm."

"What's rule number one?"

"Always, and I mean always . . . read their eyes."

155

"Thank you, Ms. Cree-Ryder."

"You're welcome, Ms. Worrell."

"I'm going to feed the horses. I can get ready on time when I don't have to put on any makeup."

"When were you not ready on time?"

"July 23, 1989. I've regretted it ever since."

Casey shoved her toward the door. "While you are out there, explain to Uncle Henry why you're deserting him today. He pouted like a three-year-old when you didn't show up to load him yesterday evening."

"What will he do when I have to go back to Indiana in a few weeks?"

"Dev . . . I don't even know what I'll do."

● ● ●

Wyoming wind greeted her at the door, and she reached for her hat, even though she wasn't wearing one. To the east, the sun had broken the horizon and was casting long shadows westward. Uncle Henry greeted her at the bottom of the porch step, then followed her to the pasture.

"Now, baby, I'm going to be gone today, so you have to behave yourself. You may not go over to Mr. Tallon's and plop on his driveway. You may not go into town and hang out at the tree in front of Mrs. Tagley's store hoping the children will give you candy." She fingered the hair between the burro's ears. "You need to stay in the yard and rest up. We'll all go riding tomorrow. If you aren't a good boy, I will have to put you in the pasture with My Maria and Popcorn. Be a good boy, and Mama will bring you back a treat."

"I hate to interrupt this mother-and-son talk."

Develyn spun around to see Cooper Tallon standing, hat in hand, ten feet behind her. She shaded the sun with her hand. The wind felt cool on her bare arms.

"Oh, Cooper . . . I didn't hear you."

"Am I intruding?"

"No, I'm afraid I talk to this burro like he was one of my children."

"It's OK, Miss Dev. I've spent my entire life alone. A man can go sour if he doesn't have someone to talk to. I used to have a running dialog with my television set until she up and ran off with a burglar."

She grinned, then folded her hands across her chest. "I hear Quint called out the troops to look for me. Sorry about that."

"Quint Burdett is a good man, but he's driven. Always pushing himself. I think he learned that from his wife, Emily. She pushed him a lot."

"I didn't know that."

"When you come from one of the premier families in Texas, you expect quite a bit from a husband."

"Cooper, I know I've spent a lot of time with Quint. But that's changing. I don't intend on reporting to him, nor do I want him to come looking for me. So, don't let him rope you into some snipe hunt for Miss Dev."

"Yes, ma'am. But all the same, if I figured you were in trouble, I'd surely want to help find you."

"I'll tell you what. Anytime you are at the cabin, I'll let you know where I'm headed so you can be the official locator of Miss Dev."

"No, I didn't mean for you . . ."

"Cooper, I need your help in this. I don't want Quint to think he has to look after me. You are my neighbor, so you get the job."

"That's fine, but I don't intend to be nosy."

She studied his gray-blue eyes, then brushed her bangs back. "I must look a fright without my makeup."

He shook his head. "No, ma'am, Miss Dev. You look as good as a potato all scrubbed up and ready for the pot."

"Eh, I don't think I've ever been told that before."

"I meant it as a compliment."

"I believe you."

He gazed across the pasture. "You are out a little earlier than usual."

"Renny Slater is coming by. He promised to show me how he breaks a wild horse."

"I hear he's one of the best. Will you be gone all day?"

"Yes, we're headed to Graybull. But I haven't forgotten about our time to sit and visit. I really haven't."

"I was just thinkin'. Maybe we could aim for Friday evenin'. I'll barbecue some ribs, and we can sit out on the porch at my place and have some supper."

"That sounds very nice, Coop."

He turned to head back to the cabins. "I'm sorry about the potato comment. It's a phrase my grandmother used. She came to this country in a covered wagon when she was three. They built a beautiful ranch house right out there near the road. Right where the cottonwoods are."

"I didn't know that."

"It burnt down, and Dad didn't rebuild it. Some day, I'd like to settle down here and build a place. But I don't think I'd want it this close to town. I'd rather have it back in the cedar hills. Anyway, we can visit about that on Friday evenin'." He jammed his hat back on. "Eh, you got purdy eyes, Miss Dev. They look like they care about people."

"That's a nice thing to say. Thank you."

"Does it make up for the dumb thing about scrubbed potatoes?"

"I believe so."

"That looks like Slater toolin' down the road. I'll talk to you on Friday."

"Yes, you will. And I will want to know all about what it was like to pioneer this area."

● ● ●

The ranch turned out to be a large brush corral just west of Graybull, at the base of the Big Horn Mountains. Next to the corral was a huge, unpainted barn. The wood siding looked like a sand-blasted sign with only the knots in the lumber that retained their original dimensions. The breeze whistled as it bounced its way through the twisted sticks of the brush corral.

With the taste of bacon still lingering from the Graybull breakfast, Develyn entered the corral behind Renny. He carried a harness looped on his right arm and a blue nylon lead rope, coiled and tucked in the back of his Wranglers.

Inside the one-hundred-by-fifty-foot corral she spied a welded-pipe round pen and a nervous black horse that shied to the far end of the arena. The dirt in the corral floor had crusted after the last rain. Develyn felt a slight crunch with each step. The breeze was sage-filled, but dust free.

Renny squatted down in the middle of the corral and stared at the horse.

Develyn crouched on her haunches beside him. "Is this squatting thing genetic in all cowboys, or is it something you have to learn?"

Renny didn't take his eyes off the horse. "It's 'cause we spend too many years too dirty to sit in chairs. Mama was particular that way." He fingered the brown nylon halter. "She favors turnin' left."

"Your mother?"

"The horse."

Develyn glanced down at the long-legged horse that stood in the northeast corner of the corral. Her rump pointed toward them, yet she craned her neck to the left to keep an eye on them. "What do you know about this horse?"

"Before I got here, I was told she's two and a half years old, nine hundred pounds. She was born at the headquarters about five miles east of here. Her mama is Mrs. Castleford's riding horse. They thought their daughter would train this one, but she decided she liked rebuilding old cars better. So they just turned it out in the pasture for two years. When she was young she was haltered and led around the headquarters. But since then, this big pasture has been home."

"Does she have a name?"

"Molly."

"So what are you doing out here?"

"Sizing her up."

"What is she doing?"

"Sizing us up. Hunkerin' down here and not moving closer for a while will help her relax."

"Are you one of those guys like in the movie *The Horse Whisperer*?"

"I don't know. I never tried to categorize myself." Renny's voice was low, soft. "But I did see the movie. Other than the morals and profanity, it wasn't too bad."

"How long does this squatting period last?"

"Until she turns around, faces us, and relaxes."

"How long will that be?"

"Between two minutes and two hours."

"You can squat for two hours?"

"Squattin' ain't the problem." Renny didn't take his eyes off the horse. "Gettin' up and walkin' afterward is the problem."

"What does it mean when she turns around to look at us?"

"That she's not trying to run away any more. Everything you see Miss Molly do today is predicated on fear. She is afraid of the unknown. Her instincts are to run away. A horse is mean only if it has been treated mean. She hasn't been treated at all, but she's scared. It's OK to be scared. It's something we all learn to deal with."

"Is it alright if I just sit in the dirt? I don't think I am quite as good at squatting as you. My mother let me sit in the chairs when I was young. Of course, there were some chairs I couldn't sit in."

"Be my guest, Devy-girl. Sorry I don't have a blanket for you to park on."

Develyn scooted down and tucked her knees up under her chin. "Renny, where's home for you? I know you have a place in Buffalo. But where were you raised?"

"Hey, is this time for the story of my life?"

"Yep, cowboy." She patted his knee. "You said we could be here a while."

"Daddy was a roustabout. He worked the oil fields when the war was over and came out to Gillette in 1951. Mama was a ranch girl. My grandparents had a modest place just west of Deadman Creek, about thirty miles east of Sheridan. Some of the church folk from that area went to Gillette in 1951 to set up a tent revival meeting to reach the souls of that rough crew of oil field workers.

"Mama and her sister sang in the choir ever' night. Not too many workers came to the meetings, and some who did showed up only as a joke. Daddy said a pal of his persuaded a few of them to go, because they were all broke and waitin' for payday."

"Did your daddy go forward?"

"Not during the first meeting. But he did go up and visit with my Aunt Paula."

"Your aunt? Not your mother?"

"He said Mama scared him to death, so he warmed up on Aunt Paula. By the second night, he was visitin' with Mama. And the third night he was saved and baptized."

"They baptized right at the tent meeting?"

"In a stock tank."

Develyn grinned. "Somehow that makes perfect sense out here."

"Three weeks later they got married."

"Three weeks? They only knew each other three weeks?"

"That's it. Grandpa said they could get married only if Daddy quit the oil field work and came and worked the ranch at Deadman Creek."

"And he did?"

"Yep. He was saved, married Mama, and went into ranching. He always said it was the best month of his life."

"Said? Has he passed away?"

"We lost him to lung cancer when I was twenty-one."

"And your mother?"

"She's still at the ranch. My brother and his family live there. He runs the place. He's a welder by trade, so he works in town some and makes a go of the place."

Renny pushed his black Resistol hat back. "Now that's probably more than you wanted to know."

"No, not at all. When you learn someone's background, you feel like you know them so much better." Develyn pointed to the far end of the arena. "Look, Molly has turned toward us."

Renny stood and helped Dev to her feet. "Walk slow and keep your voice low."

"Should I not talk at all?"

"No, I want her to get used to our voices."

They walked forward about fifteen steps, and the nervous black horse turned away from them.

"Oh, no, what do we do now?" Dev asked.

Renny squatted. "The same thing all over again. Only this time, you got to tell me about where you were born."

● ● ●

Develyn kept track on her watch. It was fifty minutes before they squatted ten feet away from the black horse. She had told Renny a short version of most of her forty-five years.

"What do we do now?" she asked.

Renny spoke in a low monotone. "Now we've shared life stories."

"We didn't tell everything."

"The details of why you left your husband is none of my business. I reckon I know enough about Develyn Worrell to realize you had a very good reason."

"Sometimes I'm not sure there is a good reason. But try as I could, I just couldn't stand to be in the same room with him anymore." Dev stared at the horse. "There, she turned around again. What's the next step?"

"Study her eyes."

"They are big and dark chocolate brown. What else do we need to know?"

"Figure out how scared she is, whether she intends to break and run, which direction she'll bolt, whether we're still a threat or just a curiosity, if she has any aches and pains, and who will win the World Series this year."

Develyn elbowed Renny's side. "You think I'm just a hick from Indiana? You think I just fell off the corn wagon?"

"A month ago you would have believed me. Stand up, but don't take a step."

When they stood, Molly began to prance.

Renny held out his hand. "It's OK, Miss Molly . . . we're not goin' to hurt you. You just need to learn a little horse sense. Now, normally your mama would have taught some of this to you. But your mama is busy packin' around the boss's wife, so you have to learn a few things from me and Devy-girl."

Without taking his eyes off the ear-twitching horse, he nudged Develyn. "OK, darlin', talk to her gentle and take two steps to the right. Set yourself there and no matter what, don't budge. She will want to break that way, but don't let her. Just keep mumbling something. It doesn't matter what, just show her that's your territory and she can't have it.

Develyn eased right. "Are you setting me up to get run over by a wild horse?"

"She's not wild. Just unbroken."

"You know what I mean."

"Take another step."

"You said two."

"I didn't know you would be so timid."

"I've never done this before."

"Neither has Molly."

"What are you going to do now?"

"I'm going to step up there and let her pet my hand with her nose."

"Don't you mean you'll pet her?"

"Nope, it's got to be her idea, or it won't work. You just keep talking."

"What about?"

"Shoot, I don't know . . . about schoolteaching. Tell me about some of your students last year."

Renny took one step toward the horse. She tried to back up, but rammed her rump into the brush corral.

"Molly, come here, darlin' . . . ol' Renny ain't all that scary . . . keep talkin', Dev. Tell me about who sits up close to Ms. Worrell . . . and why."

"Hmmm . . . somehow, schoolteaching is not on my mind. I'm trying to decide if she breaks this way, whether to hold my ground or save my life."

"Don't move at all," Renny insisted. Then he turned to the horse. "Come on, sweet Molly. Come rub your mouth on my hand. Come on, babe, you can do it."

Develyn pushed her hat back, then folded her arms. "Let's see . . . who sat up front?"

"Come on, baby . . . that's the way . . . that's the way."

Molly pointed her ears forward.

"Renny is your pal. Come on . . ."

Develyn didn't take her focus off of Molly's big, dark brown eyes. "To begin with, there is one student who spent most of the year in the corner of my room with his face to the wall."

The horse was now only inches from Renny's hand. "He's a pill, I take it. I imagine ever' class has one of them."

"Her. Shelly M–A–C–L–E–A–N. That's the way she would say her name."

"Worried about someone misspellin' it, I reckon. I got called Kenny most of my life." When the horse leaned toward Renny, he pulled back. "I want her to want it."

"Are you still talking horses?"

"Yep, and you are talkin' rebellious students." This time, when Molly leaned forward, Renny left his hand there for her to nuzzle.

"No, she wasn't a troublemaker. Just the opposite. In the classroom she would never say a word, and was so nervous she would not do one speck of work."

Renny eased his hand across the black horse's nose and began to stroke her neck. He spoke low, barely audible. "That's a girl. That's the way, Molly. Yeah . . . let me pet you a bit. You see? It's not going to hurt."

"I knew she had been homeschooled. Her mother had to go outside the home to work. This was Shelly's first classroom experience."

"Now, she's thinkin' serious of boltin'," Renny declared. "Hold your ground, Miss Dev."

Develyn wiped sweat off the back of her neck and could feel the dirt start to cake. "Shelly always brought in her homework on time. She's an extremely smart girl. But she was petrified to be in front of other children. I mean she would sit motionless until class was over."

Renny rubbed his hand over Molly's neck and flank and withers. "You see, darlin' . . . that feels good, don't it? You see what you been missin'? Devy, take one step toward her as you talk."

Develyn inched closer. "I was determined to make it work, so after several weeks of trying various things, I went to talk to her mother."

Renny rubbed Molly's back with the nylon headstall. "No, darlin' . . . think of this as a fancy necklace that will turn all those stallions' heads. Yes, ma'am . . . you are goin' to look beautiful with this on."

Molly shuffled her hooves in the dry clay of the corral.

"Shelly, her mom, two brothers, and three sisters lived in an older two-bedroom single-wide mobile home on a narrow downtown lot."

"We're approaching the moment of truth. When she feels this on her nose, she will get scared. Don't budge. She is not a mean horse. She will not harm you. But she will want to run."

Through clenched teeth, Develyn continued. "The four girls have bunk beds in one room, the two boys in the other room, and the mother sleeps on the couch in the living room."

"OK, baby . . . this is it . . . I want you to be a good girl and do everything I tell you."

"OK," Develyn murmured.

"I was talkin' to the horse," he grinned. "Go on, tell me about Shelly and her mama."

"Daddy got tired of paying alimony and moved to Alaska, they think."

"That's a good place to get lost, I hear. OK. Let's do it right now. Whatever you do, don't stop talking and don't move."

Dev clutched herself tight. "Shelly was quite talkative in her own home. She led me to their tiny room. In one corner there was a wooden TV tray and a metal folding chair."

With a motion so quick Dev couldn't follow it, Renny slipped the halter up on the horse's nose. Molly pulled back and lunged at Develyn.

"Don't move," Renny called out. "Just talk."

"The TV tray was her desk where she did all her homework," Develyn shouted. *Lord, I don't want to die like this. I don't mind going to heaven; I just don't want to be mutilated by horse hooves before I get there.* "Shelly was so proud of her little space. Renny, people in prison have more room than that."

The black mare slumped her head and relaxed her neck. Renny slid the halter up over her ears and had it buckled before she could tuck her ears back. His right hand had a firm grip on the bottom of the halter. "Keep talkin', Devy. I like this little girl."

"It was so poignant. There were her paper, pencils, and books. On the faded wall above the TV tray was a small poster

169

of Larry the Tomato and Bob the Cucumber . . . and next to that a photograph of me that she had downloaded off the school Web site."

Renny stroked the horse's neck. "You were right up there with Larry and Bob. Wow! That's quite an honor."

"It was for me. Her mother said Shelly always sat there and talked to herself when she did her homework."

"My mother talks to herself when she cooks. It's a dadgum hoot to hear her. It's as if all her sisters and brothers are there, and she has to explain what she's doing."

Develyn felt her shoulders relax, and she dropped her hands to her side. "For Shelly, talking to herself was her method of cutting out the conflicting noises of a crowded house."

Renny reached behind his back, grabbed the blue nylon lead rope, and had it snapped to the ring without Molly knowing it. He continued to stroke her neck. "So, what did you do for little Shelly?"

"I came back to school, put her desk in the corner, and told her she could sit there, face the wall, and do her work, but she could only whisper to herself."

"Molly might get a little antsy here. I'm not going to lead her, but I want to tug on this rope to let her know it's here. Hold your ground and keep talking."

"The very next week she got A's on her tests and was looking for extra work to do."

When Renny tugged straight down on the lead rope, the mare's eyes widened and her ears pinned back, but she didn't move her head. "Now, darlin', you need to yield to the lead rope. It feels better when you give in." He kept the rope tight, but the mare refused to lower her head.

"What are you going to do?" Dev asked.

"Leave it tight until she decides she likes it better when it's loose. So, your Shelly sat in the corner all year?"

"No. In March, my friend Lily invited a distant relative of hers who is training to be an astronaut to come speak at our school."

"I've spoken at a few schools," he said, still pulling on the lead rope.

"Next time you are in Indiana, I will insist you speak to my class."

Molly lowered her head until the lead rope hung limp. "That a girl . . . see how nice that is, honey." He stroked her neck. "I knew you could do it."

"I had the astronaut in my class, but I didn't ask Shelly to turn her desk around."

"How about over here to the left?" Renny said. "Turn your head this way, darlin'." Molly turned her head to relieve the pressure of the lead rope.

"She did that on her own. She was completely fascinated by his talk."

"I reckon young girls, like young horses, do some things they weren't planning to do when they get distracted." Renny tugged the horse's head right and left. Molly yielded to his lead.

"When it came time to ask the astronaut questions, Shelly's hand went up first."

"I reckon she forgot to be afraid."

"This was in March, and I believe it was the first time the other kids had ever heard anything more than a whisper from her. I know it was the first question she ever asked out loud."

"This is a nice mare. She needs to be around people more. She likes people."

"How do you know that?"

"Can't you see it in her eyes? She likes the attention. I've never met a female yet that didn't like attention."

Develyn laughed. "Am I goin' to get some more chauvinistic cowboy philosophy?"

"No, keep talking. You scoot over next to me, and I'll lead her that direction. She wants to go that way, so we'll let her walk a while. You stay beside me and continue the story."

"Does she still need to hear my voice?"

"Not now, but I want to know what happens to little Shelly M–A–C–L–E–A–N."

"After that, she decided to leave her desk facing the class."

When Develyn scooted over, Molly stepped between her and the brush corral, Renny alongside, keeping the lead rope slack.

Develyn strolled beside him. "I gave my class an assignment to design a rocket ship and assigned teams, fully expecting Shelly to beg out."

"She didn't?"

"She was so excited with the project, she agreed to work with Nickie and Treena."

"I have a niece named Trina. Katrina, actually, but we call

her Trina." Renny led the black mare to the far end of the corrals, keeping her close to the brush fence.

Develyn pulled her straw hat off, brushed back her hair, then pressed it back down. "They were about halfway through the project when the girls begged Shelly to move her desk over next to theirs so they could work on it more often." She glanced around. "Are you taking her to the round pen now?"

"Not yet. We'll circle the corral a couple of times this direction, then see if I can talk her into reversing directions. After that we'll do a couple figure eights to get her used to the middle of the corral. Then, the round pen." Renny turned the horse toward the other side of the corrals. "Now, did Shelly move her desk?"

"Yes, she agreed, but said it would only be temporary. When they finished the space ship, she was moving back."

"Did she?"

"No, she stayed with the class for the rest of the year."

"Young girls, like young mares, do learn some things."

"She is still the shyest girl in school, but what a sweetie when you take time to know her. Out of all my students this last year, I miss her most."

"And Miss Molly is stepping right out, isn't she? A little instruction, a soft voice, a little praise . . . feeling safe . . . surprising how well they respond."

"Students or horses?"

"Both. Love, kindness, and sincere concern go a long way," Renny said. He switched directions with the black mare.

"Renny, I guess it's kids like Shelly that keep me coming back every year. That's why I teach. To make a lifetime difference. It's a rare privilege, a gift from the Lord. Does that make sense to you?"

"Yes, ma'am, and it's sweet mares like Miss Molly that keep me in this business."

At that moment, the mare paused, raised her tail, then went to the bathroom.

"Oh, dear," Develyn said. "I hope that isn't her assessment of your training methods."

"That's the ultimate compliment, Devy-girl. It proves how relaxed Miss Molly is."

● ● ●

Develyn perched on the top rail of the round pen as Renny lunged Molly clockwise, then counterclockwise.

Over.

And over.

And over again.

Each time he stopped her with a "whoa," he made her turn to face him before starting again.

"What time is it, Devy girl?"

Develyn glanced at her watch. "About 12:30."

"Have we been working with her for about three hours?"

"Yes."

"Let's take a break." Renny unlatched the lunge line and replaced it with the lead. Develyn swung open the gate, and he led the horse back into the corral. Then he shoved the line into Develyn's hands. "Take her over to the stock tank, give her a drink, then tie her to the post."

"Me?"

"Now you are the one sounding like a fifth-grader."

"But what if she doesn't want to mind me?"

"Don't give her that option." Renny shoved Develyn's waist toward the stock tank. "You are the boss. She's trying to find the pecking order in this herd. All horses know they have to fit in some order. She's given me first place, now it's time for you to accept the role as second place."

"But what difference does that make?" Dev protested. "I'm not going to be around this horse after today."

"That's true, but neither am I. We don't want her to be a one-man or one-woman horse. I want her to see all people as being ahead of her in the line. Don't let her boss you. If she tries to pull back, yank the line and tell her no. When she does it right, praise her."

"You'd make a wonderful school counselor, Mr. Slater."

"That's me, guidance counselor and driver's ed. instructor."

Develyn led the mare out through the middle of the corral toward the stock tank. "I've seen you drive. Stick to counseling."

Renny veered off to the gate at the south side of the corral. Molly tried to tug free and follow him.

Develyn jerked the rope. "No you don't, young lady. You're going with me."

Molly yanked back and refused to move.

"Pretend she's a naughty fifth-grader on the playground," Renny called out.

Develyn grabbed the lead rope with both hands and yanked it. "I said, you are coming with me. I don't want any lip from you. You will be staying after school all week if you don't get off this playground right now!"

Molly dropped her head and trudged after Develyn.

"Yes!" Renny hooted. "Schoolteachers make good horse trainers."

"I haven't been doing much but watching."

"After lunch, I'll have you lunge her."

● ● ●

They sat on a bale of hay, in the shade of the old barn, out of the wind. Renny sliced cheese and Develyn sipped on a Diet Coke. The conversation bounced from school to horse training to childhood memories to failed marriages. After about an hour, they sauntered back to the waiting mare. This time, Develyn lunged her clockwise and counterclockwise.

When she stopped, she noticed Renny had littered the corral with a couple of fence posts, soda cans, newspaper, and an old worn-out steel-belted tire.

"Put on the lead rope and bring her out here."

"Why are you trashing the place?"

"This isn't trash; it's an obstacle course. She needs to learn not to be afraid of these things. She's used to a clean corral. Life isn't always that simple."

"So, you have some crisis training?"

"Just minor obstacles, so she'll learn to trust me even with something unknown."

Develyn watched from the gate as Renny led Molly around and over the posts, trash, cans, and even stepped in the tire. Over and over, he repeated the process, never taking the same course twice.

"Pick up the tire and roll it straight at her," he called out.

"Is she ready for that?"

"There's one way to find out."

The black mare didn't flinch when the tire rolled toward them. It veered to the right, then plopped down at her feet. She bent low to investigate, then stared off at the big pasture beyond the corral.

"She did good," Develyn said.

"She's getting bored. Lead her around while I get the saddle."

"Is it time to ride her?"

"No, it's time to saddle her."

Renny had Develyn hold the lead rope as he brushed Molly down, then took his time as he laid the saddle blanket on her back. The horse craned around to watch, but didn't protest.

"Should I try to keep her head straight?"

"No, let her look."

Renny picked up the saddle and looped the right stirrup over the saddle horn. "Twitch her ear."

"What?"

"Grab her ear and bend it."

"Will that hurt her?"

"No, but it will annoy her enough she won't pay attention to what I'm doin'."

With one hand still on the lead rope, she latched the other to the horse's black ear. Molly's hair felt warm, a little sweaty.

"Now, bend it."

When Dev bent the ear, Molly took her eyes off Renny. He set the saddle down with deliberate care, let the stirrups hang free, then reached under the horse and buckled the cinches.

"I'll tighten these later. Turn loose of her ear."

"Will she buck?"

"We'll find out, won't we?"

Molly cranked her head back, but didn't protest.

"Isn't this a purdy saddle, Molly, darlin'?" Renny drawled. "Why, you look beautiful all dolled up with a fine rig like this. Maybe not as beautiful as Miss Dev, but you are a real head-turner, like she is."

"Save your flattery for horses, cowboy."

Renny stopped, reached over and pulled Develyn's chin around where she had to look at him. Then he tapped her nose with two fingers. "Ms. Worrell, you are one beautiful lady. You make a man proud to be in the same room or even the same corral with you."

Develyn bit her lip. "Thanks, Renny. I appreciate those words from you. I'm in the middle of Wyoming, and you make me feel like the world is spinning around me. I always feel good when I'm with you. But I can't imagine you could say that, what with me having absolutely no makeup."

"Darlin' . . . darlin' . . . darlin' . . . there are two things I'd like to teach you this summer. Well, actually three." Renny led Molly around the arena wearing the saddle.

"Oh?"

"I'd like to teach you how to break a horse."

"I'm learning a lot today."

"Yes, you are. And there are a couple more things to teach you today. I'd also like to teach you that you have a God-given beauty that can't be covered up with cream and lotion."

"At least I can cover up all these crow's feet around my eyes."

"Devy-girl, those are trophies of wisdom and age, and ever' one of them well-earned. Wear them with pride, darlin'. You earned the right to look your age."

"I've never heard it expressed that way."

Renny stopped in the middle of the arena, grabbed the front cinch strap and yanked it tight. Then he took the lead from her hands and looped it over the saddle horn. He eased the reins over the horse's head, then clutched them in his left hand. "Now it's time to mount up."

"Do you think she will buck?"

"What do you think, Miss Dev?"

"Me?"

"Look her in the eyes and tell me, is this horse going to buck?"

Develyn stared into the huge chocolate-colored eyes. "No, she won't. I think you are right. She is enjoying all the attention."

"I agree with you, darlin', but stand back anyway."

Renny stuck his left foot in the stirrup, then pulled it out again. He repeated this several times, putting more weight on the stirrup each time. Then he put all his weight on the stirrup, stood there a moment, then let himself back to the ground.

Slater repeated this several times.

"OK, Miss Dev, here's the test."

This time Slater put all his weight in the stirrup, then with patient caution swung his right leg over the seat of the saddle. As if in slow motion, he lowered his weight on to the saddle.

Molly shifted her front hooves and stood motionless.

He stroked the horse's neck. "You are a good girl, darlin'. Didn't she do good, Mama?"

Develyn laughed. "Yes, Daddy, our baby is growing up."

He stared at her for a minute.

"That was a joke."

"I know," he mumbled. "But it sounded good, anyway. Enjoy your daughter, Delaney. Children are such a blessing."

"Do you miss not having children, Renny?"

He kicked Molly's flanks, and the horse walked forward. "There are a lot of things I miss."

Develyn stood in the middle and watched Renny ride the horse around and around the corral. When he kicked the horse again, she sped up to a trot.

"This is a smooth ridin' mare, Miss Dev. Someone is getting a beauty of a horse."

He pulled up beside her. "You ride her for a while. I need to clean up the corral.

"Are we almost through?"

"I want to teach her to back up before we're done. Then I'll call the owners to come out and take a look." In one fluid motion, Renny eased off the saddle and down to the ground. He handed her the reins.

"I'll ride this horse on one condition," she demanded.

"Oh?"

"You told me that there were three things you wanted to teach me this summer. The first was how to gentle a horse. The second was to accept the way I look without makeup. What was the third thing?"

"I figured you'd call me on that."

"You figured right. Now, what else do you want to teach this Indiana schoolteacher?"

He leaned over and motioned for her to step closer. Their noses were only inches apart. "I was hoping to teach you how to kiss better." His hand slipped around the back of her neck, and he pulled her lips to his.

Her eyes were wide open.

His were shut.

The kiss was firm, not sloppy.

On the second kiss, she closed her eyes.

Develyn had Molly at a lope when the clean, gold Chevy Silverado pulled up to the barn. "Ride her out here!" Renny shouted as he opened the gate.

"Are you sure it's OK?"

"Just walk her around and talk to her. We'll show Miss Molly off to the boss."

The gray-haired man sported a pot belly and a pleasant smile. The woman wore jeans and a long-sleeved shirt, but her long gray hair was braided and she had no hat.

The man and Renny leaned against the pickup and began a laughing, hand-waving conversation. The woman strolled over to Develyn and the horse.

"I can't believe this is my Molly. She's been snotty for a couple of years. Take her at a gallop, hon. Let me see her legs."

A gallop? Out here? We haven't given her a test in the pasture. Develyn glanced over at Renny. He was sprawled flat on his back in the dirt, under the gold pickup, explaining something to the man.

Well, Devy girl, it's time to cowgirl up. I don't even know if she'll respond to a gallop command.

Develyn slammed her heels into Molly's flanks and shouted, "Heeeyah! Giddyup!"

The black horse bolted across the brown grass and sage pasture. The leather of Renny's saddle slapped Develyn's rear. She shifted her weight to her feet.

I think she has a smoother gait than My Maria, but not as fast.

The wind slapped her face. Develyn screwed her hat tight, but kept the horse at a gallop. *This is what I like, Lord. The power . . . the thrill . . . the danger of racing a horse. This is what I remembered from thirty-five years ago. This is why I came out here. One more time . . . I had to find out if it was still the same.*

I love it . . . I love it . . . I love it.

And I'll love it more if Molly will slow down and not throw me over that fence.

Without yanking the reins back, Develyn eased them until they were taut. "Whoa . . girl . . . whoa . . ."

Molly dropped down to a lope.

"Whoa."

When Dev tugged a couple of quick jerks on the reins, Molly stopped, then started to back up.

"Good girl!" Develyn leaned forward and stroked the

horse's neck. "I suppose that felt like a back up command. Let's go to the barn before one of us does something really dumb."

When they trotted up to the old barn, Renny was still under the truck. The man was handing tools to him.

Develyn swung down out of the saddle and handed the reins to the lady. "Would you like to ride her?"

"Oh, no, honey. They have to be more than eight hours broke for me to ride them. You young gals have more courage than me."

"Thanks for calling me young. I'm Develyn."

"Nice to meet you, Develyn. I'm Frannie. You sit well in the saddle. Wyoming girls usually do. We didn't know Renny was bringing a gal with him today. I would have had you two to the house at noon for dinner. When we drove up, I told the old man, Renny has a girl with him . . . and I can bet she is a purdy thing. I was right."

"Frannie, you are full of compliments."

"Renny has a way of finding the purdy ones. Did you ever meet Lucinda Monroe? She was runner-up at Frontier Days a few years back. She was beautiful enough to be a model."

Develyn chewed on her lower lip. "That's nice."

"And then there was the movie star. Renny met her up in Alberta when he was running a string of horses for that Kevin Costner movie. That girl had the smallest waist and the biggest . . . eh, . . . ego of any girl I ever saw. I don't know her stage name, but Renny just called her Lolly."

"I didn't know Renny worked with Kevin Costner."

"Oh, I don't think they ever met. Renny just took care of the horses." The lady rubbed her full lips. "I forgot about that

185

vet from Rawlins. Now she was one tough lady. She had a rugged beauty, sort of like the Big Horns."

Develyn glanced up at the mountains to the east.

"To tell you the truth," the lady lowered her voice, "the last time we talked to Renny he said he was chasin' some schoolteacher from back east. Can you imagine someone like Renny Slater with an eastern schoolteacher? Wouldn't that be a pair? I can see he came to his senses. Where do you live, honey?"

"Right now, I'm staying down at Argenta."

"Do you know Edith Tagley?"

"Yes, of course."

"Isn't she something? My mother and her were friends in grade school. How is she doing?"

"Really well. I don't think she's changed in thirty-five years."

"You've know her that long?"

"I met her one summer when I was ten."

"Are you telling me you are forty-five?" the lady gasped.

Develyn laughed. "I'm afraid it's true."

The lady leaned forward. "I just figured the Wyoming wind put them crows feet around your eyes. I'm fifty-four myself."

I need my makeup bad! "It's probably the dyed hair that fooled you."

"Nope, I think it is that little upturned nose seldom seen in girls over twelve. I'm greatly relieved about Renny. We worry that he's not married or had a family. I told the old man the other day, Renny can do a whole lot better than some pinch-lipped schoolteacher from Indiana."

Renny dusted off his Wranglers as the two men strolled over.

"Frannie, Renny fixed my dadgum pickup." The man tipped his hat at Develyn. "Howdy, ma'am. Don't believe we've met."

"Oh . . . Frannie and Frank . . . this is Develyn Worrell."

Frannie nodded. "We've met. I don't know where you find these girls, Renny, but Develyn can ride like the wind."

"Did she take Molly at a gallop?" he asked.

"Clear across the pasture and back."

"Well, how about that." Renny's grin revealed his two deep dimples. "Not bad for a schoolteacher."

"A schoolteacher?" Frannie gasped.

"I told you about my friend, the Indiana schoolteacher, didn't I?"

● ● ●

The sun had set and only dim twilight remained when Renny pulled up the driveway to Develyn's cabin in Argenta. Uncle Henry met them at the road and followed them all the way up the drive to the dirt yard.

"Looks like your boy missed you."

She rolled down her window. "Baby, you go over there and wait by the porch. I don't want you chewing on Renny's side-view mirrors again. Go on!"

The burro meandered to the front.

"I believe Uncle Henry must have been an orphan growing up on his own. He craves attention, sort of like a grade school kid whose parents have divorced and neither side really wants him."

"I think he was given to you by the Lord," Renny said.

"Why?"

"To keep you from missing school too much."

"I always enjoy my summers."

"What do you usually do in the summer? You don't move off to Wyoming every year."

"I teach summer school, then spend a week with some friends in Michigan. The rest of the summer I, eh . . ."

"Get ready for the next year of teaching?"

"Renny, it's what I do."

"I know. Well, I'm glad you came out here this summer. You perked up my life from the first time I saw you sitting on that wagon seat bench in front of Mrs. Tagley's. I was shocked when you got in my truck and drove off with me."

"It was only a quarter mile."

"Well, it changed my life."

"I didn't know it was all that dramatic."

"Any time a friendship begins that will last a lifetime, that is pure drama. You and me will be pals forever, right?"

"Yes, we will. Even if I am a lousy kisser."

"I didn't say that."

"You said I needed lessons."

"Ever' one needs to keep in practice, I reckon."

"Kind of like team roping?" she giggled. "You need to throw a few loops every now and then just to keep on top of your game."

"Hey, I like that, Dev Worrell."

"Life is like a rodeo. I learned that from a good-lookin' cowboy friend of mine."

Renny dropped his chin and stared down at the steering wheel. "Dev, look, I was out of line for kissing you. I shouldn't be complicatin' your life. You're trying to sort things out with Quint, and I'm actin' irresponsible."

"Do you regret it, Renny?"

He looked at her and shook his head. "No, ma'am. Do you mind sittin' there a spell while I mumble?"

"I don't think I've ever been asked to 'sit a spell.' I'd like to try it. What do you want to mumble about?"

"Don't take this wrong, but you are a classy lady, and I've not been around classy ladies much."

"Renny, you've seen me filthy, without makeup, angry . . . and scared to death. How can you say I'm classy?"

"'Cause I've seen you slicked up, lookin' like ever' man's dream too. I've seen you walk into a crowd and ever' head turns . . . men, boys, women . . . I've seen you change their schedule with a glance . . . and by smiling at them, prod men to demonstrate their best behavior."

"Wow, that's quite a mouthful. I don't think I can live up to that."

"You are that way, Devy-girl. Ask Casey or Quint or Cuban or Cooper Tallon."

"Thank you very much. But why the accolades?"

"Ever since I met you, I've wondered what it would be like to kiss a classy lady like that."

"Now, I'm getting really embarrassed. You've put me on a pedestal that I can't maintain."

"Anyway, today, I was thinkin' . . . if I don't kiss her now, I may never get another chance. So I kissed you."

"And all your wonderful images of me went up in smoke, right?"

"Oh, no. It was wonderful . . . but . . ."

"I'm a lousy kisser?"

"Hardly. You see, I found out what it's like to get to kiss a classy lady, but I haven't found out what it's like to have a classy lady want to kiss me."

"Are you saying I was less than enthusiastic?"

"No, that's not what I meant. I just realized that a stolen kiss is just that, stolen. I should have waited, and I'm sorry for that."

"You are the sorriest cowboy I've ever met. I think you need some lessons yourself."

"What kind of lessons?"

"This kind . . ." Develyn scooted over, threw her arms around Renny's neck and smashed her lips against his. His arms engulfed her and held her tight against his chest.

"Alright, what's going on out here?"

Develyn looked up to see Casey standing by the open window. She pulled back from Renny's grasp. "I . . . I . . . I didn't know you were home."

"That's obvious. You didn't answer my question. What is going on out here?"

"We were doin' a little comparison experiment," Renny laughed. "Sort of a survey, you might say."

"Yeah, right. You were lip-locked and down for the count. It's a good thing I came out. If it weren't for Uncle Henry's brays, I might have missed this."

"I'll be right in," Develyn laughed.

"Right now, young lady. No daughter of mine is going to sit in the driveway and neck with some driftin', washed-up rodeo cowboy. What will the neighbors think?"

"I don't think Cooper will notice."

"Hah. You are grounded for a week. Now get in the house."

"What's got into Cree-Ryder?" Renny asked.

"Oh, once she has tasted being the countess . . . it's hard to get it out of her blood."

"We could just go on neckin' and maybe she'd be self-conscious and leave."

"Casey, self-conscious?"

"No, I don't suppose so." Renny leaned over and kissed her cheek. "Good night, Dev. It's been one of the most fun days of my life."

She squeezed his hand. "For me, too, Renny. I learned so much."

"There hasn't been this much mush since *Goldilocks and the Three Bears*," Casey sighed.

Develyn glared. "And your point is?"

"It so happens I have some really important things to talk to you about."

"About a certain bronze cowboy with an awesome smile?"

"Isn't he dreamy?"

"Yes, if I were twenty years younger."

Develyn opened the pickup door. "Renny, will you phone me tomorrow?"

"Yes, ma'am, I believe I will."

"Are you going to Douglass tonight?"

"Yep, I promised some high school boys I'd give 'em a bronc ridin' clinic."

"Take care of yourself, cowboy. There's a lot more you need to teach me."

"You do show progress," he laughed.

She tipped her hat. "Thank you, sir."

● ● ●

Casey hauled Develyn past a protesting Uncle Henry and straight into the cabin, then slammed the door behind them.

"What is this all about?"

"Here's the deal," Casey said. "How do I know when I've met the one that I should marry?"

"You've only known Jackson for twenty-four hours."

"My heart has known him since I was six."

"Did he propose?"

"Of course not."

"Did he kiss you?"

"Yeah, but not like you and Renny."

"That was just a game we were playing."

"Whatever," Casey shrugged. "I saw you jump on him. It was an enthusiastic game."

Develyn sank into a big musty chair and drew her feet under

her. "Casey, where is this going? Are you questioning my morals . . . my relationship with Renny . . . or what?"

"It has nothing to do with that." Casey paced around the little lantern-lit cabin. "It's just . . ."

"What is it?"

"Be patient with me."

"Is it Jackson?"

Casey nodded her head and bit her lip. She continued to stalk the shadows of the cabin.

"What's the matter, honey? I only visited with him for five minutes, but he seems perfect for you."

Casey let out a sob. "That's the problem. He is perfect." She held her arms across her chest and rocked back and forth.

Develyn scurried over and wrapped her arms around Casey. "What is the problem, sweetie?"

For several moments Develyn held her close and listened to her sobs, retreating only for the box of Kleenex. "Talk to me, sweet Casey."

"I'm scared, Dev."

"Are you afraid of a relationship?"

"I'm afraid of no relationship."

"You don't think he likes you?"

"He likes me . . . now. Dev, I have never wanted anything more in my life. You know my background. I've never had anyone close. Never had anyone care. In just six weeks, you have become closer to me than anyone. I know I'm just another of your many, many friends. But to me, you're the closest friend I've ever had."

"It may interest you to know, my countess, that I consider you and Lily my best friends on earth."

"Really?"

"Yes, now talk to me."

"But you are going home in a few weeks."

"Yes, and you are coming to stay with me between Thanksgiving and Christmas, remember? That is, provided that Jackson Hill doesn't change your mind."

Casey burst out in tears.

Develyn handed her another Kleenex. "Tell me what this is about?"

Casey finally quieted down enough to say, "Dev, I'm afraid I will die if I don't get Jackson. I don't care if the Lord ignores every prayer I have for the rest of my life. Just once I want the breaks to go my way."

"Honey, you pray about it. The Lord will lead you to his will."

"That's what scares me so much. I don't know what the Lord's will is . . . and I don't care. I don't want his will . . . I want Jackson. If he rejects me, I won't survive. There is only so much heartbreak and rejection a person can take."

"Dear, sweet Casey."

They hugged and swayed for several moments.

"But what if it is the Lord's will?" Dev demured. "What if he says to you, Cree-Ryder, this is your man. What if he says to Mr. Jackson Hill, this bronze bombshell is for you."

"Nothing good ever happens to me."

"I'm nothing?"

"Besides you . . ."

"And the barbecue at the Quarter Circle Diamond?"

"Yeah."

"And getting to be the countess at the LaSage mansion?"

"Yeah. OK," Casey whimpered. "Since I met you some things have gone right."

"You see, you're on a roll. Until the Lord shows you otherwise, why not assume Jackson is the Lord's will?"

"But . . . but . . . how do I keep him?"

"Delight yourself in the LORD and he will give you the desires of your heart."

"Are you quoting Scripture to me?"

"Yes, but I don't remember which psalm that is."

"Psalm 37:4," Casey said. "But I don't know how to do that."

"I don't either. Not for sure anyway. Let's learn together."

"I need to wash my face."

"Come here . . ." Develyn led her by the hand to the sink in the little bathroom at the back of the cabin. She turned on the water and let it run. "Close your eyes."

"What are you going to do?" Casey closed her eyes.

"I'm going to help you, countess." Develyn scooped up a double handful of cold water and tossed it in Casey's face.

"What! Why did you to that?" she shouted.

"Splashology, honey." Develyn tossed another handful of water into Casey's startled face.

"Oh no, you don't!" Casey shouted. "It takes two to play splashology." She shoved Develyn out into the cabin and splashed her face.

"Ahhhh!" Develyn hollered. "No, you don't . . ." She pushed past Casey and grabbed a water glass next to the sink.

Casey jumped back, and the glassful of water splashed across her shirt.

She grabbed the glass from Develyn's hand and tugged her into the front room, then dove for the sink. "Two can play that game. Maybe we'll just have a wet T-shirt contest."

"Time out, time out!" Develyn shrieked. "That's no fair. You'll always win the wet T-shirt contest."

Casey chased her around the table with a whoop. "There are no time-outs in splashology. Come here, you flat-chested schoolteacher."

A loud bang on the door froze both ladies.

Develyn scooted over to the door and cracked it open. "Coop?"

"Evenin', Miss Dev. I heard some screamin'. Is ever'thin' OK?"

"Oh, eh, we were having a little fun. We got carried away. You know how girls are. "

"Eh, no, I probably don't."

Hiding behind Develyn, Casey shoved the glass of water toward Cooper Tallon. "You want a drink?"

"Of water?"

"Of course."

"Eh, no thanks." He rubbed his square chin. "Dev, could you step out here for a second? I have something I need to tell you."

Develyn slipped out the door, but kept her arms folded across her chest. "I'm a little wet."

"Yes, I noticed."

What did you notice, Mr. Tallon?

"What do you need, Coop?"

"I heard Uncle Henry braying earlier, so I peeked out the window when you and Slater drove up."

"You were spying on me?"

"No. I mean, I didn't mean to. I have to admit I was keeping an eye out just to make sure you got home safe. You have a reputation for . . ."

"Adventure?"

"Yeah, that's it. Anyway I saw you and Renny actin', eh, chummy, which is none of my business. It's just that I wanted you to know that if the Friday night supper confuses things for you, we can just cancel it."

"Are you trying to get out of cooking for me?"

"No, ma'am, I'm just tryin' not to complicate your life. I have no intention of being a pest."

"Coop, I am really counting on Friday night, so don't you go backing out on me."

In the evening shadows, she spied a wide, easy grin. "I won't, Dev."

Develyn watched him saunter back to his cabin. *Oh, my, Mr. Cooper Fallon, it's a good thing you hide that smile most of the time.* She slipped back inside the cabin and closed the door behind her.

The entire glass of cold water splashed on top of her head.

Both ladies shouted, laughed, hugged, then danced around the room.

● ● ●

Develyn emerged from the tiny bathroom with a dry shirt and a towel on her head. The cabin felt empty.

"Casey?"

There was no answer.

She opened the front door. "Casey?"

"I'm sitting out here on the porch watching the Wyoming moon."

"Did you get on some dry clothes?"

"Yes, ma'ma."

"Can I join you, or do you want to be alone?"

"You can come out if you want."

Develyn shuffled out and slumped down on the uncovered porch next to Casey.

"Nice big moon, isn't it?"

"I don't think the Indiana moon is as big. I know it's not such a bright white. It's beautiful."

"And peaceful."

"Maybe that's why the Lord created night. To give us a peaceful break from the day's confusion."

"Dev, I've decided you are right. I might as well assume that Jackson is the one the Lord has in store for me, until he shows me something different."

"That's a good way of looking at it."

"How about you?"

"What about me?"

"Do you assume Renny is the one now, until the Lord shows you different . . . like he did with Quint?"

"I assume there is no man for me, unless the Lord shows me different."

"But what about that kissing?"

"I think I got carried away a little."

"What does Renny think?"

"He understands. We're just very good friends."

"You sure are a friendly thing."

"Thank you. But I don't think you came out here to contemplate my relationships."

"You've got to teach me everything."

"About what?"

"Manners, etiquette, speech, posture . . . you know everything about being a lady. I want to be classy, like you."

"For Jackson?"

"Yes, I want to be so wonderful and charming that he can't get me out of his mind."

"I don't think so."

"You won't teach me?"

"Honey, I'll teach you anything you really want to know," Develyn offered. "But that won't get Jackson to commit."

"Why not?"

"Jackson Hill isn't interested in me. He's interested in you."

"But if you teach me, I can sort of be like the countess."

"He's not interested in the 'countess' either. He rather likes Casey Cree-Ryder."

"But he doesn't know all about me."

"Then tell him."

"The truth?" Casey gasped.

"Yep. Tell him whatever your heart and the Lord agree to tell him."

Casey groaned. "You mean, I have to tell him about my three illegitimate children and my life as a dope smuggler?"

Dev laughed. "Six weeks ago I would have gasped and believed you." She hugged Casey. "Not now. I know my Casey."

Casey hugged her back. "He likes my hair down."

"I figured he would. I've told you. You have to-die-for hair."

"I need to wash it. It takes forever to dry."

"Wash it in the morning. You can let it dry while we ride."

"Eh, listen . . ." Casey let out a deep sigh, "about tomorrow."

"What time is Jackson coming over?"

"About 9:00. He has a pal near Casper that he's going to help shoe a rank horse, first. They'll have to drop and tie him."

"Do what?"

"Lay the horse down and restrain him."

"I've never seen that done."

"Anyway . . . when he gets done, he wants to come over."

"That's wonderful. Are you going someplace?"

"Eh . . . I thought we'd go for a ride."

"I think that's wonderful, Casey. It will give you a good environment to get to know each other better. Does he have a horse to ride?"

"No . . . see . . . I was wondering if I could ride My Maria, and I'd let him ride Popcorn. I'll take good care of her."

"Of course, honey. You two go for a ride."

"But that means you don't get to ride."

"I'll survive."

"What will you do?"

"Gather up all our clothes and go to the laundromat in Casper."

"Are you sure you don't mind?"

"Honey, you think Jackson is the one for you. I think he's the one for you. Now, all we've got to do is convince the Lord and Jackson."

"How do we do that?"

"I don't know the details, but I don't reckon anyone could stand against the Cree-Ryder/Worrell duo."

"We're sort of a female version of Butch and Sundance, aren't we?"

"They both munched it."

"Yeah, but what fun adventures they had before that."

"Which am I?" Develyn asked.

"You're Butch."

"I was twelve when I first saw that movie, and I pretended to be Katherine Ross all summer. But you didn't come out here to talk old movies."

"Dev, I really want you to teach me how to be more gracious and all that. I don't want to be phony, but I raised myself, and I just want to know the things that normal girls learn from a mama. That's all."

"That sounds fair enough. Here's the first lesson."

"Do we need to go inside?"

"No, this is just some motherly advice. You asked about how to know who to marry, and I've had a lot of time to think about it. I prepared a speech for my Delaney last spring, but she never asked."

"What did you want to tell her?"

"First, the one you are to marry will agree with your faith. Second, he will let you be you. And third, just being with him will bring out the best in you."

"That's it?"

"Yes."

"So, you don't think I need to try to be like you?"

"Absolutely not. Be yourself. He must like you for who you are."

"But what if he doesn't like the real me?"

"Better to find that out now. You don't want to put on a false front your entire life just to keep him."

"Right now I think I'd do anything to keep him."

"Sweet Casey, you can't live a lie. Trust me on that. Be yourself, but, mind you, be your best self."

"Meanwhile, will you teach me all the mama things I missed?"

"Yes, I will do what I can. Now, it's getting late. So I want you to go in there, brush your teeth, floss and gargle with hydrogen peroxide."

"I thought that was for dyeing your hair."

"The bottle in the bathroom is a mouth wash. It kills the bacteria. Then put on your pajamas and go to bed." Develyn stood and tugged Casey to her feet. "There, does that sound like I'm mothering you?"

"Yes, but I don't have any pajamas. Will a T-shirt and shorts do?"

"Definitely not. Tomorrow when I go to Casper, I'm buying you some pajamas."

"Oh, don't bother. I've never worn pajamas in my whole life."

"That is exactly my point."

"This is one of those 'mother' things?"

"Yes it is."

"The next thing I know you'll be making me wear dresses."

"Hmmmm. Are you a size 10 or 12?"

"Don't even go there. You said he is supposed to like me for who I am. And I'm a jeans-wearing, boot-stomping cowboy girl."

"I think a jewel-tone color would go so good with your hair."

"Don't you dare come home with a dress for me."

"Maybe a peasant scoop collar, modest, of course, and skirt just below the knees."

"Mother!"

"Relax, honey. I won't buy you a dress if you aren't with me."

"Promise?"

"Of course."

Casey led Develyn back into the cabin. "We do know how to have fun, don't we?"

Develyn grinned. "Each day is a new delight."

● ● ●

The sheets were cold, but clean, when Develyn turned off the lantern and slipped under the covers. The pillow felt softer than she remembered. Like a fluorescent nightlight, the moon glowed through the windows.

Lord, who am I to mother Casey? I need to be home, mothering my own daughter. I need to be mothered myself. Am I listening to my own advice? Does Renny bring out my best behavior? Does Quint? Does it matter? Do they let me be myself? I don't even know who the real Dev Worrell is. That would be a nice thing for me to learn this summer. Will the real Develyn Upton Worrell please stand? Help me discover that.

I hope I like what I find.

● ● ●

Brownie limped when he rode up out of the water. Develyn slid off the saddle to the prairie floor and walked him over by several tall, gray and green sages. "What's the matter, boy?"

She dropped the reins to the dirt and reached for his right front leg. He gave her his hoof.

"Oh, you got a rock in your frog . . ." She clutched the granite stone between her fingers and yanked it. "It's in there tight! I wish I had a hoof pick like Dewayne." She glanced around the dirt. "There's a stick. I'll use it."

Develyn retrieved a sliver of a cedar fence post and rammed

in under the rock. With a hard thrust, the rock flipped out. Brownie jerked back. Some of the cedar splinters remained lodged in the soft tissue of the upper frog.

"Oh, I'm sorry," Develyn cried out. "Let me get those."

Brownie shied back.

Ten-year-old Develyn Worrel trotted after the horse. "Wait . . . wait . . . I'm sorry . . . let me take care of you."

Every time Develyn stepped toward the big brown gelding he limped back, always keeping a distance between them.

"Stand still, Brownie."

The wind whipped sand in her eyes. Develyn trudged several feet with her eyes closed, then peered between her fingers. The horse continued to back up.

"Wait for me."

She lunged toward him. He bolted behind some tall sage. His head jerked down when he stepped on the reins.

"Don't do that! Wait. You are going to hurt yourself even more. Don't you understand?" Develyn screamed.

Brownie turned his tail toward her and grazed further away.

"I didn't mean to yell. I'm sorry."

She rubbed her sticky palm across her little, upturned nose and trudged after him.

"Brownie, I love you and want to help you. How come you are treating me this way?"

With his tail still pointed at her, Brownie stared across the prairie at the rocker arm of a distant oil well pump.

Lord, make that horse stand still. How can I help him if he's always running away?

She took baby steps as she sneaked up on the horse. When she got within ten feet, he scooted away.

Is that what we do, Lord . . . do people who are all hurting run away from you? Do they think it is you who hurt them and don't realize you only want to help them?

Develyn reached her foot out, then pulled it back. She repeated this until the gelding turned around.

"I know I hurt you, Brownie. I was trying to help. If I had my own hoof pick this wouldn't have happened. But Mother said we shouldn't waste seventy-nine cents on another hoof pick, and Dewayne said he would carry the pick and I should carry the comb. I guess it was my idea to carry the comb."

She circled around Brownie. He pivoted, keeping one eye on her.

"Come here, Brownie," Develyn motioned with her hands. "Come unto me . . . that's in the Bible somewhere."

She perched by a big tuft of brown buffalo grass and rested her hands on her hips. Brownie feigned grazing, though there was nothing but dirt under his nose.

"Do horses have to obey the Bible? How come they never teach that in Sunday school?"

Develyn crouched down behind a tall sage. On her hands and knees, she crept toward the horse. *If Mother could see me now, she would insist I not crawl around in the dirt. Daddy would get down here in the dirt and crawl with me. And Dewayne would just laugh his head off. Are the angels laughing at me? I don't even know if angels can laugh. I don't think it would be very fun to be an angel if they never got to laugh.*

For every foot she crept, the horse took another step away.

Develyn sat down on the warm, yellowish dirt. "I'm not playing that game any more. When you are ready, come over here and I'll help you."

She ran her fingers through the warm, fine dry soil, then spelled out D–E–V–E–L–Y–N by using her finger for a pen. When she glanced up, Brownie was staring at the rocker arm on the oil pump again.

"Don't pretend to ignore me. I saw you look over here. You don't fool me."

Brownie shook his head as if trying to rid himself of bridle and bit.

"I mean it. Don't you tell me no. Develyn Gail Upton does not know the meaning of the word no. At least, that's what Mother tells me."

The horse bent his neck around to look at her.

Develyn lowered her voice. "Come on, Brownie. Come to me, please?"

She turned her back on him and waited.

And waited.

But she didn't peek.

When it gets dark, Daddy will come looking for me. And I'll be sitting right here, and that dumb horse will be standing right there. We are both so stubborn. But if he thinks he can out-stubborn me, he has another think coming. I'm the queen of stubborn. I out-stared Suzanne Hillary in the school cafeteria . . . twice!

She felt his nose nudge her shoulder. *Hah! You weren't half as tough as Hillary.* The flat leather reins dangled at her ear.

207

When she looked straight up, two huge brown eyes stared down at her.

This time she wrapped the reins around her right wrist. Brownie elevated his hoof, even before she asked for it. With careful deliberation she plucked out four splinters, then lowered the hoof.

"OK, let's walk back to the road and make sure I got them all. You see, I really did want to help you. You are such a pill sometimes. That's what Mother calls me—a pill. I never know if that means I'm hard to swallow, or that I make her feel better when she's sick. You make me feel better, did you know that?"

Develyn trudged along in the prairie dirt, the horse one step behind her.

"Sometimes I wish horses could talk. Do you ever wish horses could talk? If you could talk I bet you'd say in a very, very deep voice. . . . 'I love you, Develyn Gail Upton.' I know you love me. I can see it in your eyes. Oh, sometimes you are disgusted with me. And sometimes you can act quite snotty. Not as snotty as LaRue Jordan, but no one can be as snotty as LaRue. But I see your eyes gleam every morning when I come out to the corral. So, there's no reason to deny it. Brownie loves Devy-girl. I should carve that in a tree somewhere."

She surveyed the prairie. "Provided there was a tree some place. Did you know Dewayne carved his initials in the bench in front of Mrs. Tagley's store? I hope he doesn't get arrested or something. I told him if they threw him in jail I'd write to him every day and bake him cookies once a week. He begged me not to send the cookies. I'm not a very good cook. I suppose

I'll get better someday. Grandma says I will never get a good husband unless I'm a good cook. Hah . . . I told her . . . 'Who wants a husband?' What I want is a horse."

Brownie nuzzled her shoulder with his nose.

"Am I talking too much? Mother says I talk too much. Daddy says I'm just exercising my lungs and mouth at the same time. Mother says I should exercise my brain more."

He nuzzled her again.

"What do you want? Is your foot hurting you?"

Again, he shoved her shoulder.

"What?" she glowered.

"It's Delaney."

Develyn sat straight up in bed. The only light in the cabin was the moon shining through the little window.

"What is it?" Develyn mumbled.

Casey poked something into her hand. "It's your cell phone. You didn't wake up, so I answered it."

"In the middle of the night?"

"It's Delaney. She's crying. I thought you'd want to talk to her."

Develyn's feet hit the floor at the same moment the cell phone slammed into her ear. "Baby, what's wrong?"

There was nothing but sobs.

And static.

"Dee, I'm going outside where there's better reception." Develyn scurried out to the porch. Casey leaned against the doorway. The moonlight radiated a dull glow like a distant dream. "Delaney, talk to me. What's wrong?"

More static and a murmur.

"Honey, I didn't hear that. Please tell me what the problem is. What did you say?"

"I said, I'm three weeks late, Mom, and I'm scared to death."

"But, baby, you said you weren't . . ."

"I didn't think so. What am I going to do? Should I go back to South Carolina and talk to Brian?"

No, you aren't going to keep shying away from me. I'm going to sit right here in the sage, and you will come to me. I love you, and I want to take care of you.

"Mother? Do you hate me?"

"Sweetheart, I don't hate you. I'm going to Casper in the morning. It's laundromat day. I'll stop by AAA and get you an airline ticket. Have Lily drive you to the airport. You are going to spend a few weeks with me."

"Really?"

Develyn stared up at the stars. "The air is clearer up here. You can think better. We'll figure it all out."

"Are you serious?"

"Baby, come see me. Let me take care of you."

"I will, Mom. I will."

9

Develyn toted out two cardboard boxes crammed with dirty clothes and shoved them in the back of her silver Jeep Grand Cherokee. Uncle Henry paced back and forth.

"I know . . . I have to go to town and you can't go. I told you to go with Casey and Jackson, but you didn't want to. I should just put you in the pasture. You'd have it all to yourself."

Cooper Tallon strolled across the dirt yard between the cabins.

"Mornin', Miss Dev." He tipped his cowboy hat. "You didn't go riding with the others?"

"Casey and Jackson wanted to ride, so I lent them My Maria."

"You could have borrowed one of my horses." He pointed to the buckskin and the bay in the pasture on the opposite side of his cabin. "Help yourself anytime."

"Thanks, but I do believe Casey and Jackson wanted to be by themselves."

"Jackson Hill, from up Sheridan way?"

"Yes, do you know him?"

"I know his mama. She teaches school up at Sheridan. She's a fine lady."

"I've only visited with Jackson a couple of times, but he seems very nice." Develyn nudged the boxes, then slammed the door. "I'm going to do laundry in Casper. I've been borrowing Mrs. Tagley's washer, but this is too big a mess to bother her. Do you know a convenient coin-operated laundry in town?"

"Jenny's-By-The-Park is where I take mine."

"What's it called?"

"Jenny's-By-The-Park. It's on 16th, just past the transmission shop. If you don't have time to watch the machines spin, she'll do the laundry for a few more bucks. It saves me a lot of time. In fact, if I didn't have to hurry down to Cheyenne, I'd take my laundry to town today myself."

"Go get it. I'll take it," she offered.

Cooper laughed. "No. I will not have you do my laundry."

"I'm not going to do it. I'll take it to Jenny and she can do it."

"Thanks, Dev, but I couldn't impose like that."

She shaded the morning sun with her hand. "Cooper, you and I are adults. I can certainly tote your laundry to the cleaners."

"If I were the one going to town, would you let me take your things to the laundry?"

"No," she replied. "I mean . . . some of it is OK . . . but maybe not all."

He grinned. "That's my point."

"You might be right. Laundry can be a little personal. Will you be driving down to Cheyenne?" She turned the key and rolled up the rear window.

Cooper waved his arm south. "Quint Burdett is flying down and said he would give me a lift."

"Quint is coming down here?"

Tallon studied the thin blue Wyoming sky. "Should be here any moment."

Develyn fidgeted with her keys.

Cooper rubbed his chin. "I take it you want to be gone when he gets here."

"I'm not quite sure what to say when I see him. Our last conversation was rather . . . short."

"Just listen, then. Let him do the talking."

"Do you think he wants to talk to me?"

"I imagine he does. But who am I to know? You do whatever you want, Miss Dev."

She opened the door to her Cherokee. "Are you going down to Frontier Days?"

"Quint and Lindsay are, but I need to meet with a couple of men from Denver. They made me an offer on my construction business."

Develyn slid into the Cherokee, but left the door open. "Do you build houses and that sort of thing?"

"No, it's heavy equipment. I dig trenches for oil fields with backhoes, bulldozers, and all that."

"So, you are going to retire?"

"I hadn't planned on it. But if they want it bad enough, I might sell out and build that log house I've been wanting here."

"Oh, that would be nice. Sometimes I think about retirement, usually every February. But I need about twelve more years for maximum benefits."

A buzz in the sky caused them both to scan the horizon.

"Maybe I'd better go," she said.

"Maybe you should answer your phone."

"Oh . . . yes . . . well . . ." Develyn fumbled to tug her cell phone from her pocket.

"Hello?"

"Hi, Miss Dev."

"Quint, is that you up there?"

"Yep. I'm picking up Cooper Tallon and taking him down to Cheyenne. Do you want to come with us?"

"I'm standing right out in the front yard visiting with Cooper."

"Yes, we can see you."

The airplane dipped lower. "Thanks for the invitation. I'm just on my way to Casper to do the laundry, so I'll pass on Frontier Days."

"We need to talk, Miss Dev. Even if you have decided to hate me, we need to talk."

"Quint, I don't hate you at all. I just needed some time to try to understand myself a little better."

"That's fair enough. How about you coming out to the ranch on Friday evening? We'll have a little supper and sit out on the porch and visit."

Develyn glanced at Cooper Tallon, who stood by the front of her rig scratching Uncle Henry's ear. "I have other plans for Friday. How about Saturday?"

"That's great. Thanks. I need to work on my approach now."

"Your approach is always very good, Mr. Burdett."

"Thanks, it's good to hear you laugh. I'll see you Saturday, then."

"What time?"

"Anytime before five will be fine. And, eh . . . Miss Dev . . . why don't you wear that purple shirt with the cowgirl on the front."

"Bye, Quint."

"Bye, darlin'."

Develyn tossed the cell phone on the seat next to her. *Why must he always dress me?*

"You want me to stick Uncle Henry in the pasture after you pull out of here?" Tallon asked.

"That would be nice." She closed the door, then rolled down the window. "This is your last chance. Can I take your laundry to Jenny's?"

He rapped his fingers on the hood of her rig. "It would help. This deal might get me real busy with lawyers and paperwork for a while."

She shoved the door open again. "Go get your laundry. I'll stick Uncle Henry in the pasture, and I'll give you a lift to the airstrip."

●　●　●

Quint Burdett pushed back his black cowboy hat when they pulled up beside the plane. Lindsay wore a white hat with a turquoise-sequined blouse. They walked over to the Cherokee.

"Thank you, Miss Dev," Cooper grinned. "Will you greet me at the airport when I return?"

"Oh, dear, I forgot. If you brought your truck you wouldn't have to walk back."

"Don't worry, it was worth it just to see Burdett's face when you drove me up." Tallon ducked his head and climbed out of the rig.

When Develyn got out, Quint Burdett strolled up and gave her a polite hug. "Hi, Miss Dev."

She hugged him back. "Hi, Quint."

"Saturday?"

"Yes." She refused to look over at Cooper Tallon.

Lindsay Burdett grabbed her arm. "I need to talk," she whispered.

Develyn studied the young woman's bright blue eyes. "OK."

"Alone . . ." Lindsay tugged her back behind the Jeep.

"Are you mad at me, Linds?"

"Oh no, Dev. I was puzzled a little bit by the way you set Daddy up, then dumped him. But . . ."

"Honey, I didn't dump him . . . it's just . . ."

"Then I thought to myself, Lindsay, that's exactly the way you've treated several boys over the years, and every time I had a very good reason for what I did. So I just know you have an explanation for this. Then when I saw you . . . well, it's written all over your face."

"My face?"

"Sweet Dev, there is only one reason a woman goes without any makeup or lipstick. You've been crying, haven't you? When I saw you just now . . . lookin' worn out and you know . . ."

"Old?"

"Well, sort of . . . I knew you were heartbroken. You got worried about how you could ever replace my mother, didn't you?"

"I think that was part of it."

Lindsay hugged her. "I've been thinking about that lately myself. Mother keeps getting more perfect every year in Daddy's mind. He's expecting me to live up to standards that Mother never demanded. But in his mind he's convinced she did. Does that make sense to you?"

"I hate to break this up, but we need to get back in the air," Quint called to them.

Develyn hugged Lindsay. "Yes, it does, honey."

"Can we spend some time talking? Just the two of us?"

"I'm coming up Saturday for supper."

"Why don't you spend the night? We can stay up late and talk."

"I'll see if I can do that."

"Thanks. I just knew we could work this out. When I saw poor Dev without makeup . . . it broke my heart. Bye."

Develyn stood by the Jeep and watched as the plane taxied to the far end of the dirt landing strip. Then she got inside and rolled up the windows to block the dust. She waved. Two hands waved back.

When she reached the blacktop of Highway 20, ten miles south of Argenta, she pulled over and stared at herself in the rearview mirror.

Never . . . ever again . . . will I make such a dumb dare. Old? Crying? There you have it, Ms. Develyn Worrell. Straight from the rodeo queen's lips. Lord, I've learned a lot this summer . . . and some of it's hard. I know it is vanity, but after this week, I will wear makeup until the day I die. That's just me.

Develyn pulled out on the highway toward Casper, then began to chuckle.

Well, Ms. Worrell, what a fine summer you are having! If you came to Wyoming to find yourself, you certainly succeeded. You are a neurotic, middle-aged, plain-looking schoolteacher who tries desperately to be something different. You're not a rodeo queen . . . or a Texas beauty . . . or even a buckle bunny. The males that you relate to best are all eleven or twelve years old. The rest imagine you are some-thing you're not.

When her *Eagles* CD blared out "Get Over It," she rolled down the windows and turned up the sound.

She didn't hear the phone.

But she felt the vibration, and punched off the stereo.

"Hi, Miss Dev . . . it's Renny."

"Hi, Mustang Breaker . . . how are those little buckaroos?"

"Enthusiastic, but they have a lot to learn."

"Sort of like me, and kissing?" she laughed.

"Dev, let me apologize about that. I don't mean to rush things."

"I'm the one who needs to apologize, Renny . . . I, eh . . . well, I thought it was just a little game we were playing, but it's more than that, isn't it?"

"It is for me."

"Me too, Renny."

"Can I get a re-ride?"

"What?"

"Can I start over and do a little better job?" he pressed.

"Sure."

"I could take you to supper in Casper, but Casey can't come with us this time."

Develyn watched the sage and fenceposts flash by. "Casey and Jackson are out riding today."

"That's great. Do you think they'll hit it off?"

"I hope so, but you know them better than I do. What's your take on those two?"

"Casey has changed a lot, Devy-girl. I appreciate what you've done for her."

Develyn slowed down behind a hay swather. "I don't know that I've done anything."

"That's not true, Ms. Worrell. I've known Casey for fifteen years. She's a legend around here. As you can imagine, she's the butt of a lot of cowboy jokes with the guns and knives and bravado. She's known as a half-breed hell-cat. I've seen tough cowboys cross the street, just so she wouldn't confront them. Then you came along. Casey settled down. She dresses better. Takes care of herself. Has cut down on the trash talk."

"Casey is a neat person. I really like her." Develyn pulled around the hay-cutting machine and waved at the baseball-capped operator.

He waved back.

"That's the greatest compliment of all. If Miss Dev likes her . . . well, there is something special about her."

"You are flattering me, cowboy. What is it you want?"

"Supper on Saturday night."

"Oh, rats, Renny, I already made some plans."

"OK, how about Friday night? I was hoping for a haircut before we went out, but I reckon you can put up with me shaggy."

"I'm sorry. I've got Friday plans too."

"Dadgum it, girl, who is this lucky guy?"

She tapped on the steering wheel and bit her lip. "Guys."

"One on Friday and another on Saturday?"

"Yeah, is that horrible?"

"Shoot, no. Now you sound like Renny Slater. Why don't I just pick a number and wait my turn? Actually, two different guys is better than the same one. It means you are still shopping."

"I'm not shopping at all. How about tomorrow night, Renny? I need to talk to you."

"About kissin'?"

"No. I've got some decisions to make about Delaney."

"I don't know a blasted thing about daughters, darlin'."

"I just need a friend to listen while I unload."

"That is something I can do."

"Thanks, Renny."

"I'll take you to an Italian place in Casper."

"Is the food good?"

"No, it's lousy, but there's lots of privacy," he said. "I'm kidding about the food, of course. It's excellent."

"Thanks. You might want to come over early, because I have a lot of things to dump on you."

"I like this, Devy-girl. This is the way to build a friendship."

She giggled. "Do you mean I don't get any more kissing lessons?"

"You don't need any lessons."

"Coming from a professional like you, I take that as a compliment."

"If Casey and Jackson are out riding, what are you doing?"

"I'm driving down Highway 20 to Casper. This is coin-operated laundry day. I decided to wear clean clothes for you."

"That will be different. I don't think I've ever seen you in clean clothes. Most have orange Popsicle stains, or something."

"Thanks. I guess you have seen me kind of ratty."

"Shoot, darlin', if I'd known you were going to the laundry, I'd have sent mine along."

"Join the crowd. I'm taking Coop's laundry too."

"What? Are you packin' another man's dirty clothes?"

"Yes, much to his protest. But there was no reason for us both to spend a day going to Casper."

"Devy-girl, don't you know there are some counties in Wyomin' where doin' a cowboy's laundry is like bein' engaged?"

"No wonder Cooper panicked. Besides, I'm not doing his laundry; Miss Jenny is. I'm just the delivery person."

"Jenny-By-The-Park?"

"Yes, Cooper said it was the best place in town." Develyn slowed down behind a hay truck and rolled up her windows to block out a shower of chaff.

"It's closed."

"It is?"

"Jenny closed it down last month. She got married on Memorial Day, and her hubby didn't want her doing other men's laundry."

"Are you kidding me, Slater?"

"Not this time, sweet Dev."

"I'll just have to find a different laundry."

"Don't use the one on 10th and Broadway."

"Why?"

"The dryers are so hot they melted the rivets on my Wranglers."

"I don't buy that, cowboy."

"Boy, you toughened up."

"Thank you."

"Tomorrow night?" he asked.

"I'm counting on it."

"So am I, Miss Dev. So am I."

● ● ●

Develyn had just passed the Natrona County International Airport when her cell phone rang again.

"Yes?"

"It's Renny the pest."

"Oh, did you find a better date for tomorrow night and have to cancel?"

"What?"

"I'm just teasing you, cowboy."

"It's no joke. I do have to change the plans for tomorrow night," he admitted.

"You can't desert me. I need you, Slater."

"Now that sounds good to my ears. Here's the deal. Tomorrow afternoon, as a finale to the saddle bronc clinic, we run a little rodeo over here. The boys get to show off and ride some buckin' horses. (Like a Saturday soccer game in Indiana but with all the parents watching from the railing.) But I was reminded that they are having a barbecue afterward. I'm expected to be there and say a few words about the boys."

"I'm sure it's important."

"So is being with Miss Dev."

"I'll be crushed, cowboy, but I'll try to hang on."

"I don't aim to miss a evenin' with Devy-girl."

"What's the plan?"

"How about you coming over to Douglas and watch the boys buck out? I think you would enjoy it. They are thrilled when someone besides parents come to watch them. Then you could stay for supper, and we'd find some private time somehow, even if I have to tow your rig home and we visit in the truck."

"I don't think Casey, nor Uncle Henry, would let us do that again."

"That's not what I meant. How about it, Dev? How about a little junior rodeo? I'll take you to that Italian restaurant next time there's an opening on your dance card."

"OK, Renny, but you'll have to phone me at home tonight and give me directions on how to get there."

"Thanks, you made my day. Shoot, you've already made my summer."

"Stood up by a junior rodeo. That's a first for me too."

"Oh . . . no . . ."

"What's the matter?"

"He was holdin' his bronc rein too short."

"Go take care of your boys, Mr. Slater."

"Yes, ma'am."

● ● ●

The wind died down at sunset. Develyn perched out on the front porch next to a short but stout burro.

"Uncle Henry, I shouldn't let you come up on the porch. You have to promise not to poop. Honey, I don't know what I'm going to do with you at the end of summer. I'll give My Maria to Casey . . . and I know she'd take you just to be nice, but why does she need a burro? What does anyone need with a burro?"

When her cell phone rang, Develyn sat down on the wooden box and leaned against the outside wall of the log cabin. "Hi, Lily."

"Hi, sweetie. Did you get the airline ticket for Dee?"

"Yes, she is to fly out of Indy next Wednesday. I couldn't get anything quicker that I could afford. You'll need to get her to the airport by seven in the morning. I know that's horrible. I didn't have a lot of choices."

"Did you tell Delaney?"

"Yes, she has the details."

"What did she say when you told her you were flying her to Wyoming?"

"She just murmured, 'Yes, Mom.' We both know that we need to be together, and right now Indiana has too many memories and too many old patterns."

"Where will she stay?"

Develyn stared at the shadows of Argenta. "I bought one of those inflatable mattresses like you see on TV. We'll pump it up and toss it right in the cabin between me and Casey."

"How long will she be there?"

"The ticket is for a week, but she can stay out here and ride home with me if she wants to. A one-way ticket costs more than a round trip."

"Will that dampen your style? What about the cowboys tripping over themselves to be with Dev darlin'?"

"Lily, Delaney is my number one priority this summer. I don't know why it took coming out here to understand that."

"You mean you're going to dump the cowboys?"

"I didn't say that."

"Good, because I don't have any intention of dropping a certain attorney."

"You promised you wouldn't get married until I get home."

"Don't worry, honey. He told me I had to pass his mother's inspection. I told him he had to pass the inspection of Ms. Worrell."

"How old is his mother?"

"Eighty-six."

"And he still has to have her approval?"

"You never outgrow the need for your mother's approval. You know that. But he was teasing about her approval. He just respects his mother that much. There's nothing wrong with that in a man."

"He sounds like a jewel."

"Would you like to talk to him?"

"Is he right there?" Develyn gasped.

"No, but I can give you his cell phone number."

"E-mail it to me."

"You never check your e-mail."

"I'll go down to Mrs. Tagley's tomorrow and retrieve it."

"Honey, if I can do anything for your Dee from here, you let me know."

"Thanks, Lil. Have you seen my cats lately? Delaney said Josephine, the monster, tore up the curtains in the back bedroom."

"In your bedroom."

"Mine? I thought Dee said the back bedroom."

"There too. I believe if Delaney goes to stay with you the rest of the summer, you won't have anything left standing but the exterior brick walls."

"And Smoky?"

"He sleeps in the basket on top of the hutch all day and runs for his life at night."

"I've thought about tossing her out the back door some night and seeing if the coyotes would drag her off. But I might get reported to the SPCA."

"For cruelty to cats?"

"For cruelty to coyotes. Is it dark there yet?"

"Yes. There's no wind and a very nice moon," Develyn reported.

"Do you have plans for the evening?"

"Just me and Uncle Henry waiting on the porch for my other daughter."

"Where did Casey and this new boyfriend go?"

"That's a good question, Lil'. They were to go riding all day, and when I got home there was a note on the table that read, 'Jackson wants to show me something. I'll be right back.'"

"When did you get home?"

"Around four."

"What time is it now?"

"Eight o'clock."

"Wow, that was really something he had to show her."

"That's what I'm thinking."

"Casey is almost thirty. She knows what's she doing."

"In some areas of her life, she's about fifteen."

"Oh, dear. It's too bad she's not mature and wise like we were at thirty."

"Honey, I'm not mature and wise at forty-five!"

"I suppose she's too old to 'ground' her for being late."

"She already 'grounded' me this week."

"For what?"

"I'd rather not say."

"Tell me she didn't catch you parked out in the driveway in a pickup truck making out with some cowboy."

"Lily, I think I'm losing my signal."

"I think you are losing your mind. Call me tomorrow night."

"If I can . . . sorry, Lily . . . the signal is going."

"Answer me one thing . . . who were you necking with . . . the rancher man?"

"No," Develyn sighed, "it was the mustang breaker."

● ● ●

Develyn strolled out the dirt driveway to the gravel road that led back to Mrs. Tagley's store, Uncle Henry beside her. She studied the landscape.

Lord, this is peaceful. It's eight o'clock, and not one car is on the road. People are settling down for the night. Even the dogs have called it a day. I'm grateful you allowed me the privilege of spending the summer here. I think I need a break every summer. Of course, my life will be different if I have a grandbaby.

228

I've tried not to think about it. Lord, I want to love and support Dee no matter what . . . but how will I tell Mother? She will blame it on me. Maybe she's right. Maybe Delaney is my fault. Spencer was my fault. Quint is my fault. Do I just leave a trail of ruined lives behind me? Now I'm sounding like one of Mrs. Tagley's soap operas.

Develyn drug her heel across the dusty drive to mark a shadowy line. "Do you see that line, Uncle Henry? When I step over that line, that's the start of a new me. I am going to be helpful and encouraging to all people and not leave any more messy relationships. I'll be the Florence Nightingale of relationships."

She stepped over the line.

"There, what do you think of that? Do you like the new me?"

She surveyed the silent lights of Argenta's dozen buildings. *I think my work is done for the night. Everything's quiet in my part of the world.*

"Leon, you get back in here right now!" A piercing scream broke the silence, followed by a thunderous explosion.

Develyn turned to Uncle Henry and sighed. "I see Mrs. Morton got some more shotgun shells."

She was halfway back to the cabin when her cell phone rang. "Casey, you'd better have a good explanation . . ."

"Dev, it's Cooper Tallon."

"Oh, Coop. Sorry."

"Did Cree-Ryder come back from her ride?"

"Yes, but she went off and didn't . . ." Develyn stopped. "But I'm not worried. Knowing her, she's having a great time."

"Listen, Dev, I've got a big favor to ask. Quint's not flying back until tomorrow. I ran across some pals of mine driving up to Butte, so I just hitched a ride with them. We just crossed the Powder River on Highway 20, and I realized they are on a tight time schedule. I can't expect them to drive me back into Argenta. They have to deliver a . . ."

"I'll come pick you up at the Waltman turnoff."

"Thanks, Dev, I'm real embarrassed having to ask you for a lift."

"Cooper, I don't know how many nights you went out looking for me. This is the least a neighbor can do. How soon will you be there?"

"About fifteen minutes, Dev. Thanks."

After jamming the phone back into her pocket, she picked up her pace back to the cabin. "There you have it, Uncle Henry. I'm making one relationship better. For the first two weeks of the summer, we hated each other. Now Mr. Tallon is calling me for a ride. That's what friends do. I'll go in and grab my purse, wallet, a bottle of water, and put on some makeup!"

Dev laughed out loud and barged into the dimly lit cabin.

You are going to meet a man who has seen you without any makeup, and it's dark. He won't know, and he won't care. Why do you have this thing about makeup? All he wants is a ride down ten miles of a dirt road. I could be a non-English-speaking immigrant from a Third World country driving a yellow cab for all he cares. He just needs a ride . . . not a babe.

Develyn glanced in the tiny mirror.

"But I am going to change my blouse. This is way too frumpy."

● ● ●

The Wyoming Department of Transportation had constructed a turnaround for snow plows about a hundred feet east of the Waltman/Argenta turnoff. Develyn parked in the dark at the western end so that any vehicle would be able to spot her, even at night.

She locked the doors and waited for headlights.

For over six weeks this tiny community has treated me like the visitor I am. I think this might be the first time I've felt like one of the community. Called on to give a neighbor a lift home. I like that. What would it be like to live here year round? The winters must be horrific. Wind, snow, blizzards, but if you had a big old house like the Burdetts . . . and a huge fireplace with logs blazing . . . and a strong, gentle man who smelled like spice aftershave wrapping his arms around you . . . a girl could survive . . . provided the gigantic picture of Miss Emily over the mantle didn't dishearten her.

In the dark of a Wyoming night, Develyn closed her eyes.

You know, Lord. I could survive with <u>Quint</u>. I could survive quite nicely. I could ride all the time. I could be the queen bee with the ranch hands. I certainly wouldn't worry about money . . . and <u>Quint</u> is a sincere Christian man. But I don't want to just survive. There has to be more than that. Doesn't there?

At the top of the rise, two miles east, Develyn spotted flashing lights. Then a second vehicle with orange flashing lights. Then a third.

Ambulances? Oh, my . . . must be a horrible wreck. Not Cooper Tallon, I trust. No, he's coming in from Casper so he would be behind them.

Her hand went to her mouth. Her neck stiffened. She had to grab her arms to keep them from shaking.

Oh, Lord, no! No . . . no . . . no . . . not Casey. Not Casey and Jackson. Please, Lord, I didn't come all the way to Wyoming to have my heart broken again. I'm not that strong . . . I'm just healing from Spencer's death and . . .

As the flashing lights drew closer, she recognized the running lights of a big truck.

A truck? A wide load! Those are a lead car, a trail car, and a wide-loaded semi. Thank you, Jesus.

She reached for a Kleenex and blew her nose.

I do love Casey so. You brought her into my life, Lord. I know I'm going to need her as a friend for a long time. I know she's with Jackson, but keep her safe. Eh . . . keep Jackson safe too.

The rigs with flashing lights slowed down as they approached.

I think, Lord, that was the first time I admitted to myself that I grieved Spencer's death. I know there was a lot in him that was good. I know he had such wonderful potential as a young man. I don't know where or how it got sidetracked. Forgive me, Lord, for failing him.

She splashed some water on her hands and wiped her eyes.

One good thing about no makeup or mascara . . . I can wash my face without smearing the warpaint.

She watched as the rigs signaled to pull over in the gravel turnout.

Oh, great . . . they are going to pull in here and block it so that Coop's friend can't park here. Why does everything get so complicated?

The lead car pulled up twenty feet away, headlights pointed at Develyn. She had to shade her eyes to watch a man get of the car. He sported a long, stringy ponytail, wore a tank-top and thick tattoos.

She relocked her doors.

I'll just pull up to the turnoff and wait for him there. I have no intention of entertaining truckers.

Two men got out of the big truck, but they were in the shadows. She did spot the driver of the trail car.

A woman? A very wide woman.

The two men from the truck popped into view.

Develyn continued to shade her eyes from the glare of the headlights as she rolled down her window a couple of inches. "Cooper?"

"Thanks for coming out to get me, Dev. I got some folks here for you to meet."

She grabbed the door handle, but it was locked. She hit the unlock button, opened the door, and swung her legs out, but the seat belt yanked her back. Free from the belt, she stepped out of the car, cracked her knee on the door, and staggered forward into the headlights.

Well, Ms. Worrell, that was quite an entrance.

"You were right, Coop; she looks a lot like Barb," the lady said.

"Dev . . . this is Andy Rasmussen, his wife, Carol . . . and their youngest son, Little Coop."

The man with tank top and tattoos reached out his hand. "The name's Cooper, ma'am. Only Big Coop gets to call me Little Coop."

"You were named after Mr. Tallon?"

"Yes, ma'am, but you shouldn't hold that against me."

Carol Rasmussen strolled over and hugged her shoulder. It felt like being caught in malfunctioning elevator doors. "Good to meet you, Dev. Big Coop said you were a sweetheart."

"You looked a little surprised when we pulled up," Little Coop said.

"I didn't hear the part about a big rig. I thought I was waiting for a pickup."

"I'm hauling a bridge to Butte," Andy said.

Develyn stared at the shadowy load. "A whole, assembled bridge?"

"I told Coop we could deliver him back to Argenta in the lead car, but he wouldn't hear of it," Andy added. "He's right. I do need to make deadline. The permit for something this wide is time limited."

"We specialize in wide loads," Carol stated.

Develyn bit her lip and glanced at the large lady. "I'm very happy to meet you all. Coop's been a good landlord and neighbor to me this summer. I'm delighted to help him out."

"Well, treat him good, Miss Dev. He's one of a kind," Andy said. "Let's get back on the road. We've got lots of highway to swallow."

"It's nice to meet all of you," Develyn called out.

The three trudged back to their rigs. The young man with the ponytail turned back before he slid into the lead car. "You were right about her, Big Coop . . . you were right."

Develyn stood beside Cooper Tallon and waved as the three rigs pulled onto the highway. "Mr. Tallon, your taxi is waiting."

He held the driver's door open for her, then ambled to the passenger side. His hat in his hand, he slid in and closed the door. "Dev, I can't thank you enough. Andy and Carol would do anything for me. They would drive me to the edge of the earth and back. But they had some trouble bypassing a low bridge back near Chugwater and got about an hour and a half behind schedule."

Develyn turned off the highway onto the gravel road back to Argenta.

"No problem, Coop. But you do have to answer one question."

He cleared his throat. "What did they mean by, 'I was right'?"

"Yes."

"I've got to give you the whole story about Andy and Carol. Andy and I worked our way through college driving backhoes for a contractor in Laramie. After graduation, he went to Viet Nam, and I went to Colorado. In the mid-seventies we found ourselves living near each other along the Colorado/Wyoming border. With a few other folks, we started a little church just off the highway near Virginia Dale, Colorado."

"A church?"

"That's one of the nicest Christian families you're ever goin' to meet. Carol plays the organ, and Little Coop sings tenor as good as anyone in a southern gospel quartet."

"He's in a church quartet?" she gasped.

"The long hair and tattoos threw you off, huh?"

"I suppose."

"Did you read the tattoos?"

"I always feel awkward about reading a man's tattoos."

"I feel the same way about reading a phrase written on the front of a woman's shirt, especially when the words sort of bobble up and down."

"What did the tattoos say?" she pressed.

"The one on his left arm says 'John 3:16.' On the right, it says 'I am the way, the truth, and the life.'"

"Witnessing tattoos?"

"Little Coop made some mistakes early in life, but he won't repeat them. He's a good kid."

"OK, you told me about the Rasmussens. How about you being 'right,' and who is Barbara?"

"Barbara was a lady in the church there in Colorado. Her husband had died in Nam, and she was raising two little girls by herself. She liked horses, so they lived out there in the mountains. She got some kind of pension from the army and she had this at-home job of sewing dog collars."

"What kind of job?"

"You know, the thick nylon dog collars? They supplied the machine, sent her a huge box of parts, and she sewed them together. They paid by the piece. Anyway, she was a part of that little church. She was a sweet woman."

"Does that mean that you and she were . . . eh . . ."

"No, there wasn't any romantic interest, if that's where you're headed. The thought crossed my mind ever' Sunday, but I was just putting together my business and working eighteen hours a day. On Sundays I would go to church, then sleep all afternoon, and start the week over again. She and Carol were pals. They were the children's Sunday school teachers."

"Carol seemed like a pleasant lady."

"She is a sweetie. She hasn't always been that heavy, Dev. She will do anything for anyone, anytime of the day. I've never known a person exemplify the phrase 'servant of the Lord' better than Carol. Anyway, I took a few liberties talking about you."

Develyn kept her eyes focused on the dirt road. "What did you tell them?"

"For thirty years, Carol and Andy have been trying to get me married. I cannot count the number of ladies they have introduced me too. And I don't mean losers. Most have been very nice, fine ladies."

"But not for you?"

"No. Not for me. Anyway, when we got to visitin' down in Cheyenne this afternoon, Carol grilled me about the women in my life. I knew if I told them there was no one, they would get me lined up with some more of their friends."

Develyn laughed. "So you told them that I was your lady, just to get them off your back?"

"I didn't say you were my lady . . . but I did say there was a neighbor gal in Argenta that . . . I . . . eh . . ."

"Make it good, Coop."

"I'm sorta diggin' myself a hole."

"That's your business, isn't it? Diggin' holes?"

Cooper rubbed his chin. "Oh, Miss Dev, you turned out purdy good."

"You mean for someone you disliked for the first two weeks."

"Yes, I'm glad you stayed around."

"You haven't finished your story."

"I told them you reminded me of Barbara, and I was hoping to get to know you better."

"And this taxi ride was sort of a ruse to show them you really did have such a friend?"

"Will you forgive me for that?"

"Sure. I've been divorced several years, and I can't count how many wonderful men my friends have pushed my way."

"Thanks."

She turned left at Mrs. Tagley's store. "What happened to Barbara? You spoke of her in the past tense."

Cooper was silent until they turned right down the drive to the cabins.

"There was a chimney fire in the night," he murmured.

"Oh, no!"

Develyn parked the rig in front of her cabin. Uncle Henry was sprawled out in the dirt asleep.

"She got the girls out, but was so burned doin' it that she died a few days later."

They sat there in silence.

"It's hard to understand those things, Dev," he finally said. "I asked the Lord about that one, night after night. I still don't have the answer."

"What happened to the girls?"

"Her sister in Grand Junction raised them. Some of us in that little church saw to it that they got a college education. One of them is a schoolteacher now."

"You put them through college by yourself, didn't you, Coop?"

"They lost their daddy to the war and their mama to a fire. Kids deserve better than that, Dev. But that was a long time ago. I had the funds and no family of my own to spend it on. But that's why I told the Rasmussens what I did."

"I look forward to visiting with you more on Friday night, Coop."

"Yes, I'd like your advice on log house designs."

"You're going to build it?"

"Looks like they are going to buy me out."

"That's wonderful. You'll have to tell me everything about it on Friday." She stepped around to the rear of the Jeep Cherokee. "Don't forget your laundry."

"Oh . . . yeah. Thanks again. You've been tendin' me all day. How was Jenny-By-The-Park?"

"Very happy. She got married in May."

Coop jammed his hands in his back pockets. "I didn't know that."

"Her husband made her close the business."

"She's closed? So . . . you didn't get them . . ."

"Oh, they are clean. I just took them to a coin laundry and did them myself."

"You did my wash?"

"There's nothing to be embarrassed about. So you spilt a little mustard on that blue and black shirt. It came right out with some stain remover."

He grabbed up the cardboard box. "And you folded them too?"

"You don't seem to like the wrinkled look."

The front door of the cabin banged open. "Hey, what's going on out there?"

"Casey! You are finally home," Develyn called out.

Cree-Ryder strolled toward them in the light of the open cabin door. "What do you mean, I'm finally home? I left you a note. That's more than you did for me."

"Mr. Tallon needed a lift, and I . . ."

"Sure. Here I've been worried for nothing," Casey jibed.

Cooper Tallon started toward his cabin. "Good night, ladies. Thanks for the ride, Dev, and for doing my laundry."

"You did his laundry?" Casey giggled.

"What is the big deal about doing a man's laundry?"

"Wait!" Cooper scooted off into the shadows. "I don't think I want to hear Cree-Ryder's answer to that."

10

Develyn pulled the sheet up to her chin, but she left the thick comforter folded back at her waist. "Jackson took you to see LaSage Mansion?"

"Isn't that too wild, or what? He's got this friend, Peter, whose dad works at the natural gas plant. Peter told Jackson as long he was going to be down this way, he should check out the old mansion."

"So you got to drive right in?"

"Yes, Peter's dad drove his rig down there with us. But, get this . . . the reason he wanted to take me down there after dark was to watch for the ghosts."

"Really? Two very beautiful ghosts, no doubt."

"Peter's dad said a couple of the guys spotted some apparitions at the mansion and . . ."

"Apparitions? I was hoping we got a better review than that."

"Well, those two men aren't talking about it any more."

"Too embarrassed?"

"Too rich. When they got back the other night, one of the guys in the office heard the story, so on a lark he e-mailed MoonBeam."

Develyn stared through the darkness at Casey's bed. "The supermarket tabloid?"

"They offered a thousand dollars to each of the men, plus pictures of the mansion. I guess a reporter is flying out this weekend."

"But there won't be any ghosts."

"They said that's OK; they'll use a reenactment."

"Reenactment?" Develyn laughed. "But who will they get to play us?"

"I was rootin' for Catherine Zeta-Jones and Meg Ryan."

"But who will play whom?"

"Very funny!" Casey snapped.

"It is funny. It really might be in the rag sheet?"

"Maybe not front cover, but it will be there."

"I'll have to hire someone to buy me one," Develyn mused. "I know all the cashiers in Crawfordsville, and I'd be too embarrassed to buy one myself."

Casey burst out laughing.

"What's so funny?"

"Indiana is a strange place. You walk up to some supermarket and a lady in a trench coat with a Groucho Marx mustache shoves some money in your hand and says, "Pssst! Hey, buddy, would you buy me a tabloid?"

"You cannot see this in the dark, Casey Cree-Ryder . . . but I'm sticking out my Indiana schoolteacher tongue at you."

"Anyway, there were no ghosts, but Peter's dad said we could wait down there if we wanted to. He went back to the plant. We stayed down by the mansion."

"Wait a minute, you parked in the dark of LaSage canyon with Jackson Hill?"

"Yes. We talked and talked and talked for over two hours. I think I do communication better in the dark."

"You talked, huh? Did you see any stars?"

"The moon was so bright, the stars looked dull, you know what I mean?"

"I meant when he kissed you," Develyn said. "Did you see stars?"

"Stars, bells, whistles, fireworks, flags flying . . . Dev, it was like the whole dadgum chorus of angels stood up and cheered."

"Whoa! That's some serious kissing."

"Hey, but we didn't fool around."

Even in the pitch dark, Develyn felt her face flush. "I'm glad to hear that."

"But he did . . ."

"I don't want to go there . . ."

"Put his hands on my . . ."

"Casey, hush. That's between you, Jackson, and the Lord."

"Cheeks."

"He held your cheeks?"

"My face. He put the palm of his hands on my face and just held them there. That was the most peaceful, wonderful feeling."

"Yes, well . . . among some native tribes, that means the couple is engaged."

"I know."

"I made that up."

"No, it's true," Casey insisted.

"It is?" Develyn gasped.

"No, but I just wanted to prove to myself I could still trick you."

"Go to sleep."

"I can't. Can you take care of Popcorn for a few days?"

"Are you running off to Reno to get married?"

"I don't think so. Jackson's sister, Penny, lives in Red Lodge, and he wanted me to go along."

"Overnight?"

"Over the weekend. But don't worry, he said she had a spare room for me and everything. I'll be good, Mama."

"Don't you think this is all moving kind of fast?"

"Dev, I'm almost thirty. I've never had a man be serious with me yet. Then the only guy I ever had a serious crush on wants to be with me. It can't move fast enough for me."

"I'm not your mother, Casey. I do worry about you like you were my daughter, but you are a smart girl. Don't do dumb things, and you'll be fine. I just don't want you to . . ."

"I know . . . get my hopes up and then have my heart crushed by Monday."

"Something like that."

"You know what I decided? I could be aloof . . . lose Jackson . . . and have no great memories. Or I could enjoy every moment . . . even if it doesn't work out, at least I'd have my memories. Even lost moments are better than no fun at all."

"Are you quoting Alfred Lord Tennyson to me? The old 'It's better to have loved and lost, than . . .'"

"No, it's far, far better to love and win!" Casey interrupted. "I'm not planning on losing this one."

Develyn rolled on her right side and hugged her pillow.

Casey's voice was raspy, soft. "When is Delaney coming?"

"Next Wednesday."

"I'll stay out in my horse trailer."

"Casey, you will do nothing of the kind. I bought one of those inflatable mattresses, and we'll all bunk in here. I need you with me. Having a moderator in the room always makes me think things through before I speak."

"Thanks, Dev. I look forward to meeting her. I feel like she and I are kinda related. Is she like you?"

"She is nothing like me."

"In the picture you showed me, she doesn't look like you."

"She looks like my brother, Dewayne. What time is Jackson coming by?"

"Eight o'clock. He's staying with some friends over in Lander."

"That's a long drive. He'll have to get up early to make it here by eight."

"Yes, but he said he probably wouldn't be able to sleep anyway."

"I see. I'm really happy for you, Casey."

"I'm happy for me too. And it's all because of you, Ms. Worrell."

"How do you figure that?"

"Well, you came out here this summer . . . and you showed up at the horse sale . . . and you made friends with me . . . and you wanted to stay at the mansion to avoid having to go with Quint . . . and you wanted to clean up the next day at the hot springs . . . and invited Renny along . . . and Jackson saw Renny . . . then me! And you pushed me to go off with him. If not for your memories of a dirt road town, I would have missed him."

"It sort of validates my entire summer."

"It just might validate my entire life."

● ● ●

When Develyn heard Casey's rhythmic breathing, she knew she was asleep.

It's not about me, is it, Lord? I thought this whole summer thing was about me. I came out here to find myself . . . to discover what was missing in my life . . . to ride free in the wind . . . to explore my childhood.

Me . . . my . . . I . . . on and on it goes.

But this summer is about Casey finding the love of her life. It's about Delaney needing some space to deal with a personal crisis. It's about Quint discovering that he will never replace Miss Emily . . .

246

it's about Lily, not being burdened trying to entertain me, and finding herself a nice man . . . it's about Renny and Coop and Mrs. Tagley and Uncle Henry. It's not about me.

And the summer is barely half over.

Maybe that's what I needed most in this trip. I needed to get my mind off myself. It's not about me.

Why is that so tough to do?

● ● ●

Develyn dumped hay over the fence into the pasture where Popcorn and My Maria grazed. She watched as Cooper Tallon rode up on his buckskin gelding.

"Good morning, Mr. Tallon. Are you coming in or heading out?"

"I'm riding up into the Cedar Hills to take some digital photos. I want to pick out the best place to build my log home."

"That sounds fun."

"I'd invite you along, but you said you were goin' to Douglas."

"Thank you very much anyway. When you pick a site, let's ride out and look at it."

"I'd enjoy having a woman's opinion." He tipped his black felt cowboy hat at her. "Have a great day, Miss Dev."

"You too Coop."

He rode north across the prairie.

Lord, I feel like I barely know Cooper. There seems to be a whole lot about him that he keeps to himself. I don't even know how old he is. Maybe he's sixty. But I do know he's strong and healthy and has a thirty-five-inch waist and thirty-six-inch inseam.

● ● ●

The store in Mrs. Tagley's living room smelled like cookies and bacon, a warm, nostalgic aroma that made Develyn feel ten years old. She plodded behind the counter and opened the chest freezer, then pulled out an orange Popsicle.

"It's just me . . . Devy-girl . . . Mrs. Tagley. I know I'm early today, but I wanted something cold to suck on. I'll leave your money on the counter."

"Honey, come back here a minute."

Develyn plodded to the back room where Mrs. Tagley was on her hands and knees next to the sofa. The black-and-white television blared a soap opera.

"Are you OK?"

"I'm just a little embarrassed. I can't get up."

Develyn hurried to her side. "Sweetie . . . I'm sorry. Let me help you."

With Mrs. Tagley's arm around her neck, Develyn helped her up. "Sit in this chair a minute and catch your breath. What happened? Did you fall?"

"Oh, I fell asleep on the couch last night, and I rolled over and fell on the floor. I couldn't get up. I think that scared me."

"When did you fall on the floor?" Develyn asked.

"About nine o'clock."

"Last night?"

"Yes."

"Oh, Mrs. Tagley, I'm sorry I didn't check on you sooner."

"It's a tough thing to lose some of the ability to take care of yourself. Now I'll be even more frightened of falling. I cracked my knee on the counter a couple of days ago. It just wants to give out on me."

"Honey, I'm going to come over here bright and early every morning to make sure you're OK."

"You don't need to do that. I've taken care of myself for over ninety years."

"It's time someone looked in on you. I'll only be here three or four more weeks, but I'll check on you."

"You really going back to Indiana? I was hopin' you'd stay."

"Thank you, Mrs. Tagley. That's kind of you."

"I don't say it to everyone, but you've got Wyomin' in your eyes. I saw it thirty-five years ago. I see it today."

Develyn studied the older woman's gray eyes. "What do you mean?"

"It's kind of like a hunger and a fulfillment, a longing and a satisfaction, a dream and a reality that makes your heart beat faster and every breath of air taste sweeter. It's a God-given gift, honey. He offers it to a few . . . and some reject it. But them that accepts it, never lets go. You'll either live here or long for here all of your life. But you will never get Wyoming out of your system. You know in your heart what I say is true."

Develyn bit her lip and nodded. "Yes, I think I've known that since I was ten."

The bell at the front door jingled. Develyn helped Mrs. Tagley stand.

"I've been on the floor all night, Devy-girl. Go take care of my customers while I freshen up a bit. I need to comb my hair and put on some fresh makeup."

Develyn stepped back to the store where she was greeted by a boy who looked about twelve.

"Where are your video games?" he demanded.

"They're on the bottom shelf in the side room under the videos and DVDs," Develyn said.

A man in Dockers and a maroon knit golf shirt strolled up to the counter. "I had a little car trouble, but the shop seems to be closed. The big door is open, but no one is there."

"I'm sorry, Lloyd goes to Casper for auto parts every Thursday morning. He'll be back between 9:30 and 10:00. He's quite a good mechanic."

"But the door is open."

"I don't think that door has worked in years. In the winter time, he hangs a plastic tarp."

A blonde-haired lady with khaki shorts, matching maroon golf shirt, and sunglasses strolled up beside the man. "This isn't Houston, Ryan. There is still a little trust in this world."

A little girl about ten peered around the shelves. She wore jeans shorts, a pink "Cheyenne Frontier Days" tank top, sandals, and a bright pink cowboy hat with a fake feather hatband.

"Hi," Develyn said. "What's your name?"

"I'm Hillary Ann Thompson. I'm in the fourth grade at Rayburn Middle School. I live at 34266 Hillside Circle in Houston, Texas, 77008. My parents are Ryan and Melissa Thompson, and I'm going to be a cowgirl just like you when I grow up."

Her mother grinned and hugged her shoulders.

Boots, jeans, cowboy hat and no makeup . . . I probably do look more Wyoming than Indiana.

"Good job, Mom. She knows just what to say."

"The cowgirl part just started yesterday."

"At the roundup?" Develyn pressed.

The father scratched his forehead. "No, we go to the Houston Livestock Show and Rodeo every year, so they are used to rodeos. But driving north of Cheyenne we were stopped on the highway while they moved several hundred head of Herefords from one grazing ground to another."

"One of the cowboys was a girl my age," Hillary Ann Thompson reported.

"So, she decided on being a cowboy girl?"

"A cowgirl," Hillary corrected.

"In Wyoming we call them cowboy girls."

The boy stomped back into the main room. "Your video games stink!"

"David, that's not appropriate," his mother scolded.

"But it's true."

"Is there anything I can get for you?" Develyn asked.

"We'll have to wait for Floyd for the fan belt. I'd like a bottle of water. How about you, Melissa?"

"Yes, that sounds nice. Do you have water in a glass bottle? It's so much better than the plastic."

"I don't think so, but check the bottom shelf of the pop cooler. The store belongs to my friend, Mrs. Tagley. I'm just watching it while she does a few chores in the back."

Melissa Thompson headed for the cooler.

"What about you kids?" Mr. Thompson asked.

"I want a Mountain Dew," the boy said.

"I would like to have whatever cowboy girls have," Hillary declared.

Develyn dug out an orange Popsicle from the freezer. "This is what Wyomin' cowboy girls always have."

The little girl's eyes widened. "Really?"

"I didn't even know they made Popsicles anymore," the man murmured.

"I'm going to have one myself," Develyn announced.

The lady returned with two plastic bottles of water. "It's OK. I just prefer glass bottles if you had them."

Develyn gave the man change and shoved the ten-dollar bill into the old-fashioned cash register.

"Do you mind if we wait out front on that old wagon seat?" the man asked.

"Oh, please do. Do you have a pocket knife?"

"Eh, no . . ."

Develyn reached under the counter and pulled out a

yellowed stockman's knife. "You can use this one and carve the kids' initials in the bench."

"You encourage graffiti?" the woman gasped.

"Just initials. It's sort of like a guest registry. You don't have to do it."

"Cool," the boy shouted. "Come on, Dad."

"This is a different world," the woman replied.

"Yes, it is," Develyn said. "It's a good world . . . and some people get to spend more time in it than others."

Hillary clutched Develyn's hand as they walked to the front of the store.

"Is that mule running loose?" the boy called out as he banged open the door.

"That's my watch-burro. He's a pet, like a dog. So I call him my watch-burro. His name is Uncle Henry. He is very fond of orange Popsicles, but don't let him have yours."

"A watch-burro?" Hillary squealed. "Daddy, can we get a . . ."

"No, absolutely not!"

"But you may visit with mine. I need to go to a rodeo in Douglas today, so he will be lonely," Develyn said.

"Are you going to ride bucking horses?" the little girl asked.

"Oh, I hope not, honey. A cowboy friend of mine is teaching a bunch of boys how to ride bucking horses, and I'm going to watch."

"Did you ever ride a bucking horse?" Hillary asked.

"Yes, I did."

"In front of a big crowd?"

Develyn thought about the wild horse auction. "The arena was packed."

"Did you get bucked off?"

"Yes, I did."

"What did you do then?" Hillary pressed.

"I did what every cowboy girl does. I got back on."

Hillary's eyes widened. "You did? When I grow up, I want to be just like you."

"I'm going to walk down to that corral and back to stretch my legs," Melissa Thompson declared. She turned and strutted down the stairs.

Ryan Thompson motioned to the bench. "David and I will be over here carving some initials."

"What are you going to do?" Hillary asked Develyn.

"I'm going back to my log cabin over there to get my Jeep and drive to the rodeo." Develyn turned to the man at the bench. "Mr. Thompson, could Hillary walk with me to that pasture? I wanted to show her my horse."

"Oh, yes, Daddy, please!" Hillary squealed.

"Yes, you may. You mind this nice lady."

Develyn and Hillary strolled hand in hand to the end of the pasture, licking Popsicles. Uncle Henry tagged along behind.

"Which horse is yours?" Hillary asked.

"The paint horse."

"He's beautiful."

"She's beautiful. Her name is My Maria."

"You have a girl horse?"

"Yes."

"What's the name of the other horse?"

"That's Popcorn. He belongs to my friend Casey Cree-Ryder. She's an Indian."

"A real Indian?"

"Yes."

"So that is an Indian horse? Wow . . . this might be the best day of my entire life."

Develyn squatted down next to Hillary until they were eye to eye.

"Honey, some time today or tomorrow, the Lord's going to offer to give you Wyoming."

Hillary's eyes widened. "He will?"

"Yes, and you can either say 'yes' to that gift, or 'no.' I want you to say yes."

"I will. I really, really will."

"I know, Hillary Ann Thompson. I can see Wyoming in your eyes."

● ● ●

The Broken Arrow Saddle Club loomed in the distance as Develyn pulled off the highway and onto the thinly graveled dirt road. The dust hovered like ground fog in her rear-view mirror. By the time she parked in the converted pasture, grit coated her arms, face, and lungs. Several dozen pickups and horse trailers littered the grounds. Dogs ran among the rigs.

Uncovered wooden bleachers were half full of men and women wearing jeans, boots, and cowboy hats. She spied three wooden bucking chutes across from the stands. At the far end of the arena, roping boxes stood empty.

South of the arena, shade tarps stretched tight snapped like towels in a locker room when the wind picked up. Under the tarps, smoke steamed up from a huge portable barbecue grill. Next to the grill were several tables.

Two dozen boys, ages twelve to twenty, sat on the top rail of the fence. Each sported jeans, boots, long-sleeve western shirts, and cowboy hats. They listened to the dimpled cowboy with a black Resistol cowboy hat who rode a sorrel horse.

Develyn stood by the rail and watched the cowboy.

That's Renny's element, Lord. He's home. He's out under the Wyoming blue sky with the wind in his face, riding horseback and teaching the next generation what it's all about. He looks happy. He looks at peace.

Is that the way I look in the classroom back in Crawfordsville?

I hope so.

I want to be content. I want to accept who I am.

I want to be as excited about the subject at hand as Renny.

Somehow, spelling and parts of speech don't seem as thrilling as a bucking horse. Maybe I could devise a "Rodeo of Arithmetic" where they only get eight seconds to answer a math question.

Renny's a natural teacher. Look at those boys. They will do absolutely anything he asks of them.

"And here's Miss Dev!" Renny rode down in front of her.

She pulled off her sunglasses. "Hello, Mr. Slater."

"Climb over the rail, darlin'. I promised to introduce you to the boys."

She climbed up two rungs, threw her leg over the top rail, and slid to the arena dirt. Renny climbed down off the horse and handed her the reins.

"Ride down the line and introduce yourself to the boys."

She took the reins, but hesitated to put her boot in the stirrup. "Slater, if you stick a thistle under this saddle and this horse so much as bucks once, I'll jump off this horse and murder you in the middle of the arena with my bare hands," she murmured. "Do I make myself clear?"

"Yes, ma'am. I just want you to say howdy to the boys."

She swung up into the saddle and jammed her right foot in the stirrup. "If he bucks, you're dead, Slater."

"Relax, Devy. You look younger when you relax. And eh . . ." He motioned to her face.

"What?"

"Wear your shades."

"My sunglasses?" She glanced down at him. "What's the matter, cowboy? You said you liked the no-makeup look."

"Oh, I do, darlin', but I sort of built you up with the boys."

"And you don't want me looking older than their mother?"

"No, darlin' . . . that's not it . . . exactly."

"I think I might murder you anyway. Just for general principles."

"Boys," Renny hollered. "Let me introduce you to my good pal, Miss Dev Worrell. Earlier this summer she helped me ride stock over at that wild horse sale in Argenta. The day before yesterday, she and I were up at Graybull and we worked together and gentle-broke a rank mare in only seven hours. As far as I know, she and Casey Cree-Ryder are the only ones to ride down the north end of Sage Canyon and back up again since the oil company dynamited that roadway. What I'm sayin' is, this is one tough cowboy girl. So treat her nice."

Develyn rode down the rail, and like a wave at a Colts football game, the boys' hats came off one at a time, followed by a chorus of "Howdy, Miss Dev, ma'am."

They all have dirty cheeks, smiles on their faces, and cowboy in their eyes. Where do these boys come from? Oh, my, there are some lucky little girls in Wyoming.

She turned the horse around and walked him by the cowboys again.

"Now I know what some of you boys are thinkin'," Renny said. "But Miss Dev is just a little too old for you. Besides, you'd have to wrestle me to get her hand."

"I'll wrestle you, Renny," one boy shouted.

Develyn turned back to see a boy standing on the outside of the rail. His face looked twelve, but his body looked like an NFL linebacker.

"I bet you would, Luther," Renny laughed. "Now that you've gotten a chance to meet Miss Dev, all of those in favor of my proposal, signify by sayin' 'aye'."

Enthusiastic "ayes" exploded from the boys on the rail.

"All opposed, say 'no'."

Silence.

"What did I just get voted on?" she pressed.

"You are officially elected the queen of this rodeo."

"Queen?" She glanced at the boys, and then out at the parents in the stands.

"I told them that even with all your experience with horses, you had never been elected rodeo queen. Now you have."

"Oh my, that is a wonderful honor. Boys, thank you very much. Am I supposed to make a wall run, or what?"

"At this rodeo all the queen has to do is sit in the stands and look purdy, then present the trophies and ribbons at the barbecue."

"And pose for pictures with the winners," one of the boys called out.

"I'd be privileged to do that."

"I'll wrestle you for her, Renny," Luther repeated.

● ● ●

Develyn sat all afternoon in the middle of the bleachers between Charley Rice's grandmother, Beatrice, and Cody McAllen's mother, Candy. Frank Slinisky and Candy's husband, Larry, served as pickup men. The scores were decided by Frank, Larry, and Renny with a consultation in front of the bucking chutes right after the ride. Renny shouted the score and what made the ride strong or weak.

Sinde Salvador, stopwatch in hand, was the timer. Her daughter, Natasha, blew the portable airhorn after eight seconds. Except for when she was winking at Carrie Hammer's cousin, Mason, from Rock Springs.

Each of the twenty-two boys rode two rounds. The top ten averages moved on to the finals. At the intermission after the second round, Renny met Develyn at the gate.

"How's the rodeo queen?"

"It's quite an honor. I presume I was the only candidate."

"The others were too scared to run against you."

He slipped his hand in hers, and they ambled toward the parked rigs.

"I think the whole queen thing was cooked up by my mustang breaker."

"Hey, you need to be queen just once."

"Thanks, Renny, you make every day fun."

"Good. Because I don't think Ms. Worrell has had nearly enough fun in her life."

Develyn pushed her hat back. "Can I pull off my sunglasses now, or will it frighten you?"

"Pull 'em off."

"You're probably right. I've been uptight for so long it's a lifestyle. But you and Casey and the others are helping me relax."

"Good. I was hoping that would happen."

"Look at today. It's a little girl's dream. I think I'll put it on my dossier, right after my master's degree—rodeo queen."

When they reached Renny's pickup, he opened the tailgate and motioned for her to sit next to him.

"You know what, Miss Dev . . . ?"

"What?"

"You make my life fun too."

"As an object of your jokes?"

"No, when you're around I try harder at everything. I'm more aware of things. Want to do it all a little better. You step my life up a notch just by being in the crowd. I know, I know . . . it sounds crazy. But you are a classy lady, and that's every cowboy's dream."

"That's a very nice thing to say."

"Here's the deal . . . my life gets to be such a routine."

"A routine? Renny, your life is different every day of the year."

"Oh, the jobs are different. But the manner that I go about them is routine. The same style. The same actions. Even the same jokes. And after a few years, I'm just givin' the minimum. I know what it takes to get invited back. But I don't do much more. Then here you are. I want you to see me at my best. So I don't dawdle with shortcuts and old routines. I give it the effort it deserves, whether that's breakin' a wild mare or running this camp. I think that's what I wanted most out of being married, and the thing I never got. I wanted someone to bring the best out in me. Am I making sense, or have I been bucked on my head too often?"

She kissed his cheek. "Renny, you may not know this, but you've been counseling me. Excellence in any field is difficult to maintain when you don't have anyone in the stands to witness it. In almost twenty years of marriage, Spencer never came to one of my class programs. He said I wasn't supposed to be

261

involved with his work, and he wasn't supposed to be involved with mine."

"I am sorry about that, Dev. When we are young, I don't think we understand the permanent effect of some of the choices in our lives. There are some things we can't break free of, even if we want to."

"If you had it to do all over, would you go back and marry your wife again?"

"You mean if I was eighteen again, but knew what I know now?"

"Yes."

He pulled off his black felt hat and ran his calloused fingers through his sweaty hair. "Yes, I would, Dev. I was crazy in love with her. Maybe now I know how to do it right. How about you? If you were back there, a senior at Purdue, knowing what you know now . . . would you marry Spencer again?"

"It's funny, but I realize, yes, I would. I don't know if I've learned enough to make a difference. It seems to me I still don't know enough to have kept him in my bed. But I wouldn't miss Delaney for the world. And I do think I could do a better job raising her. I'd like a chance to try, no matter how much pain I'd have to repeat."

"We're two of a kind, Dev . . . and nothin' alike."

She smiled. "The rodeo queen and the mustang breaker. We are quite a pair, Mr. Slater. A rather fetching couple, don't you think?"

He jammed his cowboy hat back on his head. "As long as I keep my receding blond hairline covered."

Develyn pushed her sunglasses back on. "And as long as I keep my crows feet disguised."

"Thanks, Ms. Schoolteacher, for comin' over this afternoon."

"And thank you, Mr. Mustang Breaker, for inviting me."

Develyn slid her hand to the back of his neck and pulled his lips to hers.

It was a soft, peaceful kiss.

Until Natasha Salvador punched the airhorn.

Develyn stood up. "Do saddle-bronc riders only get to kiss for eight seconds?"

"I think that means it's time for the finals. Besides, no one saw us over here smoochin'."

"I'll wrestle you for her, Renny!"

Develyn looked around, but couldn't see Luther.

Renny took her hand and led her back to the arena. "What are we going to do with that boy?"

"I'll walk up to him, grab the collar of his shirt, pull off my sunglasses, and say, 'I'm your worst nightmare, Luther. I'm as old as your grandmother!'"

"Be gentle with the lad. You don't want to scar him forever."

● ● ●

The coffee shop was almost empty, but the air conditioning worked. Renny and Develyn sat across from each other. He sipped on iced tea. She had ice water.

"Well, Rodeo Queen, how was the evening?"

"The light was poor enough after dark that I survived even after I pulled off my sunglasses."

"Ever' one of the boys wanted a picture with you."

"I think it was your exaggerated introduction of me."

"Everything was the truth; just not the entire truth. Don't sell yourself short, Dev. You have a wonderful personality. Those boys like being around you, even if you are as old as their mammas."

"And some grandmas. Candy is a grandmother at thirty-four. You were great, Renny. That's where you belong."

"I know. Rodeo is not just about horses and buckles. It's about self-discipline and courage and never giving up and believing you can do it."

"I'm really glad I came. I've seen you with the big crowds. I've seen you with the ladies. I've seen you face-to-face with rank horses. But I think tonight was the best. You shined with those kids, Renny Slater. I felt proud to be with you."

Renny chewed on his tongue as he stared at her. He looked out the window at the empty parking lot, then wiped the corner of his eyes. "Dadgum corral dust," he mumbled.

"Was it something I said?"

"To have a classy woman like you say that she was proud to be with me . . . well, I reckon that's the highest honor I ever received in my life."

"Cowboy, you surely know how to make a girl feel good. For the life of me, I can't understand why these Wyoming women aren't lined up at your door begging you to marry them."

A dimpled grin broke across his face. "You know, some

women are funny that way. They want a home, income, steady work, stability."

"Isn't that pathetic?" she laughed.

"Exactly my point."

"How about you? What do you need?"

"A future."

"Oh, my, that's a big assignment."

"I've always said I'd keep up this life for a while but by the time I reached my forties, I would settle down. Well, here I am, and I don't seem to be any closer to staying put." He stirred his iced tea with his finger. "What are you doing next Tuesday?"

"Delaney flies in on Wednesday, but I think Tuesday is free. I'm not sure when Casey is coming back from Red Lodge, but it doesn't matter. What did you have in mind?"

"I'd like to drive you up to my place in Buffalo. It's not much. Just forty acres and a doublewide, but it has a lot of potential. I'll have you back before dark."

"That sounds fun. I'd like that, Renny."

"Don't be expecting something like Burdett's."

"When you come visit me in Indiana, don't expect a place like Quint's either."

"You know what? I'd like to come visit you. I'd like to see your house . . . and your town . . . and your school. I'd like to sit in the back of the classroom and watch Ms. Worrell and those fifth-graders."

"I can tell you this: you show up looking like the cowboy you are, and the whole class will hang on you and ignore me completely."

"In Indiana?"

"Around our area, you have to be an astronaut, a basketball player, or a cowboy to grab the kids' attention. Cowboys are the rarest of the three."

Renny reached across the table. Develyn took his hand.

"Devy-girl, I don't reckon I know what's goin' on here. One moment I'm wantin' to get serious with you, and the next . . ."

"You want to run away?"

"No, the next moment I'm thinkin' what a naïve, foolish cowboy I am to think I'd have a chance with you."

"It's my fault. I think I'm sending mixed signals. At times, I'm confused over what I really want, what the Lord wants, and what's just a little girl's fantasy that I can't let go. I know you are always going to be a special person in my life. I'm really looking forward to going up to your place. I think the more we know of each other, the more we'll understand where the Lord is leading."

"Don't hesitate to tell me the truth. I'd rather get bucked off quick and go on with life than get bounced around and fall off right before the buzzer."

"Until this summer, I had no idea rodeo was a philosophy of life, not just a sport."

Renny stood and tossed down a two-dollar tip. "It's a narrow philosophy of life, Dev . . . but even then, I haven't always acted too wisely."

She grabbed her purse. "I have never been known for my wisdom, Renny. Ask my mother or my daughter."

"I'll get to meet Delaney, won't I?"

"Yes, and she'll swoon over your cowboy charm."

Their rigs were parked side by side in the parking lot. A slight breeze made it cool, but not cold.

"I'll see you Tuesday. Thanks for the good time, cowboy." Develyn kissed his cheek.

He put his arm around her waist. "Anytime, Rodeo Queen."

● ● ●

Develyn set the cruise control and plowed west along the dark trail of blacktop called Highway 20. An hour later, when she came to the Waltman/Argenta turnoff, she had met only six cars coming toward her and had passed one hay truck in her lane. She knew the dirt and gravel road back to Argenta, but at night she couldn't see it very well, so she bounced along at forty-five miles per hour. All the lights were out at Mrs. Tagley's.

She must have felt well enough to turn all the lights out. I'll check on her early. I need to leave myself a note. Casey is gone; just an empty cabin. It'll be great to have Dee here . . . if we can keep from ticking each other off. I think I came out here to be by myself, but you in your wisdom, Lord, you did not leave me alone. I thank you for that. I'm lousy company, that's for sure.

She parked her Cherokee next to the cabin's front porch. Even in the dark a familiar face greeted her.

"It looks lonely back here, Uncle Henry. No Casey . . . and Cooper must have turned in early. I brought you back a taste of sweet feed. A lady at the rodeo named Sharon gave it to me . . .

said it will help you and My Maria sleep better. I never knew horses or burros had trouble sleeping, but I promised I would try it."

She grabbed up a coffee can from the back of the Jeep.

"Whoa, look at this." She held up a man's white sock. "I'm sure this is Coop's. I'd better give it right back to him. I don't want to have to explain to Delaney how it got there."

The compressed feed was about the size of Develyn's thumb. She shoved it in Uncle Henry's mouth, and he chomped it like a carrot.

"So you like that, huh? Let me get the big flashlight, and I'll take some out to the horses." She lit the lantern in the cabin and grabbed the large black flashlight.

Uncle Henry stood up on the porch by the door waiting for her.

"You get down, honey . . . you will not get a reward for being naughty. I'll put this sock on Mr. Tallon's porch, then we'll go find My Maria and give her a sleeping pill. Hah . . . I need to take one of these. I wonder what they taste like. They smell like compressed weeds."

She crept up onto Tallon's porch and draped the sock through the door handle.

I might as well give his two ponies a treat too. The whole neighborhood will get some sleep.

Cooper Tallon's bay horse waited at the corral, but she couldn't spot the buckskin. She fed the bay some of Sharon's sweet feed. "Where's your pal? You're a hungry thing! Cooper feeds you or turns you out every night. I've watched him . . . what are you . . . he hasn't come back yet, has he?"

Develyn tossed some hay to the corralled horse and tromped back to Tallon's cabin. She rapped on the door. "Coop? Sorry to bother you. Are you there?"

She pushed down on the latch and swung the door open. "Coop? Are you in here?"

She shined the light around the cabin.

It's identical to mine . . . only neater. Of course, he doesn't have two women living in his. He's not home yet, but he should be. He was just going to the rim of Cedar Hills. He should have been back by noon. He could be in trouble. Maybe he got bucked off.

Coop doesn't look like the type who bucks off easy.

Maybe he had a heart attack? He's a hard-working man. Or a stroke? Or a snake bite?

It's not about me . . . it's about others. And Cooper Tallon is one of the others you put in my life. I'll call him. If he has any cell phone reception . . . maybe he's able to talk and can tell me how to locate him. He knows these mountains. He came out in the dark after me.

Develyn stepped out on the porch and flashed the light at her cell phone. She punched Tallon's number.

Ring . . . please, Lord, let there be reception . . . Ring. Ring. Ring.

"Yes! He's got . . ." She paused when she heard a phone ring inside Tallon's cabin. "Rats . . . he left the phone here. Never mind about that prayer, Lord."

She trotted back to her cabin.

"Uncle Henry, we're going to saddle My Maria and go look for Cooper. I can at least ride up to the hills and back. I won't get lost in the open sage."

She glanced up at the dark sky.

"Of course, it would be better if those clouds didn't cover the moon and stars. But I'm going to do it, because he needs someone to help him. And this summer is not about me."

She grabbed her saddle out of the back of Casey's horse trailer.

"I wish you could carry a flashlight, Uncle Henry. I know, I'll park the SUV over there and leave the headlights on to saddle by. Then I'll leave the motor running and park the rig around back with the lights on high beam across the prairie. I'll ride until the lights get dim, then I'll turn around if I haven't spotted him by then."

She ducked between the fence rails and snapped the lead rope on a startled paint mare. "Come on, girl, we have search-and-rescue work tonight. Wow, I'm beginning to sound like a real Wyoming cowboy girl, aren't I? I hope I know what I'm doing. That would be different, wouldn't it?"

11

Develyn worked in the bright glare of the Jeep's head-lights to saddle the paint mare. With the back brushed, the blanket smoothed, the saddle set, the cinches buckled, the breast collar snapped, and the stirrups lowered, she led the paint around the truck twice, then tied her back to the rail. She drove the Jeep Cherokee behind the cabin and parked it, the engine running and lights on high, across the prairie toward the distant Cedar Hills. Then she hiked back to the waiting horse. "Suck it in, girl, suck in that tummy." She yanked the cinch two notches tighter.

Suck it in, yourself, Devy-girl. This is the ultimate irony, Lord. I am becoming the one I've only pretended to be. This middle-aged Indiana schoolteacher is saddling up in the dark and riding out by myself after a cowboy. I wonder if I should take one of Casey's guns or knives? That would make a nice photo for the school home page: Ms. Worrell, with crossed bullet belts and knife in her teeth. Even Dougie Baxter would have to respect that.

She swung up into the cold saddle. If felt comfortable under her.

"OK, girl, time for a midnight ride. I know, it's only ten o'clock, but midnight rider sounds better than ten-o'clock rider. As Jackson and Buffett would say . . . 'It's twelve o'clock somewhere . . .' Shoot, it's midnight in Indiana. I ought to call Lily, but it would freak her out. She'd call the state patrol, or the mental hospital, or both."

Develyn shined the flashlight about twenty feet in front of My Maria as they plodded across the prairie, swerving around the sagebrush. Uncle Henry trotted by their side. The headlights grew dim when they dropped down into the dry creek bed, but were still bright when they lunged up on the other side.

At five minutes until eleven they reached the first scrubby cedar trees.

"We'll cut a path east for a mile, then we have to head back, girl. If we wander into the cedars, we'll lose our beacon."

A few minutes later, Dev stood in the stirrups and stared into the shadowy cedars. "Coop?"

On her second holler, she thought she heard something.

"Coop, is that you?" *Because if it isn't you, I'm going to die of fright.*

"Over here, Miss Dev!"

Yes . . . yes . . . yes.

In the glow of the flashlight, Cooper Tallon stood beside his buckskin gelding. His face was muddy, his hat battered, his shirt ripped.

"Are you OK?" Develyn asked.

"I've had worse days."

"Is your horse lame?"

"The riggin' busted on the saddle."

She patted My Maria's rump. "Come on up and ride double."

"Normally, I'd refuse to wear out a woman's mount. It's only a four-or-five-mile walk, and someone thoughtfully left headlights pointing out here."

"It's the North Argenta Search and Rescue. You search for me . . . I'll search for you. I didn't know if you needed a signal light, but I knew I would." Develyn kicked her foot out of the stirrup.

Cooper Tallon handed her the reins to the buckskin and swung up behind her.

"Grab on to my waist," she instructed.

"I'll be alright."

"If I were riding behind you tonight, you'd insist that I hold on to you."

She felt his strong arms circle her and lock fingers.

"You are a mess, Mr. Tallon."

"Yes, ma'am. It's a good thing it's dark. I have a feelin' it would look a whole lot worse."

"Would you like to talk about it?"

"No, I'd rather wake up in my bunk with indigestion and a bad dream, but you earned the right to hear the story. I can't believe you'd saddle up and ride out here."

"Do you think you're the only one who can help a neighbor?" Develyn patted his calloused hands that rested on her stomach. "Besides, I hope to be here another month, and I'm sure you'll have to come out and rescue me a time or two more. Now, what's the deal here, Coop?"

They plodded south, and Develyn turned off the flashlight. My Maria plodded for the Jeep headlights.

Cooper Tallon cleared his throat. "I took my time this mornin'. Just enjoying the quiet and trying to sort things out. All I've ever known is hard work, Dev. So this idea about selling out causes me to think about things I've never pondered. When I got up to the top of Cedar Creek, where the springs run all summer, I sat there ponderin' about things. I did a little prayin' and wonderin' if I'd made other choices in my life, how things would be different. A man needs to ponder by himself sometimes. And Cedar Creek's a great place to do it.

"When I was a young man, I lived along a canyon northwest of Ft. Collins, Colorado. Once a week or so, I'd climb the mountain behind my house and just sit there and talk to the Lord. I could see the front range, and the prairie, and almost to the throne room itself. But I moved, then got too busy being boss to do that. Dev, a man needs that kind of a place. I don't know about you gals, but a man needs that."

"It sounds wonderful, Coop. I don't know how to climb a mountain, but I would love a quiet place like that. Sometimes I go down to Turkey Run State Park and find a deserted bench and try to have a peaceful time with the Lord. Peace is the goal.

I spend most of my life with twenty-five fifth-graders. It can be fun . . . it can be frustrating . . . but it is never peaceful."

"Maybe I can show you this site before you leave. You're welcome to use it too. You can ride right up to it. This property has been in my family all my life, but I never saw that spot in that way before. Kind of strange how you discover the good things when you are older. Anyway, not far away from that spot I found a beautiful meadow on the high side of the crick that would make a perfect place for a log home. I must have spent another hour or so deciding exactly where to build the house, and barn and shop. I was kind of like a kid with a new toy. I ran around putting cornerstones where all the buildings would go."

"You definitely have to show it to me."

"I could show you the pictures, but that's where the day turned sour. I snapped a mess of digitals, then wanted one last picture of me riding the buckskin with the home property in the background. So I propped my camera on a big rock near the creek, set the timer and ran around and jumped on my pony and grinned."

"That sounds like quite a trick."

"The first time my head wasn't in the picture. The second time I only had half a horse."

"How about the third time?"

"Now, there's the problem. To get everything in the lens, I propped the camera up on pebbles and my gloves. I had just climbed up in the saddle when a gust of wind blasted through and knocked my camera over. It slid down between boulders next to the creek. I jumped out of the saddle and sprinted down there. But I couldn't reach the camera."

"Oh, dear."

"So I started digging at those boulder with my hands. Seems like ever' time I moved one, it would slip down deep. I laid on my belly with my toes in the crick, and got my hand on the camera."

"Oh, good . . ."

"No, that's the first foolhardy act of the day."

"What happened?"

Tallon gave her a squeeze. "I hope you appreciate how difficult it is for me to admit."

His lips were close enough to her ear that she could feel the warmth of each word.

"Miss Dev, I got my dadgum arm stuck."

"Stuck?"

"Don't laugh. I couldn't get my arm out from the rocks. It was something about the angle and the leverage, I couldn't yank it out. I couldn't move the rocks. It felt like one of those Chinese thumb cuffs where the harder you pull the tighter it grabs."

"Only it was made of granite rock. What did you do?"

"You mean, after I yelled at myself, pounded, and pouted? I wanted to get my horse down there. I figured I could grab onto the stirrup with my free hand, and he could step back and yank me out of that mess."

"Oh, that sounds painful."

"So did spendin' the rest of my life with my hand stuck in the rocks."

"Did your horse cooperate?"

"No. I screamed and hollered at him until he ran off."

"Coop, this is quite a story."

"I remember thinkin', 'Lord, I already had my prayer time. I don't need this. This serves no purpose in my life.' But who am I to say? The fun was just beginning."

"There's more?"

"It was three o'clock before I finally dug myself out of there. I never did get the camera. Reckon I'll go back for it another day."

"I'll go with you."

Tallon laughed. "Don't know if I want to show you the scene of my folly. Anyway, I found my horse standin' in that little creek. I gentle-talked him and waded out there. About three feet before I got to him, my boots sunk down in mud halfway up to my knees. The crick isn't six inches deep, but this was a muddy sink hole."

"Like quicksand?"

"Only this was thick, gumbo clay. I couldn't pull my boots out of it."

"What?"

"Yep, they were stuck. Oh, I could pull my feet out of the boots, but couldn't get my boots. Meanwhile, this pony, disgusted with my yellin' and splashin', hiked over to the tree and just watched.

"It's one thing losing a digital camera, but no cowboy is going to ride off without his boots. So I stood in the crick in my stockin' feet and dug in the clay mud to retrieve my boots.

One came out fairly easy, but the other was swallowed up by the clay from hell. But I fought it until I yanked it out. When I finally did retrieve it, I turned and chucked that sucker at the trees."

"Your horse was in the trees."

Tallon squeezed her waist. "See, you thought of that. But at the time I didn't. The horse was half asleep, bored by the afternoon's events. That boot caught him right behind the ear. He jumped five feet straight up, dove through the cedars, caught the saddle on a tree, busted the cinch, and bolted into the prairie dragging my saddle behind."

"Oh, Coop, you must have been furious."

"Dev, I just sat there and laughed. It was beyond belief. I said to myself, 'Well, Tallon . . . I'm glad you got that out of your system, 'cause nothin' else can go wrong today.'"

"That's a good attitude."

"It would have been fine, but things didn't get much better. I cleaned up my boots and myself the best I could. Then I went in my socks to find my pony, cause I didn't want to wear soakin' wet boots."

"That sounds hard on the feet."

"Yes, ma'am. I lasted about a mile and then put on the boots. But that wasn't much better. They were already rubbin' my feet raw when I caught up with the horse. He was not too happy to see me, having been clobbered and dragging the saddle."

"He had an exciting day too."

"Anyway, it was gettin' along towards five o'clock by the

time I secured him. He was too spooked to try to ride him bare-back, so I just balanced the saddle on his back and headed to the house."

"At five o'clock?"

"Miss Dev, I'm goin' to trust this story doesn't get past you. It's a reputation a man don't want others to remember."

"I promise, Mr. Tallon."

"Anyway . . . my feet lasted another mile, but they were rub-bin' raw and startin' to bleed with the wet socks and wet boots. I made it back to Bugler Wash, so I parked myself out of the wind and built a little sage fire to dry my boots and let my feet rest. It was kind of a tirin' day, and I dozed a little by the fire."

"That's good." Develyn turned on her flashlight again as My Maria, Uncle Henry, and the buckskin gelding dropped down into the dry creekbed and out of the distant signal of the headlights. "But I thought this was Bugler's Wash."

"It is. I was east of here a ways. You can't see town from there."

"But I found you back in the trees."

"That's where the story gets even more embarrassin'. When I woke up, it was dark. The clouds had moved in, so I couldn't read the stars. I got myself turned around and started north instead of south. I wonder if I am getting old."

"How old?" Dev's hand went to her mouth. "Oh, dear . . . did I say that out loud?"

"Fifty-six. Today, I felt a lot older. I discovered my error when I got to the trees. By then my feet were raw again. So I sat down to rest them and ponder. I was sittin' there dozin' in and out of sleep, wonderin' what in the world the Lord was tryin' to teach me and how could anything good come of the day, when I heard your voice."

"It must have startled you."

"That's the funny thing, Miss Dev. It just seemed natural. It was almost as if I was expectin' it. That must sound strange. Maybe my mind is too tired and sleepy."

"I know what you mean. When you answered my shout, it didn't startle me at all. Maybe it was the Lord's prompting, but I just knew I was supposed to saddle and ride out here. I just drove back from the rodeo over in Douglas. I noticed your buckskin was gone, so I looked for you."

"You might be right. Maybe the Lord prompted you. He does take care of fools."

"You aren't a fool, Cooper Tallon."

"Some days I feel like I'm thirty . . . other days like a fool-ish old man. And when I'm visitin' with you, I feel both."

"Fifty-six is not old."

"Don't tell my feet that."

They plodded close enough that they could hear the engine running in the Jeep. "I've got some wonderful stuff for your raw feet, but you can't look at the label. When I first started riding this summer, I wore my . . . eh . . . my derriere raw in two days . . . and Mrs. Tagley gave me some lotion that absolutely soothed everything overnight and I haven't hurt since."

"What's it called?"

Develyn rode the horse around to the front of the cabins. "You can't look at the label."

"How can I use stuff without knowin' what it is?"

"OK, it's called 'Dr. Bull's Female Remedy,' but it really works, Coop, it really does."

He released her and climbed off the horse. "I'll only try it if you hand it to me in a brown paper sack."

She swung down out of the saddle. "Well, Mr. Tallon, thank you for the delightful evening."

"This was probably more important than you can imagine. Thanks. This is a transition time in my life. Knowing you helps me think things through."

"Let's put up our horses. Ill get that ointment for your feet."

Develyn left the Jeep parked behind the cabins. Uncle Henry lay down in the dirt next to the rig. With My Maria pastured and the tack stored, she darted into the cabin and grabbed the bottle off the cluttered counter.

Cooper Tallon sat on a log bench in front of his cabin. In the dim lantern light she saw him toweling off his feet.

"I didn't have a paper bag to disguise it with, but if you sit out here in the dark, you can pretend it says NFL sports cream or something."

He rolled up his sleeve and rubbed on his right arm.

"How's your arm?"

"I think I pulled a muscle or something, trying to yank it out of the rocks. I can't lift it above my shoulder without it hurting. But it will heal in time."

She squatted down in front of him. "OK, let me see those feet."

"What do you think you are doing?"

"I'm helping my friend."

He pulled his feet back. "No, Dev . . . really, I can't . . ."

"What is it with you, Coop? Give me your foot or I'll send you to the principal's office."

"You schoolteachers are a pushy lot."

"Yes, and where would the world be without us?"

He sighed and shoved out his right foot. She squirted the lotion all over her hands, then rubbed it into his feet and ankles. "Coop, do you have any eggs?"

"Eh, yeah."

"Do you have any bacon?"

"I reckon so."

She motioned for him to stick out his other foot. "Good. I need to borrow them."

"Any time."

"I'm borrowing them right now. While you finish cleaning up, I'm cooking you some breakfast. You haven't eaten all day."

"I can't have you do that."

She stood, put the lid on the bottle, and handed it to him. "Do that again a couple of times and you'll feel better. Now, go get the bacon and eggs. I'm kind of a lousy cook, Coop. But I can stir up some breakfast."

"But, you don't understand."

"Listen to me, Cooper Tallon. I need to cook you breakfast as bad as you need me to cook it for you."

He leaned back against the cabin wall. "What do you mean?"

"The Lord has been trying to show me that this summer is not about me. It's about me helping others."

"Like the old neighbor man?"

"Not old. But I need to do this for you. I feel better about myself when I'm doing things for others."

"You don't know how hard this is for me."

"That's why you have to allow it. How often do you let someone else do something for you personally?"

"Hardly ever."

"How often have you let a woman do something for you?"

He folded his arms and stared down at his bare toes. "Never."

"Then it's time you learned, isn't it?"

"I reckon . . . but even a good schoolteacher don't give the boy five tests on the first day of school."

Develyn laughed. "Good point. If you let me cook you breakfast, I promise it's the last thing I will do for you today."

"You promise?"

"Yes, I do."

He stood up. "I'll get the bacon and eggs."

She reached down and scooped up the little bottle. "Don't forget the Remedy."

"Yes, ma'am . . ." He paused at the door. "I can hardly wait for recess, Ms. Worrell."

●　●　●

When the alarm on her watch rang at six in the morning, Develyn leaped out of bed, but couldn't remember why. She stared at the busted brass alarm clock on the counter, then shoved the button on her watch. She staggered to the propane stove, turned on the burner under the teapot, then shuffled across the cold linoleum floor to the sink. She cupped a double handful of cold water, splashed her face, and stared out the window at the cabin one hundred feet away.

We talked until 2:00 . . . it was nice. Nothing dramatic . . . nothing too personal . . . just "things." Digging trenches and teaching science and horses and Indiana summers and Wyoming winters. For two hours, I didn't think about me. That was nice, Lord. Real nice. The horseback ride was like a dream. A good dream. Not a thrilling dream. Not a scary dream. Just a comfortable dream. Like shoes that fit well and you can use them both for the classroom and yard duty.

She peered at the cabin again.

I wonder how Coop's feet are today. What an experience. Of all the people I've met in Wyoming, he is the least likely to need my help for anything. But I suppose if you stay here a while everyone will need help sometime.

A distant shotgun blast interrupted her thoughts.

Everyone except Mrs. Morton.

Develyn grabbed a bottle of water from the chest, twisted it open, and took a gulp.

I've got to go to Mrs. Tagley's for some ice today, and . . . Mrs. Tagley!

"That's why I set my alarm."

She pulled on yesterday's jeans and a T-shirt that didn't smell too bad. She combed her hair and peered at the little mirror.

"Casey Cree-Ryder, you are not here. Why do I feel obligated to keep this no makeup deal? Are you leaving your hair down?"

She's leaving it any way Jackson Hill wants it. I hope she is having a great day. Lord, I'm leaving the makeup off, just to prove to myself that I can do it if I want to.

She glanced in the mirror once more.

But I am never, ever going to do this again. At least no one but Mrs. Tagley will have to look at me, and she doesn't care.

The back door to Mrs. Tagley's house had a screen on top and wood panel below. It hadn't been painted since Franklin Delano Roosevelt was president. Develyn scooted across the back porch and cracked open the kitchen door. "Mrs. Tagley, it's me . . . Devy . . ."

"Come in, honey. Thanks for checking on me. Have some coffee. I'm in the bathroom putting on my makeup. I don't let anyone see me without makeup."

Develyn grinned and poured a mug of coffee. *You see, Lord? Even Mrs. Tagley needs her makeup. So it's not vanity. Just prudence.*

"There!" Mrs. Tagley's word preceded her entrance into the kitchen. "I never feel quite dressed until I have on my makeup. I call it my heavenly look."

"Heavenly?"

Mrs. Tagley filled a mug that read "Paris, 1936." "Oh, yes. In heaven we will be made perfect, right? So there will be no bags under our eyes, or crow's feet, or gray hair, or sagging chins . . . and other parts. Anything I can do to make myself look like I will in heaven, I call heavenly. I figure the Lord wants us to look like we will in heaven on the inside . . . in our soul . . . so why not look that way on the outside too?"

"I never thought of it that way. I like that."

The older lady sipped her coffee and stared at Develyn. "You ought to try it, honey."

Develyn laughed. "Yes, well . . . I'm trying a no-makeup experiment. I'm trying to see how many men I can scare off."

"Is it working?"

"Not yet."

"You girls don't have to worry until you get a little older. And thanks for checking on me. I'm going to open my store and turn on my soaps. Satellite reception is a wonderful thing. I get the soaps two hours early. You're welcome to stay if you want."

"I need a bag of ice."

"Help yourself. Unlock the front door and turn my sign, would you? I've got to check on Misty."

"Misty?"

"She thinks she's in love with Dr. Radford, but he's no good for her. You remember how he treated Priscilla Davenport? Misty needs to learn how to choose the right man."

"So do I."

"That's not any harder than buying new shoes. Just find one that's comfortable, yet nice enough to wear uptown . . . and keep him."

Develyn grabbed a bag of ice from the freezer, then unlocked the front door and turned over the tattered "YES, WE'RE OPEN" sign.

Comfortable shoes? Maybe comfortable boots?

A young boy stood by the cottonwood tree in the dirt yard in front of Mrs. Tagley's. He stared at Uncle Henry, who was scratching his back against the tree.

"Good morning," she called out.

He wore a black and orange Harley Davidson T-shirt. "Is the store open now? I'm visiting my grandma, and she said an old lady runs this store. Are you the old lady?"

"Mrs. Tagley is inside. She can help you."

The boy pointed to Uncle Henry. "That sure is a weird looking horse. Is it a Shetland pony?"

"It's a burro. A donkey."

"It's got ears like a rabbit. I think it's an alien."

"He belongs to me. His name is Uncle Henry."

"Does he follow you all over?"

"Yes, he thinks he's a dog."

The boy shrugged. "So does my sister."

"Well, I hope you find what you want at the store."

"Does she have any cool video games?"

Develyn looked at his deep blue eyes. "I don't think she has any good ones. I hear they stink."

"Yeah, that's what I figured."

She was out in the dirt street when he shouted, "Hey, what's your name?"

"I'm Ms. Worrell."

"My name is Leon Morton."

• • •

The morning breeze blew the clouds away. By noon the sun blazed through a thin, blue Wyoming sky. Even with a slight breeze, it was hot. The old John Deere thermometer on the front of the cabin read eighty-eight degrees, but Dev didn't know how accurate it was. She sat in a plastic chaise lounge in the dirt yard, near the pasture. One hand sported a glass of ice water . . . the other was empty, but a hardback book titled *Classroom Discipline for the New Millennium* lay sprawled in her lap.

When her cell phone rang, the book dropped to the dirt.

"Hi, sweetie."

"Hi, Lily."

"Are you out riding?"

"No, I'm sitting in the yard. Casey went to Red Lodge with Jackson, and I was drinking ice water and . . ." She glanced down at the textbook in the dirt. "Napping. It's a hot day in Wyoming today."

"Sunbathing?"

"Lily-girl, I'm in the shade. I do not need to sunbath. I'm as brown as Angela Porter's mother."

"She's from Honduras. But I get the picture. So, you had a big night at the rodeo and are sleeping it off?"

"Honey, my days are so crazy, I will need a year to sort out what I did and who I am."

"Are you bragging or complaining?"

"Bragging."

"Is the mustang breaker the right one for you?"

"You know what, Lil? I have stopped trying to figure that out. Renny packs more fun in a day than anyone I have ever known. And you should see him work with those boys. Can you imagine a cowboy version of Ed Massenet and Tom Benton rolled into one?"

"Wow, too bad he doesn't have a credential. Tom is moving to the high school."

"I didn't know that."

"And you probably didn't know that Ms. Lassiter is marrying Cory Fields next Saturday in Terre Haute."

"What? Why don't I know these things?"

"Honey, cowboy exile was your choice."

"Sometimes it feels like I've been gone a lifetime."

"Are you different, Dev? Has it changed you?"

"I think so, Lil."

"Do you like the changes?"

"I think so. But the real test will come on Wednesday. I tried to call Delaney today. She must be working."

"She's filling in for Dana at the Beef Haus. She said she wanted a little pocket money before visiting her mother in cowboy heaven."

"Cowboy heaven?"

"You are building quite a reputation around Crawfordsville. They are talking of making a new video . . . *Teacher Gone Wild.*"

"Oh, sure."

"Now, tell me everything about yesterday."

● ● ●

Develyn sat in the cabin and stared at her toenails.

OK, no makeup for a week. But I already had fingernail polish and toenail polish on. Does that mean I take it off . . . touch it up . . . or leave it ratty? That was the dumbest dare I ever took in my life. I have quite ugly toes, Lord. I'm not complaining. I have learned to accept who I am, and generally, I like your work on me . . . but the toes? Well, perhaps you were distracted that day with a world crisis or something. They need help.

"Dev, are you home?"

She padded over to the door and shoved it open. "Hi, Coop . . . I was just contemplating my toes."

He stared down at her feet. She curled her toes.

"That was the stupidest thing I ever said. It's not time for the barbecue, is it?"

"No, I was just wondering if I could park Cree-Ryder's trailer next to my porch for a wind break. I want us to eat outside, but you know how gusty it can get."

"Oh, sure. Do you want me to move it?"

"No, no. I'll take care of it."

"How are your feet?"

"I hate to admit it, but that stuff works." He pointed to his boots. "With two pair of dry socks, I can even wear my boots." He reached into the back pocket of his jeans and pulled out the bottle. "I wanted to bring this back to you."

"Oh, you can keep it as long as you need it."

"I poured some of it in another container," he said.

Develyn grinned. "You don't want something called Female Remedy in your cabin."

"Did you read all the stuff on that label?"

"Yes, I did."

"I don't even know what some of those body parts are!"

"Neither do I, Coop. But I'm glad your feet are better."

"I don't know what time the meat will be cooked for sure. I'll just come over and get you when it's ready. Maybe close to six."

"That's wonderful."

"Say, I have a favor to ask. Do you have a dress?"

"I brought one. Why?"

"Well, I never take time to dress up. I thought tonight might be a nice time. I mean, please do whatever you'd like. But I'm goin' to scrub up a bit and thought I should warn you."

"How delightful. Yes, I'll wear my dress."

"Thanks, Dev. It's kind of a silly notion, but I'm trying to think about how to live my life if I'm not married to the construction business 24/7. I hope you aren't too uncomfortable in a dress."

"Coop, I wear a dress to school every day of my life. I only buy dresses that are comfortable."

● ● ●

Develyn peered into the little mirror and applied the last stroke of mascara.

Lord, I have sinned . . . have mercy on me. She pursed her mouth and studied her lipstick. She turned from one side to the other to study her eyes.

"That's better, Ms. Worrell. It's heavenly."

She sat on the edge of the bed and pulled on her dressy beige sandals.

"I have a dozen nice pair of shoes at home, Mr. Tallon, but this is the best I have in Wyoming. And this is the first time in five weeks that I've worn panty hose. I haven't gone that long without wearing them since . . . since Delaney was born."

Well, Ms. Worrell . . . you look nice enough for . . . for parent-teacher night, or even a summer wedding at the church. Why did I think of wedding? Lord, I'm at peace with all of that. It's not about me. This summer is not about . . .

"Miss Dev, are you about ready?"

There was a sharp rap at the door.

"I'll be right there, Coop."

She peeked in the tiny mirror, searched for food particles between her teeth, then headed for the door. On the way she plucked up her cell phone.

No! They can wait.

She tossed the phone back on the bed and swung open the door.

"Oh, my . . ." she said.

Cooper Tallon sported a charcoal gray, western-cut suit, crisp white shirt, black vest, and a black onyx stud at the collar where a tie might otherwise be. His black boots were polished bright, and his black felt cowboy hat was in his hand.

"Coop, you look so handsome."

"Thank you, ma'am," he grinned. "I can scrub up ever' once in a while. You have a classy look about yourself, but then you always do."

"Thank you, sir." She curtsied. "This is fun. I'm glad you thought of it."

"To tell you the truth, Dev, I've never done anything like this before, but I've been thinkin' I should do some things different."

"You didn't go buy a new suit for tonight, did you?"

He smiled. "No. It doesn't have much wear . . . mainly weddings, funerals, and whenever I'm biddin' a government job and need to make a good impression."

"If I were governor, I'd certainly hire you to build . . . whatever it is you build."

"Dev, I don't remember which arm I'm supposed to offer you, but since my right one is nearly lame, I'll offer you the left."

"That happens to be the correct one, Mr. Tallon."

They strolled toward Casey's horse trailer that now separated the two cabins. Uncle Henry brayed and followed along behind.

"No, honey, you can't come."

The burro took another step.

"I said, 'no!' You stay over in our yard until I come home."

Uncle Henry dropped to his front knees, then plopped over on his side.

"OK, you can take a nap there, but not one step further."

Tallon shook his head. "I've seen contract acts at rodeos that aren't as good as you and that donkey."

"And I've had hundreds of fifth-graders that never minded as well."

He escorted her to his front porch.

Develyn's hand went to her mouth. "Oh, heavens . . . I can't believe this! Oh, Coop, this is wonderful." She cranked herself up on her tiptoes and kissed his leathery tough cheek. "Where did you get the roses? And the linen cloth?"

"It's just a card table and foldin' chairs. The linen cloth was in my grandmother's trunk."

She leaned over the table and smelled the flowers. "You know, to be honest, I miss the flowers of Indiana. Most all yards have such beautiful flowers. Wyoming seems too harsh for a flower garden. Now, tell me . . . where did you get the roses?"

"I had a quick trip to Casper."

Develyn studied the table setting. "China and silver? Were these in your grandmother's trunk too?"

"Yes. Last night after you left, I couldn't sleep so I sorted through that old trunk in the back of the cabin. I haven't had time to look at it in years. There are some wonderful journals and photographs."

"After supper you will have to show me."

"They are old and dusty. Mainly family things."

"I want to see them."

He pulled out the chair, then slid it under her.

"You are very good at that."

"You can thank my mama for that. She was a stickler for teaching manners."

Develyn sighed. "My mother still is."

"Before we go any further, I need to tell you two things."

"OK."

"First, I don't have any ulterior motive with supper tonight. So you don't need to sit around wonderin', *What does he really want?*"

"You are a jewel, Coop. You take the pressure off me and make me feel relaxed. I think that's why I wanted to come to Wyoming this summer. You said you wanted to tell me two things?"

"The other is, you know that sock you hung on my front door last night?"

"Yes?"

"It's not mine."

Develyn started to giggle. "You mean I had another man's sock in the back of the Cherokee?"

"Apparently."

"Oh, dear, and I don't have a clue who it belongs to."

"Well, it isn't any of my business. I once came home from the laundromat with some ladies' undergarments so risqué I had to bury them so the trash man wouldn't spy them. Now, let's eat."

He stepped inside the cabin and brought out a pitcher. "I'm not a drinkin' man, so there is no champagne, but I do have some sweet tea." He poured the glasses, then sat down. "I'll serve our food in a minute. The corn needs a little more cooking. Being on the go all the time, I've eaten more meals in the truck or on the job site than I ever did at a table. But I promised the Lord, years ago, if I am sittin' down to eat, I would ask him to bless the food."

Tallon dropped his head. "Lord, you've been good to me . . . a whole lot better than I deserve. You provided this food . . . and brought this fine lady into my life for a few weeks . . . and I thank you for it all. Give us the strength to do your work and the heart to do your will. In Jesus' name, Amen."

Develyn gazed at Cooper's eyes. She couldn't tell if they were green or gray.

"Are you staring at me, ma'am?"

"My grandmother used to say that you never really know a person until you hear them pray. I appreciate you showing me that side too."

"I'm trying to slow my life down enough to allow me to be myself."

"And I like it."

"I hope you like supper. Let me tell you the menu, then give you an explanation. I've got boneless barbecue ribs using my own sauce . . . watered down a tad for Indiana taste buds."

"Thank you, sir."

"And my own homemade buffalo chili, with roasted corn, garlic bread, and the freshest Caesar salad the market had to offer. For dessert, some homemade, fresh peach ice cream."

"My word! Cooper Tallon . . . I can't believe you did all of this."

"Now, here's my confession. This is just about the only thing I know how to cook. Once a year I toss a cookout for the men who work for me and their families, and this is the exact menu they've had every year. Other than bacon and eggs and steak, this is the full extent of my cooking ability."

●　●　●

The wind died down at dark, and the temperature dropped to a pleasant coolness. After ice cream they sat across the table from each other and sifted through the old pictures and artifacts from the trunk.

"Coop, how wonderful that your grandmother labeled them all. I have a box of pictures from my father's side of the family that I refuse to throw away, but I don't have a clue who any of the people are."

"I enjoy all the outdoor shots of the family homestead and all."

"Where was this big house?"

"Right over there where Uncle Henry is lying."

"Look at this one. They brought the pump organ and the sewing machine out in the yard and posed next to them."

"Yep, they were proud of them, no doubt."

"You know what you should do, Coop? When you build yourself that nice big log home, make sure you include a den. Save one wall for old pictures. Take the best of these to a photo shop and get them enlarged, matted, and framed. Use earth tone frames, in greens, browns, rust, even a dull gold next to a huge river rock fireplace. Wouldn't that be grand?"

Tallon stared at her.

"I mean, if you want to, of course. I guess I got a little carried away."

"I never pondered it before, but as soon as you mentioned the idea, it sounded perfect. You make me realize there's a whole lot about building this place I never considered. I can see I need a woman's input. Can I hire you to be my consultant on the design and decoration of the house?"

"You most certainly cannot. I'm not for hire. I only do such things for my very good friends. So you have to take my advice for free, cowboy. I'd be delighted to add anything I could."

"I was serious about hiring you."

"Yes, well, I would never do it for money. Then if it turned out horrible, you could sue me. This way you are just stuck with it."

"Do you have any ideas for a proper kitchen?"

"I haven't thought about it much, but you will need a large room, with a center island, floor-to-ceiling cupboards on all four walls, wrap-around counter space and two separate sinks, one of them deeper than the other."

Cooper shook his head. "I'd hate to see what you'd come up with if you pondered it a while."

"It's not too late to fire me."

"I can't fire you; you won't take any pay."

"That's true. Wait until I tell you what I have in mind for your walk-in closets."

Cooper laid his hat, crown down, on the card table. "You will let me design my own shop, won't you?"

"Only if you promise to have it insulated, well heated, and a sawdust removal vacuum system built into the walls."

"I take it money is no object?"

"You don't want to cut corners." Develyn waved her hands. "Oh . . . oh . . . I just had a great idea for glass panels on both sides of your big oak double front door. The glass on the left will be etched with an elk, and the panel on the right will be an antelope."

"Etched glass?"

"And above the door . . . yes . . . above the door in oval glass turned on its side will be etched . . . 'C. T.' you know, for Cooper Tallon."

"No C. T.," he said.

"OK, forget the C. T. What about the elk and the antelope?"

● ● ●

About midnight Uncle Henry wandered to the porch and brayed at the nicely dressed couple still sitting across the table in lively conversation.

"Your watch-burro says it's time to go home."

"Thanks for the wonderful supper."

"Thanks, Dev, for helping me clean up and all the great suggestions for the house. I've got a notebook full of ideas now."

She studied her watch. "I can't believe it's midnight. This has been the fastest night of my life."

He stood up. "I'll walk you home."

"It's a short walk, Mr. Tallon."

"That's my loss." He offered her his arm. "I don't know where tonight fits in the scheme of things for me or you. You're going to go back to teaching in a few weeks, and I might sell my business. I might move out here. And I might build myself that big log home. But one thing I know is that I had one of the most pleasant, eh, . . . enjoyable . . . eh, comfortable evenings of my life. It will hold a special place in my memory that is crammed at the moment with project cost estimates and diesel engine repairs. I thank you for that. Good night, Dev."

"'Night, Coop. This was one of the highlights of my summer." She stood on the porch, and he on the dirt. They were head to head in the dim light.

She tilted her head and closed her eyes.

He shook her hand.

12

Saturday morning broke with thunder. It showered off and on until noon. Develyn spent several hours keeping Mrs. Tagley company because she didn't watch soap operas on the weekend. Lindsay Burdett phoned about 1:00 p.m. with an invitation to fly down and give Develyn a lift to the ranch, since the roads would be slick and muddy, but she declined.

She stabbed her diamond stud earrings into her lobes and studied the little mirror in the cabin. *Diamonds and denim. Nice, but not overdressed. Sorry, Quint, it's back to no makeup today. I want only one failure on my record. Not that last night was a failure . . . it was wonderful . . . it just might have been the first time a man ever refused to kiss me.*

That's OK.

It's not about me.

Rats. I haven't even seen Coop since last night.

She grabbed her purse and her denim jacket and scooted outside. She glanced over at the burro, asleep on his feet by the fence. "Uncle Henry, take care of the place."

When she slid into the Jeep, a folded note waited on her center console.

Miss Dev, I lined up a couple of early appointments . . . (one with an architect and another with the doctor) . . . since neither usually is in the office on Saturdays, I jumped at the chance. I might not get home until later, and I didn't want you traipsing off to rescue me. I know this isn't much of an accolade coming from an old bachelor, but last night was the "date of my life" and you are a gracious lady for making it so. At times, it felt like we had known each other for years. Other times I felt like a foolish sixteen-year-old boy. Please excuse my lack of wisdom if I did or didn't do the right thing at the right time. Coop.

A grin broke over Develyn's face. She hummed along with the Eagles singing "Desperado" as she turned onto the gravel road west.

The trip to Burdett's ranch was uneventful until she reached the Cedar Hills. The road turned from packed yellow dirt to slippery red mud. Even when she put it in four-wheel drive, she had to slow down to twenty-five miles per hour. The washes and gullies ran with water. She crept through each one of them. With her sunglasses low on her upturned nose, she aimed for the driest side of the roadway.

"OK, I should have listened to Lindsay and let her fly me to the ranch. But I had a reason for this, Lord. I need to be independent around Quint. I need to be able to get up and drive home if I want to. When I'm at the ranch, I feel my life is outside my control . . . all I can do is go along with things, or act snotty . . . and I don't want to do either."

No wonder Miss Emily was a pilot. She could get in the plane and fly off anytime she needed to. I don't think I can do that. I can barely look out the observation platform at the Sears Tower. However, if a lady had to be stuck somewhere, the Burdett ranch is a good choice.

Maybe for a few months anyway.

Of course, if a lady was there with the one she was crazy in love with, it could be a permanent honeymoon. There is nothing wrong with . . .

The Jeep spun out and slipped to the side of the road.

"No, no, no . . . you can't do that! This is a four-wheel-drive Jeep. I've seen those commercials on television. I could drive this baby up the side of a cliff if I wanted to!"

The road up the hill swung to the left, but Develyn's right rear wheel was in the grade to the right, and all four tires threw mud. She took her foot off the accelerator and stared down at her cell phone.

Even if there is reception out here, I will not call. I do not want help. I have to learn to take care of myself. If I cannot get to that ranch house and back by myself, I have no business contemplating making it my home. I will not panic. I'm the queen of the rodeo, I'm a regular Wyoming cowboy girl . . . I can do this.

I can't get out and push. Someone has to steer, so that's out of the question.

I could wait a few days for the road to dry, then drive right out. But they would send the posse out after me. I am determined not to be rescued again.

It's in four-wheel drive and won't pull out of this rut. What are my alternatives?

Lord, I need a little wisdom here.

Eh, what if I see if I can back down the hill to where it is flat? Maybe I can get out of this rut and then make another run at the hill.

She put the rig in reverse and eased her foot on the accelerator.

"Yes!" The Jeep crept back down the incline. "Thanks Lord . . . I figured it out."

At the bottom of the hill, she pulled back into the center of the muddy road and put the Jeep in the lowest gear. This time she hugged the left edge of the road and crept her way to the top.

"Yes! This will work fine if no one else is stupid enough to be driving this road and barrels in from the other direction. And, if I have four hours to reach the ranch."

The open valleys and prairie between the hills was dry enough to cruise right along, but the tree-shaded inclines were all slick. So she repeated the precautions each time.

I wonder what this is like with snow and ice? You can't fly a plane in snow and ice, can you? Do they hibernate? Do they go to Texas? Do they have a place on South Padre Island?

Develyn stared at her watch. *They said arrive anytime between four and six . . . it will be closer to six . . . sixish, I suppose.*

At 6:02 she spotted the headquarters. Ten minutes later she pulled into the yard. A horseback Cuban greeted her. She rolled down her window.

"Welcome back to the ranch, Miss Dev."

"Hi, Cuban. You didn't saddle up to come find me, did you?"

"The old man was gettin' worried. I knew you'd make it."

"Thank you for your confidence. It was worse than I thought."

"Yes, ma'am, I can see that. You got more mud on your Jeep than a Nebraska homestead."

"I was determined to drive. Us schoolteachers can be very stubborn."

"Yeah, that's what the ol' man said."

"He did?"

"More or less."

"Is he upset with me?"

"More or less."

"Thanks, Cuban. I'd better get to the big house. Will you and the other hands be joining us for supper?"

"Oh no, Miss Dev. This is a private deal tonight."

Develyn parked the Jeep near the back door of the big house. Though the twilight sky was clear, the grass still glistened from the rain. The sanded parking area felt spongy as she stepped out. She stared at her Jeep.

That is the most disgusting filth I have ever seen. It's like a moldy bacteria gone wild. This rig could be the main character in a remake of The Blob . . . *but who would they get to take Steve McQueen's place?*

"Hi, Dev . . ."

When she glanced up, Lindsay Burdett stood at the top of the stairs. "Hi, Linds. Sorry I'm a little late."

"I'm glad you made it. You'd better hurry. Daddy has been worried about you."

"I just hadn't experienced that beautiful clay mud before. It looks like I'm taking five hundred pounds of it home with me."

"I know. You get used to it. Sort of."

Develyn followed Lindsay through the screened veranda and into the kitchen.

"I got to do all the cooking tonight. Go join Daddy in the dining room, and I'll serve."

"Thank you, Lindsay."

The blonde twenty-five-year-old scooted over next to her. "Dev, listen . . . no matter what you and Daddy discuss or don't discuss, I have to talk to you in private tonight. It is really important to me."

Develyn noticed tears in Lindsay's eyes.

"Honey, what's wrong?" Dev whispered.

"Later . . . OK?"

"I promise I will not leave the ranch without you and me having some time to talk in private."

"Are you going to spend the night?"

"I don't think I want to drive that muddy road in the dark."

"It will be dry by morning if the wind blows."

"We'll talk later."

●　●　●

The Burdett dining room table could seat twelve. Three antique hutches lined the interior wall, each crammed with dishes. Two places were set side by side near the door that led out to the front veranda. The door was open, and Develyn felt a cool breeze when she entered the room.

Quint Burdett greeted her. "Miss Dev, you look wonderful. You had me worried, of course, but we only worry about ones we love, I suppose."

"Thanks for your concern, Quint. I wanted to test my ability to navigate these roads."

His long-sleeve blue western shirt was buttoned at the collar, but he wore no tie. "You've caused me to do a lot of thinking this week. I've looked forward to tonight. I believe we have a lot to talk about."

"I think you're right."

"But, first, you have to eat my gourmet meal!" Lindsay rolled an oak serving cart into the room.

● ● ●

The private meal and conversation stretched two hours.

The leather chairs on the front screened veranda felt soft as a featherbed as Develyn and Quint finished up the raspberry mousse. He reached across the wide arm of the brown leather chair. She took his hand.

"I wondered if you'd do that," he said.

"Quint, you are a wonderful man. I am privileged to have your friendship."

"But, something . . . ?"

"I don't know how to say this."

"Just blurt it out."

"Try as I may to be otherwise, I don't think I'm right for you."

"Miss Dev, as I have told you, you are the second most wonderful woman I've ever met. You are an incredible lady, a charming lady, a fun lady . . . and if a man my age may be blunt . . . a very sexy lady."

Develyn laughed. "That's a first."

"It's true. I believed, and still believe, that you and I are quite compatible and could build a very good marriage."

"But not a great marriage?" she probed.

"Probably not. I think you are right about that. It must be why you've shown caution this past week. I've been praying a lot about it. That part was good. I want to understand why I was so sure, and so anxious to pursue you."

"Did the Lord answer you?"

His sigh was so long and so deep, Develyn bit her lip until it ended.

"Miss Emily holds me tight, Dev." His voice started to crack. "And I don't want her to let go." He shook his head. "I don't know what else to say."

She squeezed his hand. "The love you two shared is inspiring. You're right. No one could ever compete with Miss Emily. Quint, you have a lot of love to give. There are many women in this world who would be satisfied with the love you could give. They would cherish it, cling to it, and adore you for it."

"But not you?"

"I need the Miss Emily kind of love myself this time."

"I know. And you deserve that."

"You know what I think, Quint? I don't think you would be happy with yourself unless you gave the Miss Emily kind of love to me . . . or anyone else. You would always feel you weren't doing enough, and yet you wouldn't be able to do more."

"That's exactly the place that I came to." He clutched her hand tight. His voice softened. "Your grace and love helped me learn that lesson. I could have gone out and ruined my life, and Lindsay's life, and Miss Emily's memory by doing something foolish. You are a gift of the Lord this summer to help me understand myself. It is a gift I neither deserved nor can ever repay."

Develyn couldn't hold back her own tears. "Will you promise me that you will be my good friend forever? I need you in my life, Quint Burdett. And I need to be reminded of your love of Miss Emily."

"That's a promise I know I can keep with all my heart. Even Miss Emily would approve of that. You would have liked her, Miss Dev, oh, you would have liked her."

"I know I would have."

"You will always be welcome to stay here at the ranch when you come to Wyoming. You have a permanent invitation to the yearly barbecue."

She released his hand, but rubbed the top of it. "I certainly intend to come back, that's for sure."

"I know. I can see it in your eyes."

"That's what I hear, I'm hopelessly in love . . . with Wyoming."

"You know, Miss Dev, I need to talk to you about something else. While I was fuming and praying and trying to figure things out this week, it dawned on me that part of the push to pursue you was for Lindsay's sake. She doesn't want to leave her daddy until he has someone to look after him."

"That's commendable."

"But stifling. Look at the isolation back here. When Miss Emily was alive, they flew all over the country together—a play in New York, or a concert in L.A. They attended parties in Dallas, reunions in Austin. But since Miss Emily died, Linds seldom leaves. In the back of my mind, I had the notion that I needed to settle down, remarry, and turn her loose."

"Where would she go? What would she do?"

"She's been offered a position as assistant director of public relations for the University of Texas at Austin. It's her major, and a great place to develop her career."

"And find her man?" Develyn probed.

"Exactly. But I don't know how to talk to her about it. She's going to think I don't want her around . . . or that she can't take care of me . . . I've been waiting for her to make the break, but she seems so content to be here. I'm scared to death to mention anything."

"You need to talk to her, Quint."

"She really likes you, Miss Dev. Could you approach the subject for me? Give me a woman's opinion. I've never had to be a single parent until the last couple of years. I surely miss a woman's wisdom and guidance."

"I'll be happy to visit with her, but sooner or later it's got to be father and daughter."

"I know, Miss Dev . . . I know. I believe the Lord might have brought you out to Wyoming just to help the Burdett family."

● ● ●

Develyn sat on the edge of the queen-size bed as Lindsay roamed her cavernous bedroom. Lindsay's blonde hair curled halfway down her back.

"You and Daddy talked a long time."

"Your father is a very easy person to talk to."

"That's what Mama always said, but a lot of people feel intimidated by him."

"He can be a very dynamic, forceful man. I can see how that might happen."

"How come you're not intimidated?"

"I'm too naïve," Develyn said. "By the time I realized who he was, we were already friends."

"I didn't listen in on you guys. Daddy said I was banished to the kitchen."

"We had some private matters to discuss."

"You turned him down when he asked you to marry him, didn't you? I could see it in his eyes when he walked you to the door."

"He didn't ask me."

"He didn't? But he had Mama's ring resized for you when he was up in Powell."

"I didn't know that."

"He planned to take you out to a surprise supper in Cody and ask you to marry him."

"I didn't know that either. No wonder he was so insistent that I go to Powell with him."

"I guess I always knew he would change his mind."

"Linds, your father is a wonderful man. I believe your mother brought out the best in him like no other person on earth. I believe he will love her until the day he dies."

"Yes, so will I. But I hope to get married. Why would you have turned him down, had he asked you?"

"Two reasons . . . the first is that I just couldn't compete with Miss Emily. I would always be a disappointment and cause many regrets even though your dad would be gracious and loving. That would cause him to hold back, and that kind of reserve would disappoint me."

Lindsay continued to prowl the room. "What's the second reason?"

"I'm an Indiana schoolteacher . . . that's my identity . . . my passion . . . my calling. This is the most beautiful ranch I have ever seen in my life, but it's too isolated for year-round life. I would shrivel up and die back here. If your father loves me at all, and I believe he does, he loves the Indiana school-teacher. When that part of me died, it would be difficult for him, and impossible for me."

Lindsay stopped in front of her dresser mirror and studied her long blonde hair. She folded her arms across her chest and looked at Develyn's reflection in the mirror. "You are right, of course. I guess I knew all of that too. But I hoped it wasn't true. I really like you, Dev. I wanted it to work so much."

"Honey, that's a wonderful compliment. You're a talented and beautiful lady. I count it a privilege to be your friend. I will die if I'm not invited to your wedding."

"My wedding? I don't even have a boyfriend."

"You heard me. Do I get an invitation?"

"No matter when or where?"

"I'll be there."

Lindsay grinned and scooted over to the bed. "You see? You are so sincere and caring, just like Mama. That's why I wanted it to work. Can I be real honest?"

"I think I know what you're going to say."

"You do? Mama always knew what I was going to say. Daddy said the two of us could communicate all evening and never say a word. What am I going to say?"

"That you can't live up to Miss Emily's image, either. And you hoped I would marry your father and take care of him, so you could move someplace else and have a career."

"Is it that obvious?"

"Only tonight. Was I right?"

"It was supposed to be different. My brother was going to marry some ranch girl and move back here with Mama and Daddy, then I could go out and find my place in the world. When my brother died, that changed the plans. When Mama died, it changed everything. Now, it feels like I'm dying on the inside. Every girl in my high school class . . . every one has been married at least once. I don't even have a boyfriend. I don't have any girlfriends either. I have Daddy and the ranch . . . I love them both, but I've got other things to do in life. I got this offer . . ."

"Assistant public relations director at the University of Texas in Austin?"

"How did you know that?"

"Your father told me."

"Why?" Lindsay quizzed.

"Because he thinks it's a wonderful opportunity and wishes you'd take the job. He wants you to give it a try."

"Daddy said that?"

"Yes, he did."

"But what about him? Dev, he's always had someone to take care of him."

"Honey, he has to learn what kind of life the Lord has in store for him now. It's a process. I think he and I have worked out some things. Now it's time for you and him to learn. The Lord has an abundant life in store for your daddy, even after Miss Emily is gone and you are on your own. That's what makes you, your daddy, and me so much alike. We're searching to see what the rest of our lives should be like."

"You're sure Daddy's OK with me moving to Texas?"

"He'll cry when you go, and miss you terribly when you're gone, but he wants you to do it."

"You think if I went to talk to him right now, he'd cry?"

"He probably would."

"The only times I've ever seen him cry are when my brother and then my mama died."

Develyn bit her lip. "And the only time I've seen him cry was tonight when he talked about his Lindsay."

● ● ●

The sky draped deep blue.

The cedars reflected dark green.

The air tasted like fresh, clean sage.

The road back to Argenta was dry enough not to stick to the tires, and just wet enough to suppress any thought of dust. Develyn had both front windows rolled down, Brooks and Dunn music turned up loud.

Lord, I haven't been this happy since I first drove to Wyoming. It's been a good summer . . . a great summer . . . and . . .

She reached over and turned off the stereo.

I miss my Delaney. I've been taking care of other people. I've been taking care of myself. I need to be taking care of my baby. Maybe, her baby. Oh, Lord . . . help me to accept your will in this matter.

When she crossed the railroad tracks, her cell phone registered a signal and she glanced at her watch.

It's ten o'clock in Indiana. That's plenty of sleep.

She punched the speed dial and waited for the ring.

On the fifth ring, there was a sleepy "Hello?"

"Hi, baby, it's me."

"Mother, what's wrong?"

"Nothing, Dee, I just called to check on you."

"This early in the morning?"

"It's 10 a.m., isn't it?"

"Yes, but I put in a double shift yesterday, and helped them close. I didn't get to bed until two. I want to sleep until noon."

"A double shift? Honey, take care of yourself."

"I made $112 in tips. Cool, huh?"

"Yes, it is. Now go back to bed."

"OK. Mom . . . why did you really call?"

"I was missing you like crazy and wanted to tell you I loved you."

"Yeah, that's what I thought. I love you too Mom."

"See you Wednesday, baby."

● ● ●

She fed Uncle Henry and the horses before she went into the cabin. She noticed Cooper Tallon's pickup parked in its usual place. She pulled off her boots and her socks and wiggled her toes on the cold linoleum floor. Then she grabbed a plastic bottle of water. When the phone rang, she stepped outside to answer it.

"Hi, Devy-girl."

"Casey, how are you? Where are you?"

"I'm at Jackson's sister's place in Red Lodge. We are getting ready for church. You haven't got married yet, have you?"

"Me?" Develyn laughed. "Of course not. Have you?"

"No way. But I did have a question. What is your last day of school next year?"

"Next June?"

"Yeah."

"I don't have my calendar. Why do you ask?"

"Jackson and I are trying to pick a date for the wedding, and I want you to be my maid of honor . . . or is it matron of honor?"

"You what? You . . . you . . . you've only known him three days."

"Why is that such a big deal?"

"You can't agree to get married after three days."

"How many days does it take? Thirty? Forty-two? Sixty? Is there a law or something?"

"There's no law; it varies from couple to couple . . . but you can't . . ."

"Good, Dev. I think Jackson and me are one of those rare three-day couples."

"Casey, you can't do this. You can't get engaged so soon."

Develyn heard Casey holler. "It's no good Jackson, Mama won't let me marry you."

"Wait . . . wait . . . wait, honey . . . I didn't say . . ."

Casey burst out laughing.

"Were you trying to give your old mother a heart attack?"

"I had you going, didn't I? You are so easy to tease."

"I guess it's my gift . . . to others."

"I need you to get a phone number for me."

"This whole call was about you needing a phone number?"

"Yeah, Jackson's sister is looking for a dressage horse. Becky Trimmons has one over in Gillette, but I don't remember her number and it's not listed. Can you get my address book out of my red gear bag?"

"I'm still tiffed over that wedding ruse."

Develyn went inside the cabin and read Casey the phone number.

"So, that's all you wanted?"

"That's it. Thanks. I'll be home Tuesday."

"I'm going up to Buffalo with Renny on Tuesday, but I won't be late."

"Are you and Renny a number?" Casey asked.

"No, we are just friends. Real good friends. How about you and Jackson? Are you two a number?"

"Yeah, I think we are. I've never been a number with anyone before."

"Do you like it, Casey?"

"Yes, I do. I really like it."

"Are you still planning to go with me on Wednesday to pick up Delaney?"

"I'm countin' on it, Dev. Listen . . ."

"Yes?"

"I really do want to know what your last day of school is next summer."

13

"hat's the best place for breakfast between Billings and Cheyenne," Renny said. His black hat was pushed back, a wooden toothpick hung from his dimpled smile.

"It's incredible how much food they serve you." Develyn leaned against the seat of the pickup and studied the out-stretched parallel ribbons of Interstate 25 north. "I didn't quite understand the name of the place."

"It hasn't always been called 'Earl's or Else.' When I first started eatin' there it was called 'Earl's & Elsie's.'"

"Elsie was his wife?"

"Yep."

"What happened to her?"

"She went home."

"To her parents?" Develyn asked.

"To her husband and kid."

"I thought you said she was married to Earl."

"She was. She was a mail-order bride from China. Earl went through this agency in Seattle. Paid to have her come over, and married her. He gave her the name Elsie. She was quite an excellent cook. You should have seen the place before she moved in."

"But she got homesick and returned to China?"

"Turns out her daddy was some political prisoner over there and they needed to ship all his family out of the country. When things changed, it was time to gather them all back. So one day, a big black limousine with foreign embassy plates pulled into Earl's & Elsie's and off she went. Turns out she had a husband and a son back in China. All he gets is a letter and a picture of her kid ever' Christmas. He was just goin' to white out the '& Elsie's,' but it tossed the sign off center. So he changed it to Earl's or Else."

"Or else . . . what?" Develyn asked.

"Or else you have to eat somewhere else, I reckon."

"I would have never guessed by looking at the outside that it had good food. In fact, there's no way I'd ever stop there on my own."

"Yep. I always say that Earl's sort of looks like a cross between an auto wrecking yard and a Mexicali brothel. You know, that rundown, cheesy look."

She sat up and laughed. "You said that just to get me stirred up. I'm not falling for that, cowboy. I know for a fact you've never been to such a place."

"Shoot, Devy-girl, I've never even been to Mexicali. I visited Juarez once and been to Calgary a dozen times. That's the extent of my international travels. How about you?"

"I've been to Europe a couple of times with my mother, and . . ."

"Hold on, Devy-girl!" Renny shouted.

Develyn clutched the handhold as Renny slammed on the brakes. They shot out into the wide dirt median that separated the interstate lanes.

"What is it?" she yelled.

"Ivan's in trouble."

The pickup bounced and lunged as the left tires raised off the ground when Renny cranked a hard left and roared up on the southbound lanes.

She fought to catch her breath. "Who's Ivan?"

"Look!" Renny pointed to a horse trailer on the right apron of the Interstate. A man tried to get a kicking, panicked horse out of the silver trailer.

Renny pulled over fifty feet behind the rig and jumped out of the truck. "Come on, we've got to help!" he hollered.

We? I don't have to cross a border to be in a foreign land.

"Renny, you're a sight for sore eyes!" the man shouted. "Geraldine was gettin' close to deliverin' the baby, and things got complicated . . . I didn't have time to wait for the doc . . . so I was rushin' her to the clinic but it don't look like we'll make it."

A little boy stuck his head out the pickup window. "Daddy, the baby is crying."

"Honey, you help her settle down."

"She wants Mommy!"

"I know, hon," Ivan shouted. "But Mommy's stuck in the front of the horse trailer."

Develyn's hands went to her mouth as he tried to peer in front of the flailing horse. *Oh, my Lord, no . . . a pregnant lady is stuck in the front of a trailer with a panicked horse?*

"Ease up on the rope, Ivan!" Renny shouted.

"She'll surely kick you to death if you get in there, Renny."

"You'll lose your wife, your horse, and the little one if I don't get her out now."

Take a deep breath, Dev . . . you are OK . . . if you faint, no one will even notice. Stay calm. You can do this. Everyone's going to die.

A big truck blasted by so close the wind almost spun her around.

The horse kicked at Renny. The bang of the hoofs on the walls of the trailer sounded like lightning striking. Renny waited for the second kick, then dove into the trailer for the horse's head stall.

I can't watch this . . . he'll be kicked to death.

Renny's right hand caught the head stall, and he hung on like a dead weight. "Yank on the lead rope now!" he shouted.

The tall, thin cowboy with the battered straw hat waved at Develyn. "I need some help."

She ran and grabbed the rope. *No one has ever needed my strength before. They've never even asked for it.*

The rope burned her hands as she and Ivan yanked. The horse struggled and fought, but first one hind leg and then the other left the trailer. After another kick at Ivan and Develyn, the horse backed out of the trailer and tugged Renny like a ball and chain. A woman limped out behind Renny. She sported a torn flannel shirt and had sweat dripping down her face.

Ivan and Renny led the horse to a spot between the freeway and the fence. The flashing lights of a Wyoming state patrolman caught Develyn's attention.

"Slater, what's going on here?" the lawman shouted.

Hatless, but still clutched to the halter of the horse, Renny waved a frantic arm at the trooper. "Bobby, call Dr. Bradford in Casper and tell him to get out here right now. We've got a breech birth coming any minute, and we'll lose the horse and the foal if we don't get help."

The woman stepped up to Develyn.

"The horse . . ." Develyn mumbled. "The horse is the one giving birth?"

"You didn't think it was me, did you?" The lady stuck out her hand. "I'm Lovie, Ivan's wife. You are so pretty and clean you must belong to Renny."

"I'm Dev Worrell. We're good friends."

Lovie rubbed her thigh. "I'll have a major bruise there tomorrow. I'm lucky that was the only time I was kicked."

"What were you doing in the trailer?"

"Tryin' to keep Geraldine quiet until we got to the vet. She's my mare."

"I'm glad you didn't get hurt more."

"I never prayed so much in my life." The woman watched as Renny and Ivan looped a rope around the horse's leg.

"What are they doing?"

"Lying the horse down. You do know that there isn't another man in Wyoming that would have dove in there and grabbed that halter. Renny will put his life on the line for his friends . . . shoot, for complete strangers . . . time and again. I don't know how he's lived this long. He's a godsend, that's for sure."

Above the roar of freeway traffic, Develyn leaned over and whispered. "Lovie, your shirt's ripped, and your bra's showing a little."

"Lovie, we need you over here!" Ivan shouted. "Hold her head down."

"Mommy! The baby needs you," the boy cried from the truck.

She squeezed Develyn's hand. "I suppose my bra is the least of my worries right now."

"I'll get the baby," Develyn offered.

"Thanks. Take them over by the fence." Lovie ran down the embankment to sit on the flailing horse.

Develyn hiked up to the muddy gray Dodge pickup. A little boy about five had his head out the window. "Is Geraldine going to die?"

"Your daddy and mommy and Mr. Slater are taking care of her."

"Who are you?"

"I'm Ms. Worrell. I'm a friend of Mr. Slater."

"I'm Buster."

"I'm glad to meet you." Develyn glanced inside at a whimpering infant strapped into a car seat.

"What's your sister's name?"

"Naomi."

"Buster, your mommy asked me to get you and Naomi and stand over by the fence. Is that alright with you?"

"OK."

Develyn wiped the eyes of the six-month-old, cradled her in her arms, then wrapped her in a thin, pink, burp-stained blanket. She took Buster's sticky hand, and they walked down to the fence. Several more pickups then parked behind the patrol car.

"It's Renny!" Buster shouted.

"Yes, the one putting on the rubber gloves is Mr. Slater."

"No, it's not!" Buster shouted. "It's Renny!"

You have quite a fan club, Mr. Renny Slater. "What's he doing?"

"He's going to reach up inside of Geraldine and try and turn the foal's hooves," Buster reported.

Develyn sucked air.

It's OK, Ms. Worrell . . . sit down in the dirt . . . put your head between your knees. Breathe deep.

"Buster, let's just sit here in the dirt. It might take awhile."

"Yeah, and we get to see everything!"

Develyn glanced down at the big brown eyes of the baby. Little Naomi clutched her fingers. "Honey, you and me don't have to watch if we don't want to."

● ● ●

The vet never arrived, but the brown colt did.

Several dozen people who had gathered on the shoulder of the Interstate applauded. While the colt tried out his new legs, Renny and Ivan cleaned up. After a long walk with Buster and Naomi along the fence line, Develyn returned to find the horses trailered. Only Ivan and Renny's rigs were left.

"Well, Devy-girl, I'm a mess."

She looked at his wet, filthy shirt and jeans. "Yes, and I don't want to know what it is you have smeared all over your arm."

"You and Renny were surely angels amongst us today," Ivan said.

"You have wonderful children," Develyn reported.

"Yes, ma'am, I'm a lucky man." He turned and slapped Renny on the back. "Partner, you saved me today. I can't repay it, but you got supper and a place to stay anytime you're in our area. You know that for a fact."

"Thanks, Ivan. You would have done the same for me."

Ivan looked right at Develyn. "No, I wouldn't. I would have helped all I could, but I don't have the guts or the timing to dive for that halter."

"Or the foolishness," Renny replied.

"No, you knew what you were doing," Ivan replied.

"Sometimes a man's brave because he doesn't have much to lose."

Renny and Develyn hiked back up to his pickup. "Well, Ms. Worrell, that's a little excitement I didn't expect to show you this morning."

She smiled and peered over the top of her sunglasses.

"Mr. Slater, life with you is never dull. There's always something new."

"Here's another thing new. I am too messy to even get in my truck. You are going to drive across the median to the northbound lanes and head up there two miles to a rest stop. I'll hop in the back of the pickup."

● ● ●

With a fresh, clean long-sleeve green shirt and Wranglers, Renny Slater slid back behind the steering wheel. "Is that better?"

"You scrub up well, cowboy."

"Have you had enough excitement for the day?"

"I've had enough for a lifetime."

They took the exit just south of Buffalo and angled west toward the Bighorn Mountains. Blacktop gave way to gravel, then to dirt as they approached a large green square in the otherwise brown prairie.

"That's my forty acres." Renny pointed straight ahead.

"You have it irrigated."

"Yep. Rod Clements is a well-driller and owed me some favors. So I let him sink a couple of wells for me. All together I have over a hundred gallons a minute, which is pretty good for the east side of the mountains. It allows me to grow a little hay if I rotate it around."

"Are those your horses back there?"

"Eight of them are mine. The other four belong to various friends who by now have probably forgot where they left 'em."

They pulled under a big log gate carved with a circle RS in the middle.

"Is that your brand?"

"I have several registered. That's my horse brand." Renny stopped next to a huge, half-built barn.

"This is quite a building project," Develyn said.

He got out and walked with her to the entrance of the building. "Yep, but its completion is hampered by time and money."

"A two-story barn?"

"The top story will be my house. Two bedrooms, den, kitchen, office, two baths, and a veranda that faces the mountains."

"It sounds wonderful."

"Someday, Devy-girl, I'll get it done . . . someday. Until then," he pointed to the other side of the barn, "it's me and my double-wide."

"Your yard looks very neat."

"Yeah, don't that surprise you?"

"No." She slipped her arm in his. "I have learned one thing about Renny Slater. He can do anything he sets his mind to. I bet you built every bit of the barn yourself."

"Oh, I get a friend to hold a board up once in a while. But I fenced the place and built the arena all by myself. I like workin' by myself, Dev. It's kind of like therapy sometimes."

"The arena has a couple of bucking chutes and roping boxes," she said.

"There's always someone stopping by who wants to practice. I'm surprised no one's here now."

"They just pop in and use it anytime?"

"Yep. That's what it's for."

Develyn stared into the shadows of the half-built barn. "You have a cat."

"Yeah, don't that beat all? A cowboy with a cat and no dog."

"She looks very . . ."

"Sturdy."

"Is she tame?"

"Nope. Strictly a barn cat. She moved in as soon as I built the first storage building, and has lived here ever since. I call her Jezebel. I give her a little dry food whenever I get a chance, and she takes care of the mice. But don't get too close to her."

"Does she run off?"

"No, she'll attack you."

"Oh, heavens, she is wild. But you're right. I am stunned that you don't have a dog."

"I had two when I moved here. Cougars came down off the mountain and got them both."

"But they left Jezebel?"

"Cougars aren't dumb." He pointed toward the double-wide. "Would you like to see my place? Got some Cokes and shrimp salad waiting in the refrigerator."

"Shrimp salad? Mr. Slater, how in the world did you . . ."

"Well, don't be too amazed. I picked it up at the super-market last evenin'. It looked good, and I haven't had shrimp for a while. I was trying to guess what a schoolteacher might like. It was either shrimp salad or frozen foot-long green chili burritos."

They strolled to the grassy area in front of the gray mobile home with forest green trim.

"I love your roses!"

Renny pulled off his hat and brushed back his thinning blond hair. "People in town claimed that roses wouldn't grow out here."

"So you had to prove them wrong?"

"Something in me likes to do that."

"That's quite a pottery menagerie."

"Most of them are horrible looking. Ever' last one is a gift. I'm afraid to toss 'em 'cause whoever gave it to me will stop by and ask. So I confine 'em to the north side. In the winter time they stay covered with snow. But it looks like the coyotes got in here, 'cause most of them are turned over."

Renny ambled into the yard of small animal figurines. "I reckon I'll set them upright, but I'm not sure that looks better."

"Do you mind if I go on inside and use the ladies room?"

He shoved the key ring toward her. "It's the big silver one."

A brass sign above the doorbell read, "Lord, bless this home with love and laughter." Develyn fumbled to get the key in the door and found it was unlocked.

Somehow that doesn't surprise me. Nothing about Renny Slater surprises me.

The living room furniture was leather and oak. The spring on the self-closing door was tight. When she released it, the door slammed hard.

"Renny, darlin', I'm in the kitchen washin' my hair," a woman's voice shouted.

Develyn froze. Her neck stiffened. She wrapped her arms around her chest.

A woman wearing jeans and a white sports bra appeared at the kitchen doorway with a white towel wrapped around her wet, red hair.

"Oh! Is Renny with you?"

"He's outside," Develyn mumbled.

"I'm Mary."

"I'm not."

"Oh, don't worry, honey. I'll just dry my hair and scoot to the back room so you and Renny can . . . well, whatever."

Develyn opened the front door and shouted. "Slater, get in here."

Renny bounded through the door, hat in hand. His dimpled grin faded when he spotted the woman with the towel.

"Mary? What are you doing here?"

"You invited me, remember?"

"I what?"

"You said if Walt ever beat me up again, I could always come over here." She dropped the towel to reveal cuts and bruises on her neck and ear. "He came home drunk and came after me with the rake."

Develyn held herself and began to rock back and forth.

"Your place was locked but I found the spare key finally, under that little hideous yard frog. I had blood in my hair, so I washed it. Who's your friend?"

"Mary, this is Dev Worrell. Now go back in there and get your shirt on."

"Renny, I can go out to the barn if you two want to visit."

"Just get your shirt on, darlin'. I'll take care of this."

"Renny, don't send me back to Walt. Not today. Let me spend the night here." She started to cry.

"You know I won't send you back. I'll figure out something. Go get dressed."

The woman wiped her eyes on the towel, then looked at Develyn. "I used to be purdy like you." She shuffled back into the kitchen.

"Dev, the master bathroom is down the hall on the right, if you still need it. I need to make a phone call, and then explain this to you."

"Are you calling the sheriff?"

"Not yet."

● ● ●

Develyn stood in front of the mirror of the tidy bathroom and dried off the water she had splashed on her face.

Lord, Renny's life is one emergency after another. It's all I can do to keep from fainting. I don't know what's really going on here. I don't know if I want to know.

Mary was sitting on the couch when Develyn returned to the living room. She could hear Renny finish a phone call.

He ignored Develyn when he returned and pulled up a chair in front of Mary. "Darlin', when did Walt get back in the area?"

Mary's voice softened. "Two weeks ago."

"You promised me you wouldn't take him back next time."

"He didn't have anywhere to stay, Renny."

"What happened to the money he got workin' that oil rig?"

"He said someone stole most of it."

"Do you believe that?"

She dropped her pointed chin to her chest. "No."

Develyn could see more bruises around her neck.

"What's he been doin' for two weeks?"

"Drinkin'."

"Where did he get the money for the booze?"

"He took it out of my purse, I reckon." She began to sob.

Renny scooted over on the couch next to her and cradled her head against his shoulder. "Darlin', listen to me. No one can help you unless you want help. Do you want help?"

"I want him to love me and not hit me."

Now tears streamed down Develyn's face.

"You have to answer me, darlin'. You are still the purdiest redhead in Johnson County. Do you want help?"

"I want to stay with you, Renny."

"You didn't answer me."

"Yes," she whimpered. "I want help."

"Then you have to do what I tell you to do."

"If I mind you, will you let me stay here? I'm a good cook, Renny, you know I'm a good cook."

"I have somethin' much better in mind for you than stayin' here."

She clutched on to him. "Don't ever turn me loose."

Develyn heard a rig pull up in the driveway.

"Don't let him get me, Renny," Mary wailed.

Develyn peeked out the window. "It's a man and a woman."

Renny stood, with Mary still clinging. He shoved her back. "Mary, go get your things. That's Pastor Tim and his wife, Barb. They have a safe place for you, and they know exactly how to handle this."

"But," she sobbed, "I wanted to stay with you."

"Darlin', in your heart you knew I'd never be able to let you do that. Get your stuff."

Within minutes, Pastor Tim and Barb drove off with Mary and her two paper sacks of belongings.

Develyn and Renny sat outside on the front step.

"How did she get here without a car?" Dev asked.

"She said she hitchhiked."

"In that condition?"

"About a year ago Walt beat on her. I remember at the time thinkin' I would surely regret offerin' her help. I just didn't know what else to say. Walt is OK when he's sober. He's a good oil rig worker because he can't get to a bar or liquor store. He was in jail ninety days last time. They let him out because he was going down to Louisiana to work the rigs in the gulf. He even sent Mary some of his pay." He took a big breath, then sighed. "I don't know what to do in that kind of deal."

"Are you going to call the sheriff?"

"Pastor Tim said he'd take care of it. They are good folks." He patted her knee. "Must have been quite a shock walking in the house and seeing her."

"Yes, I take back what I said when I mentioned nothing would surprise me."

"Well, Devy-girl . . . it startled me. When you screamed, I figured there was a snake in the house again."

"Renny, is your life ever quiet and peaceful?"

"You see those mountains back there?"

"Yes."

"Sometimes I have to ride off in them and get lost for a few days."

"By yourself?"

"Yep. I just stay out there until the solitary eats me up and I need to come back."

"It must be quite lonely, camping by yourself."

"No more so than the rest of my life."

"Renny Slater, are you saying you are a lonely man?"

"Devy, I know most ever'one in this half of the state. They know my name, and they'll welcome me in their home, any day or night of the year. But none of them are close. Do you know what it's like to be right at the hub of all the activity and still feel alone?"

"Renny . . . I've known that since I was twelve."

"I figured you had. It's one of the things that draws us together. That, my irresistible dimples, and your little upturned nose seldom seen in a girl over twelve."

She turned and slugged his arm. "Don't you start in on my nose."

"Are you still hungry?"

"I was promised a shrimp salad."

He stood and tugged on her hand. "Come on, Ms. Worrell. I've got a surprise for you after lunch."

"I don't know how many more I can stand in one day."

"Maybe that's not a good word. How about a unique gift for you?" His grin revealed two deep dimples.

•   •   •

"Where did you get it!" she giggled. "I love it!"

"I got a friend in Billings who has a trophy shop."

"The Golden Thistle Award. How fitting," she said.

"I figured you'd want a token to remember the first day you met Renny Slater."

"This is the same thistle?"

"I jammed it in the side pocket of the truck. It's been bouncin' around in there all summer."

"Renny, this is wonderful. It goes right on my desk in my classroom."

He scratched the back of his neck. "I don't like to think about you goin' back to Indiana. Not just yet. I'm gettin' mighty fond of you being here in Wyoming."

"I agree. I do want to enjoy every day. Teaching brings its own set of problems. I'm not ready to face those yet."

"I got something I want you to read." Renny retrieved a letter stapled to an envelope from the top of a cluttered desk. "Tell me what you think of this."

Develyn read each word with care, then glanced up. "Wow . . . Renny Slater, college professor. That sounds great."

336

"Can you imagine me at a college with a bunch of eighteen-to twenty-year-olds?"

"Yes, I can."

"You mean that, don't you? I can see it in your eyes. And you know what . . . if I had the right woman with me, I probably could do it."

"Where is the College of Southern Idaho?"

"It's a junior college in Twin Falls."

"Would you coach both the men's and women's rodeo teams?"

"Yep. I'd have a gal for an assistant."

"What kind of contract? Year round?"

"Nine months. I'd have my summer to come home and work on the place, if I wanted to. The salary is pretty dadgum good. But still . . ."

"You sound hesitant."

"Can I just blurt something out, Dev?"

"Of course."

"I daydreamed a little about what it would be like, you know . . . if I were to marry a certain Indiana schoolteacher and we settled down in Twin Falls. You teachin' fifth-graders and me with the college."

"I'm flattered, Renny. I don't know if I've ever been someone's daydream before. What did you conclude?"

"Even if we were crazy in love, I'm too stubborn and you're too old."

"Oh, dear . . . I went from daydream to old in just seconds."

"Devy, I think I could learn to be a good husband, if I had a wife who would take the time to school me. I know you could do that. But I also would like to be a good daddy. Now, my forty-two isn't too old to be a daddy, but I reckon your forty-five is too old to be a mama again." He reached out for her.

She took his hand. "You are right about that."

"Yet, I can't remember having a more fun summer than this one with you, Ms. Worrell."

"Mr. Slater, I'm sure nine out of the ten most exciting times in my life have been with you."

He laughed. "What about that tenth one?"

"I was just leaving it open for speculation."

Renny disappeared to the kitchen. Develyn reread his rodeo team coaching offer.

She heard a knock at the door. She waited for Renny to come back. When he didn't appear, she opened the door.

A huge unshaven man wearing a Houston Astros baseball cap glared at her.

"Who in hades are you?" he grumbled.

Develyn folded her arms across her chest. "I'm . . . eh, a . . . a friend of Renny's."

"Get out of the way. I'm here to fetch my wife."

The man started for the doorway.

"Mary is not here, Walt," Develyn blurted out.

He stepped back. "How do you know who I am?"

Develyn felt Renny's hands at her waist as he tugged her aside.

"She's right, Walt. Mary isn't here."

The red-faced man waved his hands. "She ran away, Renny. I want her back. I want her back right now."

"Of course she ran away, Walt. You hurt her."

"She deserved it."

"No, she didn't. I've told you that before. No woman deserves a beating."

"She ain't here?"

"No."

"I'm goin' to look around." He shoved Renny back a step.

Renny dove his head into the big man's chest. Walt staggered back, tumbled off the front step, and sprawled on his back in the grass.

As he struggled to his feet, he yanked out a revolver. "I'll kill you, Slater. I'll kill you!"

Develyn could feel her entire body begin to shake. *Oh, Lord Jesus . . . no . . . no . . . no.*

"You aren't going to kill me, Walt. Give me the gun," Renny demanded.

"I sure as hades will." He pointed the gun at Renny's head. "Where's my wife?"

Renny kept his voice low. Calm. "Give me the gun, Walt."

"I'm killin' you, Slater! This time, I'm killin' you!" the man screamed.

"Give me the gun and sit down on the step with me. Let's talk. We've been friends a long time. You don't have many friends, Walt. You need me. Give me the gun."

The big man's shoulders slumped. "You won't call the sheriff?"

"No, I won't call the sheriff. Let's talk. Now give me the gun."

"Who's that woman?"

"That's my good friend. She's a schoolteacher from Indiana."

"She don't look like no schoolteacher. She looks like a barrel racer."

Renny stuck out his hand. "Give me the gun."

Walt hesitated. Then he dropped his chin and sighed. He handed the gun to Renny.

Develyn wiped the sweat off her face with her fingers.

"Let's sit down, Walt."

The big man motioned at Develyn. "Have that buckle bunny come out here and sit down too. I don't want her sneakin' back there to call the sheriff."

"Dev, come sit next to me."

Walt, Renny, and Develyn lined the step.

The man rubbed his face into his massive hands. "What am I goin' to do, Renny?"

"You need some help."

"Jail don't help."

"It keeps Mary safe for awhile. If you can't think of somethin' better, that's where you'll end up. I think you need to quit workin' the rigs."

"What do you mean?"

"I've got a friend who's got a special kind of ranch outside

Silver City, New Mexico. He helps men like you, and you get to ride horses and do some ranch work."

"You talkin' about dryin' me out?"

"Rehab, it's called. I know some boys it really helped. But you have to sign up for twelve weeks, and you don't get to leave."

"Three months is a long time."

"You've got a pretty big problem, Walt. Besides, think about how pleased Mary will be when you are sober all the time and slicked up handsome."

"I do scrub up good."

"Yes, you do."

"Does that New Mexico place cost a lot of money?"

"It ain't cheap, but I can get you a scholarship. For some students, they will pay everything."

"How do I get there?"

"Let's let Johnson County worry about that."

"How do I do that?"

"What if you contacted the sheriff's office and asked them to come pick you up? Tell them you need some help and you're willing to do rehab in New Mexico, if they get you there."

"You think they'll do that?"

"They don't want to pay your room and board at the county jail."

"You goin' to tell them about the gun?"

"What gun?" Renny replied.

Walt dropped his head in his hands. "You're the only friend I got left, Renny."

"You get yourself cleaned up, you'll be surprised how many friends you have. You want me to get that phone for you?"

"Will you or the rodeo gal call them for me?"

"Nope. We promised you we wouldn't. You got to make the call. I'll dial it for you."

"You'll wait with me 'til they come?"

"You know I will."

"You'll see that my truck gets home?"

"We'll drive it for you."

"How about my gun?"

"Why don't I keep it until you get home from New Mexico? You ready for the phone?"

"I'm ready for things to be different, Renny. I truly am."

● ● ●

The sun lowered over the horizon when Renny pulled into Argenta and drove past Mrs. Tagley's. Uncle Henry met them at the road and trailed behind to the cabin.

"Well, Mr. Renny Slater, you sure know how to show a girl a good time."

Renny shook his head. "Dev, I don't know what to say. I'm sorry for the danger I put you in."

She leaned over and kissed him on the lips. "Renny, you are the bravest man I have ever known. Being with you is like riding in the Old West with my cowboy hero. Whether you are diving after a panicked horse, or standing down a drunk with a gun, you are awesome. It's a privilege to call you my friend."

"What do you think about that college coaching job?"

"I don't know. I'll pray about it. I think it's a great opportunity for some stability for you. But I'm not sure you're called
to have a stable life. Where would Ivan and Lovie and Little
Buster and Naomi and Mary and Walt . . . and all those kids in
Douglas be if they didn't have their Renny? You are needed
here by hundreds of different people in hundreds of different
ways. You can do some things that no one else can. Wyoming
needs you, Renny Slater."

"How about Ms. Worrell?"

Develyn laughed. "I was told that I am too old. But I do
have a cherished trophy. You will be my good friend forever.
I'm going to need you too. A cowboy girl always needs a hero."

"The schoolteacher and the mustang breaker. We make a
pretty good team, Devy-girl."

This time he kissed her on the cheek.

● ● ●

Before she pulled the wrapper off, Develyn pressed the
orange Popsicle against her forehead. She plopped down next
to her brother on the wagon seat in front of Mrs. Tagley's store
and stared out at the bright Wyoming day.

"I didn't know it could be so hot out here. Before we came,
I thought Wyoming was all mountains covered with trees and
always cold."

Dewayne held half his Popsicle in one hand and the other
half in the other. He rotated his licks from one to the other.

"It's windy every day. Daddy says Wyoming is the air freeway that connects the west and the midwest, and there is always a lot of traffic going both ways."

Develyn lapped at the bottom of her Popsicle. Three drops had already hit her pink T-shirt. "Did I tell you that I'm moving to Wyoming?"

Dewayne chomped off half of one Popsicle with a single bite. "When?"

"After I graduate from college."

He traced his carved initials with a clean-licked Popsicle stick. "I thought you were going to be a schoolteacher."

"I am," she said.

"You going to teach school in Wyoming?"

"No, I'm going to teach school in Crawfordsville."

"So, how are you going to live in Wyoming at the same time?"

"I will have two houses. I'll spend summers and vacations here. And during the year, I'll stay in Crawfordsville. Mrs. Ralston has a house in Wisconsin. So I'll have a house in Wyoming."

"What if your husband doesn't want to do that?" Dewayne pressed.

"I cannot imagine a husband not wanting to do everything I ask."

"Neither can I." Dewayne stood up as he finished his second half of the Popsicle. "But I don't think it's as easy as that."

"Where are you going?"

"Daddy said Mr. Homer traded a Ford transmission for a filly. I wanted to go look at it."

Develyn slurped at her Popsicle and watched it drip on her bare knee. "The transmission or the filly?"

"The filly."

"I want to go too."

"You don't have on any shoes."

"My feet are tough." She trotted down the wooden steps and into the dirt yard after him.

"Devy-girl, I'm going clear to the corral, and I'm not going to carry you on my back."

"And I'm not going to carry you either, Dewayne Upton. I'll race you."

"You can't outrun me even if you had on your shoes."

"Hah!" she yelled, then took off and raced west down the dirt road.

● ● ●

The eight-month-old gray filly pushed her nose through the rails of the corral fence when Dewayne staggered up, toting his twin sister on his back.

"I knew I'd have to do this," he grumbled, then shoved her down.

"I stepped on a sticker." She pointed to her toe, then bent over and peered between the rails. "Isn't she cute?"

"She looks like a regular horse, only smaller," Dewayne mumbled.

"Posh. She's adorable." Develyn stroked the horse with a sticky hand. "You are a very pretty girl. Are you hungry? Would you like something to eat?" Develyn held the dripping orange Popsicle in front of the filly's lips.

The horse slapped it to the dirt with one swat of her long thin nose.

Develyn stared at the Popsicle lying in the powdery corral dirt.

Dewayne burst out laughing.

Her hands on the hips of her pink shorts, Develyn bit her lower lip and fought back the tears. "That was terribly, terribly rude!" she cried. "I hope your mother teaches you some manners."

"Horses don't need manners," Dewayne insisted.

"Well, this one does." Develyn stared at the big dark brown eyes. "But she's still a baby. She has a lot to learn."

"I think I'll go fly my kite."

"I've jammed a sticker in my toe. You'll have to carry me back to the house."

"I pulled the sticker out."

"It still hurts. Good-bye, honey," she said to the horse. "I'll come back and see you when you learn some manners." Develyn reached over to stroke the filly's nose.

The horse turned her head sideways and bit Develyn's finger.

"Ouch! Did you see that? She bit my finger! That hurt," Develyn wailed.

"Then you won't notice the pain in your feet when you walk to the cabin," Dewayne said.

"I try to be nice, I try to do things for her, and look what she does. That is terribly, terribly rude!"

"What is terribly, terribly rude?"

"Her mother needs to teach her more than manners."

"Whose mother?"

There was an abrupt shaking of Develyn's shoulder.

"The . . . eh . . . Casey?"

"Were you dreaming of horses again . . . or your Delaney?"

Develyn sat up in the yard chair, then toweled the sweat off her forehead. "I don't know." She gazed at the sun, halfway across the afternoon sky.

"You were mumbling about someone being rude."

The shotgun blast followed by a shout, "Leon, you get back here!" brought Develyn to her feet.

"What time is it?"

"Time to go to the airport and get Delaney. Ms. Worrell . . . are you ready for your daughter?"

Develyn shoved her sunglasses high on her nose. "Casey, I've never been more ready in my life."

THE HORSE DREAMS TRILOGY
BY STEPHEN BLY

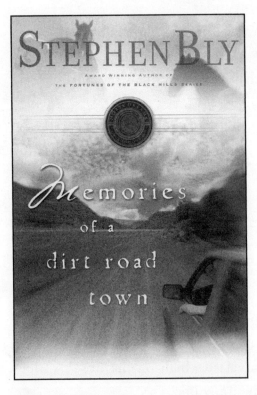

ISBN 0-8054-3171-3
Trade paper, $14.99

In *Memories of a Dirt Road Town*, Develyn Worrell discovers her past, present, and future revealed through an assortment of new friends, including a paint mare, who help her get her life back in focus. Develyn soon finds the peace, confidence, and acceptance she's been missing.

Don't miss the first book in the Horse Dreams Trilogy, *Memories of a Dirt Road Town*.

For more books by award-winning author Stephen Bly, look for these titles at bookstores everywhere:

The Fortunes of the Black Hills series:

Beneath a Dakota Cross 0-8054-1659-5
Friends and Enemies 0-8054-2437-7
Last of the Texas Camp 0-8054-2557-8
The Long Trail Home 0-8054-2356-7
The Next Roundup 0-8054-2699-X
Shadow of Legends 0-8054-2174-2

BROADMAN
&HOLMAN
PUBLISHERS
www.broadmanholman.com